SOULCERESS

Linsey Hall

Copyright 2014 by Linsey Hall
Published by Bonnie Doon Press LLC
Paperback Edition 1.0

Linsey@LinseyHall.com
www.LinseyHall.com
https://twitter.com/HiLinseyHall
https://www.facebook.com/LinseyHallAuthor

BONNIE
DOON
PRESS

ISBN 978-1-942085-10-2 (eBook)
ISBN 978-1-942085-11-9 (Paperback)

Books by Linsey Hall

Braving Fate
Soulceress
Rogue Soul
Stolen Fate

DEDICATION

For my parents, who've always supported me.

ACKNOWLEDGMENTS

Thank you so much to all of the people who put their time and effort toward helping me with this story. As always, thank you Ben for helping me create this book. Emily Keane, for reading every story I've written, no matter how busy you are. And to Doug Inglis and Veronica Morriss for your help and support when this particular story hit a rough patch. Thank you to Carol Thomas for reading this story and always being there for me.

Thank you to Valerie Hayward, Shelley Bates, and Jena O'Connor for various forms of editing. The story is much better because of your expertise. And thank you to Simone Seguin for writing wonderful back cover copy.

Thank you to my beta reader, Charisma Cassidy. I appreciate so much that you volunteered your time and expertise to help make this story the best it could be, especially the epilogue.

Dear Reader,
Warren and Esha's story has a special place in my heart, as does the secondary hero, Chairman Meow. I hope you enjoy them as much as I do.
Happy reading,
Linsey Hall

GLOSSARY

Aether - The invisible substance that connects the afterworlds and earth. It is both nothing and everything.

Aetherwalking - A method of traveling through the aether to access the afterworlds or different places on earth. Some Mytheans have this power and can bring another person with them.

Afterworld - A heaven or hell created by mortal belief. Mortals can access them only through death. Some Mytheans can aetherwalk to them.

Immortal University - An organization created thousands of years ago to protect Mytheans and keep them secret from mortals. It was initially founded as a true university, hence the name, but over time it morphed into an institution with greater power and responsibility. The university's primary goal is to maintain the secrecy of Mytheans and to keep the gods from warring to obtain more followers. They do this primarily through diplomacy. The university also provides services to Mytheans that they can't get elsewhere, lest mortals figure out that their clients never die. Things like education, health services, and banking.

Mortals - Humans. They are unaware of the existence of Mytheans or that all heavens and hells truly exist. They are immortal in the sense that their soul will pass on to whatever afterworld they believe in.

Mythean - Supernatural individuals created by mortal belief. They are gods and goddesses, demons and monsters, witches and other supernatural creatures. They are immortal in the sense that if they live on earth, only beheading or grievous injury from magic can kill them. If they are killed their soul will pass on to an afterworld. Secrecy from mortals is one of their highest priorities. Some Mytheans, particularly species of demons and some gods, are trapped in their afterworlds. Others have access to both earth and the afterworlds.

Mythean Guardians - Powerful mortals made immortal, or other supernatural beings who serve at the Praesidium. They protect those mortals and Mytheans who are important to the fate of humanity.

Otherworld - The Celtic afterworld. The Celtic gods are forbidden from traveling to earth because they believe that they are required to be in Otherworld to keep it functioning.

Praesidium - The protection division of the Immortal University. Mythean Guardians work here. Their job is to protect those important to humanity and maintain law and order by keeping Mytheans secret from humans and keeping the gods from warring.

Soulceresses - Mytheans who fuel their power by draining the immortal power of other Mytheans' souls. When fueled by the power of others, they can manifest their magic with a thought. They are hated by other Mytheans because of this. They also have the ability to see the evil in a person's soul.

CHAPTER ONE

"Can you repeat that?" Warren Campbell asked, his head buzzing.

"The witches are losing control of their prison." Cadan, his friend and colleague, looked grim. "They think the barrier will break within the week."

"A week?" Warren's stomach pitched.

"Aye. The only prisoner is too powerful to contain any longer. A soulceress called Aurora."

Aurora. The name made the blood pound so hard in his head that his eyes throbbed. He hadn't heard anyone speak of her since she'd stolen his soul more than three hundred years ago.

"You all right, mate?" Cadan asked.

Warren blinked and met his friend's dark gaze. He was spacing out—back to the past when he'd fucked up his entire life.

"Aye." He shook his head, then surged to his feet. He had to get his act together. "I'll go see them and figure out how we can help."

"I'll come too."

"Ah, doona worry about it. You've done enough by telling me." More than that, he didn't want Cadan to know the truth about him. Closest friend or not, the fact that Warren was a monster without a soul was something he didn't want to share.

"Aye, well, you know the witches. Prideful lot. Won't seek help 'til it blows up in their faces."

Which made his job a hell of a lot harder. As the head of the Praesidium, the security division of the Immortal University, it was Warren's job to keep things like this from happening.

Intent on doing so, Warren strode out of his office and down the beautiful old hallway of his building on the university campus. Cadan kept pace with him, ignoring Warren's assertions that his help wasn't needed.

Cadan was a Mythean Guardian, as the warriors who worked for the Praesidium were called, and was tasked with protecting the individuals most important to humanity while keeping the dangerous Mytheans like Aurora in check. He was also his closest friend and nosy as hell.

Which meant he was right on Warren's arse as he strode through the great atrium that marked the entrance to the Praesidium's building and pushed out through the heavy wooden doors.

"You're acting damned strange. What the hell's the matter?" Cadan asked as they descended the stone stairs leading to the cobblestone courtyard.

Warren ignored him and focused on the stone buildings rising on all sides of the courtyard, their gray faces dour on this *dreich* day. The sun couldn't beat its way past the heavy gray clouds, and it suited his mood just fine. He strode across

2

the courtyard toward the rolling green hills surrounding the main part of campus. The witches kept to themselves in cottages near the forest. Private, but still within the protection of the university.

"Seriously, mate, what the hell is wrong?" Cadan demanded. "You look like death."

Where would he start? With the fact that the soulceress who owned his soul and could use it to power her own evil magic was the one who would be released? Or perhaps with the deaths he'd caused that had landed him in this mess? That everything he'd worked for was about to come crashing down around his head? That he lacked any humanity at all?

No. He'd kept those secrets for years and would continue to keep them. The life he'd created here at the Immortal University wasn't perfect, but it was something good he'd worked hard to create out of the ashes of his past. Aurora might have made him into a soulless monster, but he'd tried to do good with his life in the years following the loss of his soul and his humanity.

"I'm fine. Just doona like the idea of this soulceress getting out, that's all," he said.

Out of the corner of his eye, he saw Cadan shrug. His friend didn't buy his excuses, but Warren couldn't bring himself to care.

They arrived at the lushly gardened section of the university that housed the witches' cottages and strode down the path leading to the main cottage in the middle. Roses climbed up the gray stone, pink and red and yellow, all vibrantly in bloom despite the fact that it was a dreary November day. Smoke drifted from a chimney that speared up from the side of the slate roof and the windows were aglow with golden light.

Good, they were within. He banged on the wooden door, meeting his friend's eyes as he did so. Concern tightened Cadan's brow, and Warren realized he probably looked crazed. He tried to flatten his features into calm even as his insides roiled.

"Be quiet," a voice hissed from within.

Warren turned to see one of the witches peering through a little slot in the door. Her eyes blazed green and threatening.

"I'm here to talk about the problem with your prison in the aether," he said.

It was the only prison of its type, a jail without bars or stone. It floated within the aether, that ephemeral substance connecting earth and the afterworlds—known to mortals as the heavens and hells of their religions. It was between here and nowhere, and as such was impossible for him to manipulate. Only the witches had access because they had created the prison.

"We're working on it. Right now, in fact. And you're going to screw it up. Come back tomorrow."

"Now." Warren's voice rumbled.

The witch squinted, glowering. "Tomorrow. We're in the middle of a containment spell. You're going to screw us up. We're trying to shore up the boundaries and you're messing with our concentration. *Come back tomorrow.*"

Warren frowned, but the seriousness of her voice penetrated. A flash of light bursting from the windows convinced him. If they were doing what they could, he wouldn't interfere.

For now.

"Tomorrow," he said.

She slammed the little slot in the door shut.

Warren heaved a frustrated sigh and pinched the bridge of his nose. A huge part of him wanted Aurora to be released so that he could hunt her and retrieve his soul. *No.* The risk to others was too great if she was released. She could aetherwalk away from the university as soon as she escaped, free to wreak havoc anywhere she chose. There was no telling how long it'd take him to find her, or what she could do in the interim. He'd made a vow to protect others when he'd joined the Praesidium. Serving his own selfish needs at the expense of the safety of others was not an option.

He met Cadan's worried eyes. "We're done here."

Cadan nodded. "Come on, let me buy you a pint. Work day's almost over."

"Thanks, but nay. Go back to your Diana."

"I've got time. She'll be in the library for another couple of hours."

Warren liked Cadan's woman, an American scholar who was the reincarnate of Boudica. But his friend would be happier with her this evening, no matter how much he protested. Warren was shite company right now.

"I've got some things to take care of. Give my best to Diana." He clapped Cadan on the shoulder, then spun and strode away, desperate to get some space and clear his head.

The possibility that Aurora might escape made his skin feel like it was stretched too tight over his muscles. He felt trapped in his own body, torn between duty and possibility. He spun on his heel, changing direction and heading to his house instead of back to his office. All he needed was some space.

He told himself he'd do the right thing by seeing to it that she stayed in prison.

But he couldn't say if he believed it.

CHAPTER TWO

"It's a freaking miserable night to be hunting rogues," Esha Connor whispered to Chairman Meow, her feline familiar.

They crept silently through the darkened tunnels of the Edinburgh underground, each dodging the deepest puddles in the worn dirt floor. Unrelenting rain had leaked through the porous ceiling, which was actually the street above, and Esha could feel the Chairman's foul mood. It matched her own, which was the reason she'd leapt at the job to kill the rogue demon who'd been lurking down here.

She caught sight of a cluster of remnant shadows to her left and gave them a wide berth. Shadows of old evil that lingered after the death of the evildoer were thick down in the underground—one of the reasons Edinburgh was considered the most haunted city in Europe. She could have banished the shadows, but the shadows were relatively harmless and any magical activity might alert her prey.

Anyway, she kind of liked Edinburgh's reputation.

A soft rustling noise made Esha and the Chairman freeze. Esha squinted into the darkness, knowing the

Chairman did the same. She hadn't wanted to alert the demon to her presence before they managed to find him, so she carried no light.

Instead, she instinctively followed her connection with her familiar, whose night vision was far better. But the Chairman was antsy in the unusual damp of the underground, and her skin almost crawled in empathetic annoyance.

It was turning out to be a shitty night.

The rustling grew louder and the smell more rank. Like dead bodies and misery. She covered her mouth and nose with the sleeve of her shirt. The Chairman crowded up against her legs. With a tinge of dread, she held out her right hand and willed a bright fireball into existence in her palm.

"Ugh," she said at the sight of her prey.

The Chairman hissed. In less than a second, she took in the small cavern that opened up from where they stood. A tall but spindly red demon crouched along one wall, some kind of body part—she didn't want to dwell on which—gripped in its claws. Red splattered the walls and more unidentifiable pieces of gore littered the floor.

The Chairman's revulsion, combined with her own, made her gag.

Disappointed, she pumped more power into the fireball and flung it at the demon. It shrieked. She flinched.

The Chairman turned to smoke, becoming incorporeal so that the noise and other earthly threats couldn't hurt him.

Bile rose in her throat as she watched the demon burn. She made herself watch so she could be certain that she'd accomplished the job, even though she wanted to turn away to save her appetite.

When the demon was nothing but ash, she waved her hand and forced a cleansing wind through the dark space. It was the wind of time, which she used rarely, and never in the presence of another except her familiar.

Time accelerated within the wind — in this case, enough to disintegrate the gore into dust, as though a hundred years had passed.

She felt grief for the mortal families who would never know what had happened to their loved ones, but she couldn't leave the bodies down here to be discovered by mortal police. They were unlikely to find the place since they didn't know it existed, but she couldn't take the chance.

Remaining secret from mortals was a Mythean's number-one priority and one of the main goals of the Immortal University, her employer. To ignore the importance of secrecy made one a rogue. A lesser criminal than the one she had just slain, but a rogue nonetheless. If one alerted the mortals to the existence of Mytheans—creatures from myth made real by mortal belief—then one would be targeted for imprisonment or death.

In which case, Esha was sent to deal with the lawbreaker.

"Come on, let's get a drink," she said to the cat and turned to make her way out of the underground. After that, she sure as hell needed one. She'd been in a pissy mood lately, and this rogue hunt had been an opportunity to get some aggression out.

It was one reason she liked her job as a mercenary for the university. Esha was a soulceress, the only one in Britain, and she was perfectly suited to her field, given her ability to see the shadows of evil that lingered around a person. Without a doubt, she could determine if the one she'd been sent to kill was deserving of death.

Since they were no longer worried about running into a rogue, it didn't take long for Esha and the Chairman to get out of the underground. They exited through an opening in the cliff beneath Edinburgh Castle, close to the Grassmarket and some of Edinburgh's older pubs.

A quick sprint through the rain and soon she strolled into an ancient little pub, looking for a man to take her mind off things. Stormy winds slammed the heavy wooden door behind her as she shook the raindrops off her short, honey-brown leather jacket.

"Who do you think we'll find tonight?" she whispered to the Chairman, who had turned to smoke again when they'd entered the mortal-run establishment.

He glided along next to her, invisible to all eyes but hers. He couldn't answer her, but no matter. She knew what she'd find at The White Stag. A willing man to make her forget *him*. She didn't go for one-night stands often, but since a real relationship was out of the question for her kind because soulceresses were reviled, she'd gotten used to making do.

"A pint of Tennent's," she told the bartender.

As he pulled her pint, she turned and leaned back against the worn oak bar and scanned the wooden-walled room that was crowded with little tables and small leather-backed chairs, searching for a guy who looked dangerous enough to be intriguing but shallow enough not to mind a one-night stand. And definitely mortal. He had to be mortal.

Her brows shot up when she caught sight of a table of giggling witches in the corner of the pub. Their familiars had turned to smoke as well.

"Damn," she muttered, and turned around to lean on her elbows on the bar. What were they doing here?

Mytheans didn't normally come to mortal pubs. She hadn't expected them to be here since they generally liked to keep to their own kind, especially when drinking. It was one of the reasons she liked to hang out in mortal pubs; she didn't have to be reminded why she was alone. Like a high-schooler who didn't have a lunch table full of friends, she found it easier to go to the library when the lunch bell rang. Or a mortal bar, where she didn't expect there to be other Mytheans cringing when she walked by.

"Bunch of losers and half-rate spell chanters," she muttered to the Chairman.

When his warmth pressed up against her leg, she looked down to see that he'd gone corporeal for a moment to comfort her. Then back to smoke. A small smile pulled at her lips, but it faded as soon as she peeked over her shoulder at the other witches. Still laughing, like girls in movies always did when they were out in a group.

She spun to face the door and head out, then stopped. She didn't give a damn what they thought. The bartender finally handed over her beer, and she figured she might as well get half of what she'd come for.

Anyway, she wouldn't have to worry about steering clear of the other witches because there was no doubt that they'd steer clear of her. Smart. She'd suck the power right out of them and enjoy every second. Oh, they'd regenerate it eventually, but no immortal liked giving up their energy to a soulceress.

It wasn't like she could help how she collected power, but no one cared about the details when they felt the extra power that made them immortal slipping from their souls. They didn't actually become mortal, just weaker for a little while as they temporarily lost whatever special ability their species possessed.

She sidled down the bar toward a towering man at the end. "Hey, handsome," she said, giving him a bold once-over. Not bad, for a mortal.

He returned the gesture, apparently liking what he saw, if his grin was any indication. "Hello, lassie. American, are you? On a bit of vacation?"

She smiled when she heard his rough brogue; he was a local. And a damn fine one, at that. Not that she'd keep him around past tonight. Relationships between mortals and Mytheans always ended in disaster. The life-span differential was a bitch. But he'd do fine for her purposes.

"Sure am." The lie slipped easily off her tongue. After they'd slept together and he'd chipped away at the despicable block of loneliness sitting in her chest, it would be easier to say she had a flight to catch than to explain that she didn't date. Mortals eventually died on you. And it hurt. "What do you do?"

What the hell was *she* doing here?

Warren's eyes were glued on the entrance to the pub where Esha stood, shaking the rain from her jacket. When she unzipped the leather, she revealed a plain cotton shirt that was too tight for his peace of mind. He swallowed hard and looked away.

Within seconds, his gaze was dragged back to her. She glanced around the pub, her amber eyes bright. She didn't see him in the darkened corner, and he sat back, no longer intent on leaving.

There was nothing he could do tonight to ensure Aurora wasn't released, and the idea of twiddling his thumbs at home had been unbearable. He'd come here because he wanted a place to think that was far from the university and devoid of Mytheans.

The White Stag had been fine for all of ten minutes. Then the witches had shown up. Initially, he'd been annoyed. They should be hard at work shoring up the aetherwalls of their prison. But then he'd noticed that they were the youngest witches in the coven. Still in training and likely more of a distraction than a help with difficult spells.

Either way, they ruined the anonymity of the place. As he'd been getting up to leave, Esha had walked in.

Now, his eyes tracked her as she sauntered across the pub toward the bar. He liked the way she walked. It was very *her*, with her chipped-shoulder, couldn't-give-a-shite attitude. Her hips swayed in jeans molded to every inch of her. She was tall and lean, all strength and supple muscles that made him think she'd give as good as she got.

He shook his head. Not that it fucking mattered. He couldn't let it matter. She was hell on his celibacy and peace of mind. Iron control kept him sane. She threatened that, and he did his damnedest to avoid her because of it. He'd been pretty successful for the ten years that she'd been at the university.

Until their work had thrown them temporarily together a month ago. Once, she'd asked him why the signals he sent were so hot and cold. She could see that he wanted her as easily as she could see that he resisted it. And she wanted him back. That day, they'd come so close to kissing that he could still feel the heat of her breath.

But he'd pulled away. He'd been an arse to her when she'd asked why. He'd thrown her species in her face. Blaming his rejection on the fact that she was a soulceress was a lie, but it had come out easily, pushed by the panic over what he felt for her.

He could still remember her words. *"Always with the soulcery business. Like I have the fucking plague or something. I really thought you were different, Warren. What's your problem, anyway? You're a damned mystery monster. I don't drain your power, so what have you got against me?"*

He hadn't known how to answer, and his words had only made it worse. He'd hurt her feelings, he knew that much. She'd said that she didn't need him, that she didn't need anybody. He'd almost believed it.

Warren snapped out of his memories of the past at the sight of Esha sidling up to another man at the bar. No matter how bad an idea it was, he couldn't stop himself from becoming jealous. Which was a gods-damned worthless emotion, when everything between them was not only fucked up, it was impossible.

Though Esha lent one ear to the rumbling brogue of the man she'd approached at the bar, her attention was dedicated to scanning the room for enemies. It was a hazard of the job, but she didn't mind, because it wasn't like she left any of her assignments living. She smirked at the thought. But they sometimes had partners in crime who'd like to exact a little vengeance, so keeping a wary eye out was just good business.

She felt the smirk slip from her face when her gaze connected with that of a man sitting alone at a table in the corner of the pub.

No way.

Warren. The man she'd wanted for almost the entire ten years she'd been at the university.

Her heart shivered and goose bumps rose on her arms at the sight of him. The light from a cheery fire cast shadows over his harshly beautiful face. His fierce gaze was trained on her—probably had been since she walked in—and she kicked herself for not noticing.

The voice of the man speaking to her became nothing but a buzz. She licked her lips nervously, but managed to lean back against the bar and glare at Warren. What the hell was he doing here?

"Lassie." The sexy Scot tapped her shoulder and she jerked back to attention, blinking stupidly up at him as her brain returned to the present. She should focus on the hot man who actually liked her, not on the elusive Mythean who treated her like a bug.

Because the mortal doesn't know what you are.

But as she stared up into his handsome face, she could feel Warren's gaze burning into her. Impossible to ignore. She really should try to make him jealous, but her heart wasn't in it.

"I'm sorry. You know—" Shit, she didn't know the Scot's name. Whatever. "It was nice talking to you."

She tried to smile at him, but all she could think about was the man whose gaze continued to light her up from across the room.

She wasn't going to go over there. Avoiding him had been working out really well for her.

But she felt herself turning and her feet carrying her closer to him, her body weaving around raucous pub patrons. He was like a giant planet and she some puny little moon, helplessly drawn to him.

She'd thought there could be more between them, had wanted there to be. From what she could tell, he kept to himself and focused almost all of his energy on work. Where her isolation was forced on her by others—their loss—his was self-imposed. He was the only person she knew who was more isolated than she; it intrigued her.

And it had been a shitty night. If anything, he would distract her. True, he'd kicked her to the curb less than a month ago, and it had hurt, yet she'd slapped a bandage over that wound. She'd suffered worse.

As she made her way to him, she took in the olive sweater stretched over broad shoulders, which tensed as he watched her.

Good. He tied her up in knots; it should be mutual. His otherworldly stature and confident mien made him stand out among the other pub patrons. Golden hair glinted in the firelight, too angelic for what he was capable of.

It was such a contrast to the dark shadows that always hovered at his feet. They were the shadows of evil deeds, visible only to a soulceress. Normally, she'd only see them on rogues or other evil beings, where they clung like a black mist.

But on Warren, they hovered around his ankles, like they couldn't stick to him.

Why would he have them? Was it because she couldn't see his soul? She'd heard of some Mytheans who used magic to hide theirs. Because a Mythean's power originated from his soul, it was closely guarded, even hidden at times.

The whys of his shadows intrigued her. They didn't mesh with the decent guy she knew him to be. He might be a jerk to her, but overall he was good. Too good to have the shadows.

She sank into the chair across from him, holding his green gaze and propping her feet on the chair closest to him. He was so big she could almost feel the heat of him. At nearly six and a half feet, his head would probably brush the low ceiling of the pub, hitting the decorative copper mugs that hung from it.

"So, boss, what brings you here?" she asked, her eyes racing over his face, taking in the features that had haunted her dreams. A strong jaw, full lips, and a loaded gaze. It was a face that had seen a lot of bad. The shadows that hovered around his feet were sometimes reflected in his eyes. She didn't know what he'd done to get those shadows, but she wanted to.

"No' your boss, Esha."

Right. Thanks for the reminder. She was only a consultant, not a full member of his team. She was powerful enough that no one wanted her working against them—hence the invitation to join the university staff and eventually his department, the Praesidium—but her method of collecting the magical energy that fed her power made everyone loath to include her as an actual team member. Not that she cared, of course.

"Semantics." She sipped her beer and looked at him over the rim of her glass. His expression was unreadable, nearly unwelcoming. But she hadn't made a mistake in coming over here; she didn't make mistakes.

"What's with all the Mytheans in a mortal pub?" she asked. He ranked higher than she did, so maybe he'd know.

He shrugged. "What's your reason?"

"Here? I come here all the time." She gestured to the crowd behind her. "Easy pickings."

A disgusted sigh escaped his strong throat. "To replenish your power from unwitting victims?"

She ignored the disgust. She had to, to survive. "Please. Mortals don't have enough to speak of."

It was one of the reasons she usually slept with them instead of the immortal Mytheans. Her unconscious power collection didn't cause mortals the shivery sense of powerlessness that Mytheans felt in her presence. What felt like a hit of glorious energy to her felt like a siphoning of strength for any immortal with whom she came into contact.

Except for Warren.

"So, why is it that I never feel your power? You don't have enough to speak of?" she asked.

Everyone hated her for something she couldn't control, but he was the only one who didn't like her out of spite, because he wasn't even affected by her.

He shrugged again, but she saw a flicker in his eyes.

"You know why I can't feel the power of your soul, but you won't tell me. Cat got your tongue?" She snickered and looked at the shadow that was the Chairman, lounging on a chair next to her.

"There's no' a fae's chance in hell I'm going to tell you."

She frowned as she searched his eyes for any hint, but saw nothing. "Does it have anything to do with the fact that you have shadows that don't stick to you?"

His eyes iced over, but still, she swore they beckoned. She was clearly mad, but she couldn't help herself. "I have no idea what you're talking about."

She shivered. She was pushing him, but she couldn't stop herself. He was a mystery that she'd wanted to solve since she'd met him. "You know, you're pretty much the only one at the university who has shadows. You're different."

Their place of employment was committed to maintaining balance between the heavens and the hells and to protecting earth. Someone evil wouldn't give a damn about keeping the power balance. So if Warren wasn't evil, why did he have shadows?

CHAPTER THREE

"You know nothing of my soul." Warren's fists clenched. But she did, he realized. Not the details, but the cocky soulceress sitting across from him saw enough to know that he'd done such monstrous things that if he still had his soul, it would be as black and empty as space. All the attempts at atonement in the world weren't going to wash him clean.

"I think that no matter what you said before, you want me," she said. "You've been watching me since I walked in here."

True, his subconscious whispered, as her gaze caught and held his. Her eyes captured him. Not merely their shape and color, but what swirled within them. Something unidentifiable, but familiar. Like a window not only into her soul, but into himself as well. Except that he had no way to decipher their contents, no context for the messages they might send. He knew little of her except that she was brave and brash—a cocky mercenary who took no prisoners and asked questions later.

"I want any hot pieces of ass that I see." His tone was harsh, the words a lie. Such a ridiculous lie, but pushing her away was the only way to keep himself sane.

Esha was the one he thought about at night.

"Maybe," she said, and leaned back in her chair.

"Why are you here?" he asked.

"I already told you that."

"No, you dinna. You changed the subject. Why are you here at my table? You were mad as hell last time we spoke." He'd been an arse then, for the same reason he was being one now.

"How insightful of you to notice."

"Just being honest."

She laughed. "Honest that you don't like what I am. Here's the thing, though, that doesn't bother me since I know that you want me. No Mythean likes my species, so why should you be any different? And it's not like I want much from you. Just a distraction."

The smile she gave him told him exactly what kind of distraction she was looking for, and gods, he was tempted. Though her tone was confident, he thought he could see a shadow of something in her eyes that belied the claim that she didn't care. He hated that she expected so little of others. So little for herself.

Gods, she was probably as fucked up as he was. It made him feel less alone.

These were dangerous thoughts. He surged to his feet and skirted the table toward the door. "I'm leaving. Have a good night."

"Good idea." Her voice came from behind him.

She was following him outside.

The pub was small, and they were out the door in seconds. Wind and rain pelted them as he grabbed her arm and swung her into the small alley to the left of the entrance.

He pressed her up against the wall in the darkness and growled, "Why are you following me?"

"How do you know I wasn't heading home?" She pushed at him, then clutched at his sweater, as if she couldn't make up her mind what she wanted from him.

The darkly sensual scent of her pushed through the wet stone smell of the city and coiled around him, reached inside of him, and tugged. So foreign, the smell of a woman this close. Dim street light glinted off coal-black hair and amber eyes. She laced a spell around him. It was the only explanation for his obsession.

He squeezed his eyes shut, knowing that he should look away. Walk away. But he couldn't. The unfamiliar touch of another, something he'd gone without for so long, kept him still. He wanted her touch, her softness, her warmth, so badly that he ached.

In the darkness behind his closed lids, he felt her finger drag over his lips. His cock swelled until it was achingly hard and he barely stopped himself from sucking her finger into his mouth, so desperate was he to taste her.

He hadn't had a woman in so long he'd forgotten how they felt. But that was the point. The forgetting. The simplicity of a life that helped him forget the things that he'd done and that had been done to him. She offered a release from the self-imposed iron cage of control that kept his demons at bay. But he shouldn't want that release.

"I doona want you." His voice was ragged, his shaft thrusting painfully against his fly.

He opened his eyes to see her smiling at him, a devious grin that indicated she recognized his lie.

"No, you don't *want* to want me because of what I am. That's very different from not wanting me."

One of her kind had stolen his soul and made him a monster. He shouldn't want her. He shouldn't like her. He shouldn't feel at all, not if he wanted to keep the demons of his past from howling until his mind cracked.

Good feelings—like those associated with being near her—gave context for bad. His rigidly self-enforced control led to its own kind of peace, which he desperately needed.

Esha fucked with all of that. He should turn around and walk away. Now.

Instead, he leaned closer, his mouth hovering a hairsbreadth from hers. He wanted to be close to her, just for a second. Just long enough to know what it would feel like to be with her. So that he could pull out the memory in the dark loneliness of the night.

Her breath feathered over his lips and he gripped her hips, reveling in the feel of her beneath his hands. She was hot and soft against him and smelled so good that his mind—

"Oh, check it out." A giggling voice filtered into the alley.

The sound of laughing witches disappeared down the street, but rational thought snapped back into place, cold as the Arctic. He pushed away.

"What?" Confusion and lust clouded her eyes as they searched his face. "Why'd you stop?"

Warren's breath heaved out of his lungs as his mind scrambled to understand what he'd almost done. "Because it's a bad fucking idea. You're a damned power leech. A mercenary who's spent decades selling your loyalty to whoever pays the most."

The words were true, but too harsh. He'd said them to remind himself of what she was and why he shouldn't want her. With Aurora nearly on the loose, he couldn't be distracted by Esha.

Comprehension cleared the confusion from her eyes. Hurt and anger followed. Her jaw hardened. "Fuck you, Warren. I came here for a lay. I figured you were just as good as the next guy. It's not often that I get to fuck a Mythean."

Jealousy tore through him at the idea of her with another, but he crushed it. "I'm the only immortal you canna destroy and I'm no' interested. Go find yourself a mortal to play with."

CHAPTER FOUR

17th century, Scottish Highlands

"All I knows is, there's witches here. In this very town."

"Aye. I heard that red-haired Megan is one. Only a matter of time afore they catch her."

Warren slouched farther into his seat in the dark little pub and tried to ignore the voices behind him. It was all the same these days—villagers grumbling about witches and ridiculous hysteria about black magic. None of it existed, of course, but it didn't stop the cruel idiots from buying into the madness that was being imported from Edinburgh and farther south.

He gripped the tankard in his hand and focused on the amber liquid within, having to forcibly repress the desire to stand up and smash it over the heads of the bastards behind him. Their prejudice cost good lives. Had cost the life of his grandmother, a batty old woman, but not a witch. It hadn't stopped them from putting her on the pyre, though.

"You'll want to loosen your grip there, lad, before you lose your drink." The deep voice knocked him out of his foul memories and he looked up to see Bruce.

"About time you got here," he said, and loosened his grip. He couldn't do anything to the bastards behind him. Like cockroaches, there were too many of them. Kill those and a dozen more with the same deadly, moronic beliefs would replace them. And he'd be hanged for murder, unable to do what good he could. Because even if he hated the type of bastard sitting behind him, he loved his clan and wouldn't watch their women burned.

"I've got a pregnant woman who needs to make it to the port," Bruce said under his breath. "Tomorrow night."

Warren's lips tightened. A pregnant woman. Bloody hell. Would the horrors never cease?

"From our village?" He didn't know of any pregnant women being targeted as witches. As part of a covert band of individuals who helped smuggle women to safety once they'd been labeled witches, he should know of her if she were from here.

"Nay. From the other side of the mountain. She's got kin in America. Now that she's only a trial away from going up on the pyre, she's decided to join them."

Warren couldn't laugh at the dark joke. It hit too close to home. The trial would find her guilty. If his comrades smuggled her to him, he'd get her through the forest and to the port. Safely, if they could stay out of sight of his fellow citizens.

The next night arrived moonless and rainy. A terrible night to try to get through the woods. Worse, the pregnant woman, called Avera, looked to be about a day away from giving birth. Wrapped in a dark cloak, she was slender but for the great belly that slowed her walk to a waddle.

"Are you sure you can do this? We have miles to go through the forest," he asked her as the rain pounded down upon them. They stood on the side of the road where his colleagues had delivered her to him.

"I've no other choice."

A rustle from the farm cart behind them drew his attention and another cloaked figure climbed out, apparently done talking to the driver.

"Mother, let me go with you," the figure said as she approached. Warren caught sight of golden eyes and a strong face. The woman looked too old to be the daughter of the pregnant woman.

"Nay." Avera's voice was hard. "You won't survive in the New World. There's no' enough power there."

Warren frowned at the odd turn of phrase.

"How will you survive?" There were tears in the younger woman's voice.

"I've no choice, you know that. You canna protect me. You'll die trying, and I won't have that. In a few years, if more of our kind go to the New World and you can survive there, I'll send for you. But for now, you must look out for yourself without me to burden you."

The woman reached out to grasp her mother's arm. "But—"

"No! You're at risk as it is. This man will protect me. Go home. I'll send for you." Her voice brooked no argument.

Still, the younger woman tried. Finally, she huffed and turned to him. In a flash, her face hardened. In a dark voice, she said, "Protect her. Or I will come for you, and you will regret it with every fiber of your being."

A shiver ran through Warren as the girl turned from him and hugged her mother before climbing back into the farm cart. Lantern light glinted off her face. Her eyes flashed, changing color to pitch black. He didn't believe in magic, but as he watched the cart rumble down the dark road, the chill wouldn't leave his bones.

He shook it away and looked at the woman who stood cloaked before him. She was his responsibility, a role he took seriously enough without the daughter's eerie threats.

"Come," he said. "We must make it through the forest by dawn. Are you meeting someone at the port?"

"Nay. I'll meet the father of my child in the New World."

"Excellent. I will get you there."

She nodded and they set off toward the port. It was the worst journey he'd made by far, the dark and the wet making the travel rough and miserable. They had to avoid the road, however, or risk facing the witch hunters who had figured out that someone was smuggling suspected witches to the port. They hiked for hours, though it felt like days.

"Fucking rain—we'll never find them." The voice carried through the forest, so quiet that Warren wasn't sure of the words.

"Shite. Avera, you need to hide. Quick, near these rocks." A chill ran over his skin as he doused their lantern and tried to hide Avera among the rocks. How many were there? Were they looking for this woman?

When she was crouched against the rocks, nearly invisible in the dark, Warren withdrew his sword and hid himself behind a large oak a dozen feet in front of her. He wouldn't draw their attention, but he'd be ready if they found him.

A light appeared in the forest, small but growing larger as the men approached. Five of them. Bloody hell. His breath grew short in his throat, and he had to force himself not to gasp raggedly.

"Oy, I think I hear something," a man said, and Warren stiffened at the proximity of his voice.

A sword was pointed at Warren's throat a moment later. No more hiding. He raised his own blade and the clash of steel echoed through the forest. The battle was fast and hard, and when the lantern dropped from the hand of the smallest man, near dark crashed around them. He couldn't make out a single face as he felled two opponents, but he felt the slice of their blades and the keen edge of victory when their bodies hit the ground.

He was on his knees in the mud when a sharp scream broke out over the clash of swords. Sick fear for Avera welled in him, crushing the dark joy he felt in slaying his enemies. He had to get to her.

On a spurt of blind luck, he sank his blade into the gut of the man looming above him. He staggered to his feet, tripped over the body of one of the other soldiers he'd slain, and immediately collided with a fourth.

He gripped his sword more tightly, ignoring the blood that dripped down his arm, and slashed it across the middle of the man in front of him. The hooded figure, more apparition than reality, stumbled but didn't go down. Damn bastard was tough, but it had been a good night for Warren. Three kills, but he'd make it a fourth and get Avera back and to the port.

Warren parried, blocking the other man's strikes, before sinking his blade into his opponent's neck. The harsh gurgle of breath was music to his ears as he jerked his blade free. He'd always liked killing these idiots. He was doing the human race a favor.

He'd just spun on his heel to race to Avera when pain exploded in his head. The last thing he remembered was falling like a great tree in the forest, filled with fear that he had failed Avera.

When he finally opened his eyes, pale golden sunlight filtered through the trees above and turned the raindrops to glittering diamonds. He groaned and pressed a hand to his head. A lump crusted with dried blood twinged when he touched it.

The memories of the pregnant woman that he'd failed pierced his brain, and he jerked upright, too distraught to curse at the pain in his head. He glanced around frantically, but saw nothing except the bodies of the four men he'd felled last night.

There must have been a fifth, or more, who'd taken Avera. He staggered to his feet, intent on tracking them and tearing the heads from their bodies. The sight of one of the fallen men caught his eye and he turned, his breath caught in his throat like a boulder.

The cloak was pulled back from the face, now illuminated by the morning sun. The sight hit Warren like lightning, knocking the foundation of his life out from beneath his feet. He stumbled backward

Alan. He'd killed his own cousin.

Warren raised his hand, stared at the blood that coated it. He swallowed hard, stumbled, and looked for the next body.

His feet carried him to it, though he wasn't even sure if his brain consciously gave the command.

When he stared down at the face that had been hidden by the night's pitch black, a buzzing started up between his ears that drowned out his sense of self.

Donal. Alan's brother. Something hot trailed down Warren's face as he stared at the face of his cousin, the boy who'd been like a brother to him.

Dread wedged into every corner of his body as he looked at the other two bodies. They lay close, their crumpled forms near enough to make out their features.

Warren's knees gave out and the ground rose up to meet him.

Eoin and Gus. Four brothers. His cousins. He'd killed them. When had they become involved with the witch hunters? His own efforts to save the falsely accused were a secret, but witch hunters were usually not so secretive in their dealings.

But he'd killed them, and the dark was no excuse. Pain and regret surged within him, a tidal wave that swamped rational thought and tore a roar from his throat.

When he returned to himself, minutes or hours later, he remembered that Avera was still missing. Pregnant and very likely within the grasp of witch hunters.

He could barely feel his body as he stood. His cousins deserved a proper burial, no matter that they'd been involved in evil at the time of their death. He deserved just punishment for their murders, no matter what the light had been like when he'd killed them.

But first, he had to find Avera. Before it was too late.

It took two days. Two miserable days of combing the three nearby towns—*nearby* meaning something different in the Highlands than it did elsewhere—to stumble upon a scene more grisly than the one he'd left behind in the forest.

The crowd screamed and cheered, a riotous mob of mindless hate swarming a pyre in the middle of the square. His stomach pitched, but far worse was the sight of the woman on the pyre.

Avera. Bound by harsh rope to the post behind her, her black hair whipped in a wind he couldn't feel. He pushed his way through the crowd, desperate to free her, when her voice rang out over the screams of the mob.

"Release me! Release my daughter! Or you shall all die!" Her shriek was unholy, terrifying in its intensity and volume.

Warren was close enough to see her eyes turn black and her hair whip ever faster around her head. He realized then that there was no wind. Whatever force surrounded Avera, it was not natural. The man holding the flaming torch ignored her warning and tossed the brand onto the kindling at the base of her pyre. Three more did the same.

He pushed forward through the crowd, determined to free her and her unborn child. She shrieked as the flames grew, and as he neared, he saw that her belly was far smaller than it had been. The wail of a baby drew his attention. To the left of Avera stood a woman cradling an infant.

"Your devil's spawn shall go after you," cried the man who'd thrown the first torch.

Avera's head whipped toward him then, her eyes pitch-black holes in her skull. "Die!" she shrieked, and the man fell to his knees, clutching his neck. Her head whipped toward another man who had thrown the torch, and she screamed her bloodthirsty call again. He too fell to his knees, clutching his neck.

By now, the flames had reached halfway up her body, and Warren was still too far away. She was shrieking, but she'd channeled her pain into cries of "Die!" that she directed at members of the jeering audience until more than a dozen of them were on their knees or fallen altogether.

A true witch. Conflict rose in Warren's heart, but he pushed on all the same, knowing even now that he was too late. She was consumed by the flames, her screams silenced.

He reached the pyre finally, a minute from saving her. It had happened so fast. He had no idea if she was good or evil, but she was dead and it didn't matter.

But her child was not.

He charged around the pyre, intent on reaching the babe clutched under the arm of a terrified woman who bent over a fallen man. It was the work of a moment to pull the babe free. One look at the amber eyes of the squalling infant told him it belonged to the witch. The eyes were no normal infant's blue.

Confirmed that the baby was Avera's, he clutched it to his chest and sprinted across the back side of the square, away from the villagers who screamed and cried over the bodies of their loved ones. They'd stop him if they caught him stealing the witch's child. He had only one chance to get it to safety.

When he reached the quiet of the forest that surrounded the village, he stopped, the breath heaving in and out of his lungs as the infant cried.

What the hell was he to do now? He had a day-old infant. Nay, maybe hours old. It would die if he didn't find a wet nurse. It would die if anyone knew the identity of its mother.

Should it die? Had Avera been evil? Was this child?

He looked down into the face of the newborn. He had no idea. But he couldn't hand it over to its death without knowing. So he took it to the port, a place large enough that he found a poor woman to nurse the baby.

After arranging payment, he left the woman's humble home and set out onto the street of the port. He would find the sister and turn over the babe. He stopped in his tracks. Could he trust the sister, or was she a witch too? She had been fierce when he'd met her, her eyes flashing black like Avera's. And, witch or no, how the hell would he even find her? He had no idea where she lived.

He spun on his heel in the middle of the crowded little street, miserable and lost. The babe had a father in the New World, he remembered. It was the only thing that would work.

He ran to the docks and was relieved to find that Avera's ship had not yet sailed. A quick conversation revealed that it would sail the next morning. This was safest. The sister couldn't be trusted. He would find a wet nurse to travel with the babe and get it out of Scotland. It wasn't safe here, and though life in the New World was uncertain, it was better than a place where the babe with strange amber eyes would be hunted.

It took the full night to find a nurse to go with the babe, and nearly the entirety of his wealth, little as it was. He watched the ship until it was but a pinprick in the distance, then set off along the forest road to his village.

He was nearly home when he came upon the woman in the forest. His steps stuttered, then stopped. She stood twenty feet away, golden and light, her shining blonde hair and amber eyes bright in the dimming light.

"Warren." Her voice belied the lightness of her being. It was dark and heavy and her eyes changed to match. "You are called Warren, I have learned. I am Aurora."

He said nothing and reached for his sword.

She laughed, a crazed sound, and her eyes blackened to coal. "That won't help you."

"I tried to save her." She had some kind of inexplicable power. Powers she'd spoken of with her mother in the forest when he'd met her.

"You let her die." Pain twisted her face as tears spilled down her cheeks. "It was your job to protect her when she couldn't protect herself. The baby sapped her power, and she relied on you! We trusted you!"

He flinched at the volume of her scream, and the pain in it. Her golden hair whipped around her head, borne on that unnatural wind that had surrounded Avera when she'd worked her magic. Two great oaks that stood behind Aurora cracked down the middle and toppled over. The ground trembled beneath his feet.

"This isn't possible," he said, shaking his head.

"Oh, but it is. My mother forbade me to collect the power of souls for fear it would draw the attention of bloodthirsty mortals. But she is dead, and I have no need of her rules!" She flung her arm out and more trees toppled. "I've killed those who burned her, and I shall kill you too. You turned my mother over to those beasts!"

Rage welled dark within him. "Turned her over? I killed my kin to protect her!"

"Lies!" she screamed. Her eyes were black and crazed. She trembled, from grief or from the power raging through her, he couldn't tell. "Perhaps I should burn what you love!"

"No!" Warren gripped his sword and stepped forward, but she'd already thrown out an arm and a jet of fire shot from her fingertips. It licked at the damp underbrush, igniting so quickly that it was clearly propelled by evil.

He lunged back as the fire roared high and hot, devouring the land and charging in the direction of his village.

Nay. He'd already killed his family. Not his village. Not because of him.

"Doona do this!" he yelled, now separated from Aurora by a wall of fire. He could see her through the flames, tears streaking down her face and her eyes black with madness and rage.

"Anything! I'll give you anything!" he yelled.

"You have nothing I want!" she screamed, and waved her arm again. The fire shot hotter and higher, and he fell to his knees.

"Anything!" The smoke was choking his lungs and burning his eyes. Had it reached the village yet?

It felt like an eon, trapped in the heat with visions of his village burning, but eventually her voice carried, dark and powerful, across the flames. "Your soul. You'll give me your soul."

CHAPTER FIVE

Warren jerked out of the trance into which he'd fallen, his breath sawing in and out of his lungs. The taste of smoke lingered, now only a memory but too real for his sanity. He scrubbed his hands over his eyes and looked around the room.

He was still seated on the floor of his office in the quiet corner by the window. He used it for meditating when the memories of the past became too much, and although it normally cleared his mind and helped him find a bit of quiet, in this case it had sucked him back into his nightmares.

He heaved out a breath and stood. Perhaps he'd drifted off. It was still early and he hadn't slept well after the encounter with Esha, but he'd never before fallen asleep sitting up. Hell, he might be losing his mind as Aurora had. More likely, Aurora's near release was just dredging up the things he'd tried to pack away.

He was a soulless monster. Neither mortal nor Mythean. Mytheans were born to be immortals on earth, with varied powers. Only decapitation or grievous magic could kill their bodies and send their souls to an afterworld. But he was an aberration. A Mythean with no soul and no humanity. Without his soul to take him to an afterworld, he could not die. To many, it would be a blessing. To him, it was a curse.

The university had invited him to join them shortly after his transition. They'd tracked Aurora's destructive magic to his village and found him where he'd passed out in the midst of the fire. He'd been totally unharmed by the blaze, and they'd explained what he'd become.

He'd accepted their invitation because he had nowhere else to go. His clan would realize he was immortal, and he couldn't stay among them as a monster who'd killed his kin. There was no escape from his deeds and no way to return to his home.

When he'd arrived at the university, barely able to comprehend everything he saw there, he'd learned that Aurora had been imprisoned for stealing too many souls. The university couldn't make her return the souls, but they could imprison her for her crimes. They would have executed her if they could have, but she was too powerful and too dangerous. The imprisonment spell had allowed them to maintain their distance but contain the threat.

He'd spent the last three hundred years so close to her and his soul, yet so far away. He'd have killed her to get it back if he could have, but with her locked away, it was impossible.

If the witches couldn't maintain the aetherwalls of their prison and she escaped, he could kill her to get his soul back. But it would be a dangerous hunt, one during which Aurora would be free to wreak whatever havoc she chose.

He'd found a second home here when he'd had to leave his clan. More importantly, he'd found a purpose. Protecting

Mytheans and mortals from the misery that had befallen him had become his life. He would uphold his agreement to put the university and the safety of other Mytheans before himself. Without his soul, his word was all he had.

With that in mind, he checked his watch and saw that it was late enough that he could visit the witches. He left his office and strode down the quiet corridors of the Praesidium, then through the early morning stillness across the rolling hills to their main cottage. When he found no one there, he checked the greenhouse that sat at the edge of their little collection of buildings. They often worked there, as well.

"Hello?" he said as he ducked inside the little glass door.

"Back here!" a musical voice called.

He walked through the vibrant green oasis, the scent of flowers and dark dirt permeating the warm air.

Behind a group of fig trees he found Cora, the one he sought, and several younger witches. An orange tree behind Cora exploded when an errant spell hit it. Fragrant orange juice dripped down the glass wall.

The witches preferred to have their workspaces and living quarters on the farthest edges of the campus for this very reason. Practicing witches couldn't always be sure where their spells would land, and the young witches he'd seen in the pub last night were currently destroying the orange tree.

"Hi, Warren," Cora said, her American accent so similar to Esha's that he had to shake his mind away from the soulceress. "Thanks for meeting me here. Sorry I wasn't at the cottage. Why don't we talk over there?"

He followed her to a more secluded corner, where they took seats on wooden boxes.

"You're here about Aurora," she said. The marmot riding on her shoulder stared at him, unblinking. He looked away from it to meet Cora's eyes.

"Aye. Can you keep her locked up?" He asked it even though, selfishly, he wanted Aurora to be released so he could hunt her. But keeping her locked away was the right thing to do for the university—she was far too dangerous to be released. She was better off in the witches' aether prison, that dark nowhere that kept her away from humanity.

"That's impossible," Cora said.

"Seriously? There's nothing you can do about it?"

"We tried everything, but the barrier to our prison will break within the week. Aurora is too strong, and we just aren't as powerful as we used to be." Cora shoved her pink hair off her forehead and scowled. "She's the only one in the prison, but we still don't have enough power to keep her there."

"Why not? You're the ones who locked her up in the first place."

"Sure, the Witch Council locked her up, but only a few of us were alive at the time. Calista, the one who created the spell that put the barrier on the prison, passed on to her afterworld a few hundred years ago. We've been struggling all these years to keep the boundary closed. Without her, and with the passing of several of our most powerful witches, it's become too much. We have to recast the original spell, but without a Mythean like her, we can't."

"Like her?"

She nodded, reaching up to snag a lizard that ran across a draping petunia hanging above her head. The little creature scrambled across her knuckles before leaping onto her other shoulder and perching there. "Calista was a soulceress, the only kind powerful enough to lock up another of her species. With our help, of course."

"Witches hate soulceresses." The rivalry between the two most magical beings was legendary. "Why would you work with one of them?"

"Well, yeah. But she was different. She agreed to work with us in exchange for protection from the Burnings, which was great because she could do things we couldn't. Haven't had anyone as strong as she was in years."

Warren nodded. Calista had been wise to join the university to avoid the Burnings. The mortal witch hunts had incited a similar frenzy in Mytheans. If witches were the bogeymen to mortals, then soulceresses were their Mythean equivalent because of their ability to siphon off the power of others' souls. They'd fallen prey to the frenzy and used it as an excuse to hunt those they feared. The university didn't support the Burnings because it was contrary to the law and order that had become their model for staying under the mortals' radar, but most Mytheans didn't care. They hunted soulceresses anyway. Nearly every soulceress in Britain had been killed during what had become known as the Burnings.

"So you need another soulceress to shore up the boundary to her prison," Warren said.

"Exactly."

Warren rose. "I'm going to see if I can take care of that for you."

"I know whom you're thinking of. Trust me, we've thought of it too. But she'll never help us."

"It's her job." He'd gone to the effort of getting her to work for the university, and damned if he wouldn't make sure she did her job.

Though it wasn't surprising that Cora doubted Esha. Ten years ago, when word of a soulceress come to Scotland had reached the university, they'd sought her out and watched her. She'd been a free-market mercenary, killing only Mytheans, and while she hadn't killed any pregnant mothers or schoolchildren, she wasn't particularly picky about her contracts. He'd invited her to join the university because she was too dangerous not to have on their side. When everything in him had screamed to leave her be, to keep her away from the university because of what another of her kind had done to him, he'd found the will to remember his vows to do what was best for his job.

"You really think she'll agree to help us?" Cora's words shook him out of his thoughts.

"I'll see to it that she agrees. She'll come to you. Tonight."

"All right, if you say so." Doubt and hope warred in her brown eyes.

"I do." Warren turned and left the sticky heat of the greenhouse, wishing there were any other soulceress he could ask for help.

There was no reason she would want to help him, not after he'd been such an arse to her, but she was his only hope.

CHAPTER SIX

Esha leaned on the sill of her open window, nursing bad coffee and an even worse hangover. The bright noon sun burned cruelly into her retinas as she gazed out at the university campus.

She lived in a tower on the north side, which gave her an excellent view of the rolling green hills and the massive stone buildings of the university in the distance. The tower had once been a guard tower, but the space at the top had been modified into a flat long before she'd joined the university staff.

Last night had been such a bust. She laughed bitterly. But it *was* both entertaining and horrifying that she, Esha, queen of the outcasts with no court, was mooning after one of the most respected members of the university. And that she would choose to pursue her infatuation in such a spastic way.

But she was so done with that. After he'd left her, she'd gone back into the pub, picked a spot in the corner, and switched from beer to whiskey. Contrary to popular belief, the whiskey had actually cleared her head.

Warren wanted her, but he was too much of a coward or an asshole to admit it. And she was an idiot who had tried twice to convince him to give her a chance. *Twice.*

Embarrassing is what that was. She needed to get her act together.

The Chairman meowed, deep and low, as if he could read her thoughts and agreed.

"Oh, shut up," she said, glaring at him.

He just watched her with knowing citrine eyes from where he lounged by the little fire.

"Be nice or I'll extinguish your fire," she said.

He gave her a look that said *as if.* But he was right. She was all talk. She'd never douse his beloved fire, and it was evidence of how screwed up Warren made her that she would even suggest it.

Esha looked back out at the emerald green of the lawn and the sapphire blue of the sky. Everything was shot through with jewel tones today, as if the earth didn't know that she was in a shitty mood. She tried to focus on the beauty in front of her, but was instead drawn into her memory, to the time when her vague interest in her distant colleague had bloomed into stupid infatuation.

A few years ago, she'd just finished making a contracted kill in Edinburgh and had been walking back to her car through the quiet city streets. It had been a Sunday, hence the quiet lull, which had made it easy for her to spot a familiar figure ducking into the Veterans' League.

Curiosity had tugged at her. What was Warren doing at the Veterans' League? It was for mortals, not Mytheans, and the two rarely mixed.

Because it had been a drizzly gray morning and his head had been bowed, he hadn't noticed her. But she'd never mistake him for anyone else. Determined to figure out what he was doing, she'd crept into the alley at the side of the building and peered through the rain-streaked window to see Warren in a makeshift workshop with a couple of other men.

The others were younger, boys almost, and one was missing a leg while another wore some type of brace on his back. From the wars in the Middle East, she assumed, since it was one of the few places that British mortal soldiers were fighting. They'd been building beautiful wooden furniture in the workshop, and Warren looked to be helping the men with their projects.

He was teaching them?

Esha had returned every Sunday for a month and peered through the same window, never making contact with him. She'd eventually confirmed that Warren was some kind of mentor to injured soldiers suffering the effects of war, and the medium he used to help them was woodworking.

But he had also benefited. His step was a little lighter, and the lines around his eyes a little less deep when he left.

She'd forced herself to stop going after she figured out what he was doing. As much as she liked watching him, stalking him was just weird.

Her phone buzzed and jerked her out of the past. Gratefully, she shook the memories away and turned from the window to find her phone.

She scowled when she saw the name attached to the text message.

Warren. Of course. And it was about work, so she couldn't ignore it.

She sighed, disgusted and annoyed with the way her day was going, then glared at her coffee and chugged it. It was lukewarm and kind of gross, but she needed the caffeine if she was going to face him with this hangover.

An hour later, after standing in the shower and staring at the wall for twenty minutes mulling over what an idiot she'd been, Esha tromped across the rolling campus to Warren's office. The last of autumn's leaves crunched beneath her boots.

"Why do you think he wants to meet with us?" Esha asked the Chairman.

Though the Chairman didn't answer, she was pretty sure she saw him shrug his little cat shoulders. She took it as a sign to continue talking as they reached a cluster of stone buildings. She might as well. He was her sounding board when her only other friend, Ana, wasn't around.

"I wouldn't even be doing this if it wasn't for work." But Warren's parting jab about loyalty had stung. He was wrong. She stuck by her commitments, and she'd made one to the Praesidium when she'd joined.

The Chairman meowed his support. She glanced down at his disheveled black form. Nah, that hadn't been support. He just wanted tuna.

"Later, dude," she told him. "First we've got to see what Warren wants."

They arrived at the main cobblestone courtyard that sat in the middle of the biggest buildings on campus. She ran up the expansive stone steps, through the great wooden door to the building that housed the Praesidium, across the sunlit atrium and down a wide, wood-paneled hallway.

The oak door of his office was closed, but she didn't bother to knock. "You rang?" She asked as she strolled in, the Chairman trotting at her heels.

"Doona like to knock?" He glared at her from behind his desk and dragged a hand through his rumpled hair.

Unable to help herself, she admired the way his gray t-shirt stretched across his broad chest. His green eyes were tired, but the rest of him looked tense, muscles bunched and ready to pounce on any threat that walked through the door. Though she'd never actually seen him fight, he had a dangerous air that was unmistakable and hard not to like.

Stop it, you moron.

She jerked her gaze away from him and looked around the room. The book-filled office was dim, the kind of light that someone with a headache would prefer. Coffee cups littered the desk. "Not sleeping much?" she asked.

"No, damn it."

Had he not slept because of last night? But he didn't mention it and was playing this professionally, and her pride demanded that she do so too. "Fine. Why did you call me up here?"

"I've got an assignment for you."

A warm little rush passed over her at the words. Self-preservation crushed it. "Oh?"

When he'd asked her to be a consultant for the Mythean Guard a few weeks ago, she'd jumped at the chance to be part of a team. She wasn't used to working with one, had initially been shocked by the offer and had almost turned it down. But with a little thought, it sounded damned appealing. This would be the first assignment he'd given her.

"Aye, the Witch Council needs help with a particularly difficult spell."

"Those losers? Don't they have enough power in their little club to pull it off?" Well, there went professionalism.

"No, they doona have anyone as powerful as you."

"So true." She smiled. "Normally I don't mix with witches, though."

"It's your job now."

"True." And truth be told, she liked that she was part of the Praesidium. Part of a team. "When do I go?"

"Tonight would be best. Sooner, the better."

She had no problem with that. No plans tonight anyway. "Okay. Anyone else from the Praesidium going to help?"

"No, they said witches only, or I'd be there."

So she'd be alone. With the witches. But she didn't need any help. Hell, partners from the Praesidium would only slow her down.

"This is important, Esha. You canna screw this up."

She glared at him. Out of the corner of her eye, she caught sight of the Chairman arching his back, disheveled midnight fur sticking out at all angles. "Screw this up? Tell me, Warren, when was the last time I screwed anything up?"

He ignored the question, no doubt knowing he had no answer. "Let me know how it goes."

"Fine." She stood and walked toward the door. The Chairman slunk after her. "Tell them that I'll be there at nine."

CHAPTER SEVEN

A girl could only take so much, Esha thought as she stomped toward the Witch Council's section of campus later that night.

The Chairman stalked along beside her, the cold autumn wind ruffling his fur and making her tug up the zipper of her short leather jacket. She loved this time of year, when the leaves blew off the trees and swirled through the crisp air. It wasn't enough to save her mood today, though.

Her friend Andrasta appeared straight out of thin air, and Esha jumped.

"Damn it, Ana, a little warning next time." But she grinned at her friend, who had just broken through the aether from Otherworld, the land of the Celtic gods. The aether was an ephemeral substance that connected everything and allowed certain individuals to use it as a medium for immediate travel. Esha used it to aetherwalk, which Ana could do as well

"Gimme a break. You know I can only sneak out of Otherworld when the other gods are occupied. And it's not like I can call you to let you know I'm coming." Ana smiled at her before she began to twirl in the moonlight, hopping around like a demented fairy. Her accent suited her persona— the odd mixed Celtic of Otherworld's gods combined with the modern movies she cherished. "Earth totally rocks."

The moonlight highlighted the petite frame and shining blond hair of the Celtic goddess of victory. Esha had always thought that Andrasta, with her leather breastplate and the bow strapped over her shoulder, fit right in with the haunted-house setting of the university at night better than she ever did. Esha's customary uniform of jeans, boots, and a leather jacket were meant to blend in with the world outside of the campus, since she spent so much time there.

"Ah, that feels great," Ana said, as some of her immortal power flowed from her body and into Esha's. Esha shivered as her skin tingled from the transfer. There was no way to control it—it just happened whenever she was around another Mythean. Because Ana was a god, she provided a huge surge of power.

"Damn, I feel like I could throw a fireball the size of the moon right now." Esha shook her hands to get rid of the tingles.

"You should. That's some grade-A god power," Ana said.

Esha grinned. Ana had been mortal before she'd been made a god. She'd spent the last thousand years pining for life on earth. Having her power drained by Esha made her feel more mortal. It was the only time that another Mythean actually appreciated Esha's ability.

Mytheans normally hated the feeling of having the power of their immortal souls sucked away, even temporarily, to fuel a being who could use it to manifest any of her desires. The ability made Esha's one of the most reviled species that walked the earth.

"It's been weeks since I've seen you. How did you get out this time?"

"Cernowain's golden boar has escaped again. Everyone is trying to grab a golden bristle."

Esha grinned, thankful that Ana had skipped out and come to earth. Her friend always made her feel better. Ever since Esha had run away from her witch school in America three hundred years ago, she hadn't had any friends other than the Chairman.

Not that she needed them. But meeting Ana a few years ago had been a godsend. Literally. She snickered at her own joke.

"Didn't want to stay for the show?" Esha asked.

"Nah, gets old after the first four dozen times. It's probably the only interesting thing that happens in Otherworld, but I'm over it by now. Where are you going?" Ana fell into step next to Esha as they set off toward the witches' part of campus.

"Got an assignment for the Praesidium."

"Ooh, how's that superfox Warren?" Ana pulled an arrow out of the quiver at her back and twirled it idly between her fingers.

"Ugh, a jerk. Every time I see him, I reach for the vinegar instead of the honey. No question, I'm an idiot. But he's worse." Esha kicked at the low mist that had begun to hover over the ground.

"So, is he actually a jerk, or do you poke him until he snaps?"

"You know me too well. But both, probably. He hates what I am. Really hates it. He seems so perfect and nice. I actually thought we had some kind of connection. But he's been a real jerk. It's a mess."

"He has to have some kind of issue. I mean, he's a total upstanding citizen and all, but anyone that perfect has something really weird about them you can't see. This can't go anywhere good. You've got to quit mooning over him."

"I have." *I haven't. Have I?*

"Liar."

"Whatever—you killed the dude *you* liked."

Ana stopped twirling her arrow and glared at her. "Don't remind me."

"Sorry, low blow. I'm in a shitty mood, and I shouldn't take it out on you." Ana had become the goddess of victory by killing Camulos, the previous war god. It had been an ugly mess that Esha didn't fully understand, only that Ana had liked Camulos but had been in a bad situation with the other gods. To protect her family, she'd had to kill him.

"Fair enough, it's true. But enough of that. You're down here on earth. You've got a shot at a real relationship! All the men! I mean, sure, you've been mooning over Warren for about a decade now, but he's clearly got too many issues. Maybe you should start looking for someone else, for a real relationship." Ana's voice was wistful. Esha had a feeling that Ana might live vicariously through her.

"As if I care." *Liar.* "Anyway, even if I did, where am I going to find someone for a *real* relationship? Mytheans hate me."

"Brian was a freak, you know. He didn't deserve you."

"Quit being so insightful." Her friend *would* get to the heart of what was bothering her.

"It's true. I get that having your first love turn on you can do some serious damage. Trust me, I do. But it was a fluke. He was a jerk."

He was, though he hadn't started out that way. He'd attended the boys' school across the lake from her own all-girls witches' academy, the North American Academy for Immortal Magics. She shouldn't have been at a witch school, but it was the only place for an orphan soulceress to go. The Burnings hadn't been a problem in America, so it had been safe enough, and baby witches were basically like baby soulceresses. Until they came into their powers.

It had been a good fit, until it hadn't been. During the good times, she'd had all her friends and eventually Brian. They'd dated for two years. Two years of blissful young love. Love that might have made it.

But then she'd come into her powers as a soulceress, which normally happened around adulthood. It had started over the summer, coming in bits and spurts. When her friends figured out that she was sucking their powers away from them, they'd turned on her.

Brian had promised he wouldn't.

But eventually the disgust of their fellow students and the pressure of his prejudice had driven him away. The more desperate she became and the more she tried to cling to him, the faster he withdrew. She'd had no control of her powers or of herself at the time, had been floundering with no life raft, and it had been the last thing that she could bear.

With no friends and Brian gone, she'd left the school before graduation. She'd learned the hard way what happened when she let down her guard.

"I can't believe I told you about all that," Esha said.

"Of course you do. We're friends, idiot. And I love you even if that asshole didn't." Ana punched her.

"Thanks. Really."

"What about a mortal, then?"

"Mortals die."

She'd tried that too, when she'd been too young to know any better and wanted to bury the memory of Brian. The mortal she'd fallen for had been lovely and kind. She'd loved him. Had even been stupid enough to dream of a life with him.

Until he'd died in a carriage accident from which she'd easily walked away. It had pulled her world out from under her.

Since then, she'd never tried for something permanent because her options were only mortals. She didn't even know how she'd go about having a real relationship. She had no practice, only a long series of one-night stands and rejections by her own kind.

Their loss.

"So, what's this job like?" Ana asked.

"Gotta help the lame-o witches. They're in over their heads." She was looking forward to it. A chance to show those bitches up.

"Do you know what it is?"

"No. Something that Warren told me not to screw up."

They'd reached the beautifully wild garden surrounding the witches' cottages and greenhouses. Even now, well past dark and at the height of autumn, fluffy bunnies and cute cats roamed through the flowerbeds. Other animals would be about as well—raccoons and deer, badgers and voles. They were drawn to the Animus witches, who, likewise, were drawn to them. No one hated a witch who drew her power from the happy feelings of a kitten. Esha scowled.

"Fates," Ana said when a bunny hopped up to her to sniff at her leg. "It's like a Disney movie."

"I thought you liked Disney movies." Ana loved all movies. Anything that showed life on earth was her bag.

"Not like this I don't. Don't even think about it," she said to the bunny.

Esha laughed, but it made her vaguely ill too. Give her rogue Mytheans creeping through the underground any day. As a mercenary, she didn't spend much time around bunnies. Not that they weren't nice, but there was something about this place that put her off.

"Don't worry," she told Ana. "There are still plenty of witchy creepy crawlies."

And there were. Insects and snakes loved the witches as much as the bunnies did, but they weren't as easy to see in the dark.

Ana looked up from the bunny, who was now nibbling on the lace of her leather boot. "I'd better get back. You've got work to do, and I bet the debacle in Otherworld is almost over. Good luck with the sparkle witches."

Esha smiled. "Thanks. Try to sneak out again soon. We can go out."

"Sure. See you later!"

Without a sound, Ana left and Esha stood alone at the entrance to the gardens.

Now or never. She strode through the wrought-iron archway and caught sight of an illuminated cottage at the back edge of the garden. Night-blooming roses climbed up trellises in front of the stone walls and fireflies lit the way down the path. The Chairman hissed, and out of the corner of her eye she saw a bunny scamper off. Esha grinned.

In moments, she was knocking on the wooden door of the cottage. It swung open to reveal a small witch with a marmot riding on her shoulder. Esha resisted rolling her eyes.

"Welcome—come in!" The pink-haired witch's voice was cheerful.

The warm greeting took Esha aback, but she entered. The brightly lit little cottage was clearly a workspace and not a home. Shelves of books and crystals lined the walls, and a few chairs and tables were scattered about. But otherwise it was empty, save for a dozen witches, who smiled at her when she entered. Esha stared back, uncertain what to do. They'd never acknowledged her before. And they'd certainly never smiled.

"So, what do you need help with?" she asked.

"Um, a binding spell that we can't do without you. But can I get you something to drink first?"

"No, thanks."

"Oh my gosh, I love your jacket," the youngest witch in the room burst out.

Esha glanced down at the short, honey-brown leather jacket. It was a good one. Maybe these witches weren't so bad, with their compliments and drink offers.

"Thanks," she said, then turned to the marmot witch. The woman had come a bit too close and flinched when Esha turned to face her. Disgust and fear glinted in her eyes.

Right. So that's how it was, same as always. Nice on the surface when they needed her, but underneath it all was the usual bullshit.

When she looked more closely at the witches surrounding her, she saw the strain around their eyes that hadn't at first been evident when she'd walked into the room. Except the complimentary witch. She just looked a little addle-brained. Maybe she didn't know enough to be afraid of Esha.

"Anyway," Esha said. "Let's get started."

"Okay. Come over here, if you don't mind," the marmot witch said.

Esha crossed the wide wooden floorboards to the table in the middle of the room. A slender ceremonial dagger lay on it, along with a few other things.

Esha rubbed her hands together. After the hit of power she'd gotten off Ana, she could do anything. In fact, she'd barely drawn any from these witches since she was basically full up. Jeez, they shouldn't be so nervous. Like she wanted their piddly power anyway.

"So, what do you need me to do?" Esha asked.

Much of the magic practiced by these and most other witches was a group affair. But she doubted it would be this time, if she'd been called in. A soulceress wasn't a witch because she didn't need spells and her power wasn't innate, but she was similar. Unlike the witches, she was able to work solo only because of the immense amount of power she could borrow from other Mytheans.

She listened as they told her about the prisoner who was locked up and how she would wreak havoc if she were allowed out again.

"So you want me to cast a spell that will keep her locked up forever? That seems pretty harsh. What'd she do?"

"This is the right thing to do," one of the witches said, terror on her face. "The prisoner is evil like I've never seen before. The soulceress who locked her up before was the only one strong enough to do so. She'd have locked her up for longer if she could have."

Soulceress. Esha wondered who it had been. She'd never met another of her kind before, but she'd always wanted to.

Again, her eye caught the dagger lying on the table. Silver glinted in the light, and realization hit her. They wanted not only her power to bind the witch, but her blood as well. Esha's head swam. That meant that they wanted her to imprison one of her own kind. Not a witch at all, but a soulceress.

Not only that, blood rituals were a big freaking deal. She would give away some of her ability permanently when she gave her blood for the ritual. It would leave her able to draw less power and manifest less magic.

"Holy shit," she murmured.

Though some might call a soulceress a witch, what with the magic and all, these bitches knew better. They expected her to lock up her own kind. Forever. And to sacrifice part of herself to do so.

The witches had backed away from her a few feet. Esha was vaguely aware that the Chairman was stalking erratically in circles around her. She swayed a bit as she realized that she might have an opportunity to meet another of her kind. And that the witches had lied to her.

"Whoa, ladies. No way am I helping you with this," she said.

"What?" The marmot witch's voice sounded strangled. "You have to."

"No." Esha shook her head and turned in a circle, taking in the sight of the twelve frightened witches surrounding her. "No, I really don't. Were you going to tell me I was locking up another soulceress?"

Esha could see in their faces that they hadn't intended to. Did they think she was stupid?

"Right, then. I think we're done." She turned to leave, the Chairman already ahead of her and waiting impatiently at the door.

"But... why?"

Esha didn't bother to turn around to answer the question. "Please. She's probably no more evil than I am."

CHAPTER EIGHT

In his office, Warren paced in front of the fireplace. Despite the autumn wind that howled against the mullioned windows, the hearth lay cold. His mind was a jungle of tangled vines, the only thought he could grasp was that of Esha's coming task. He hadn't been able to eat or shower. The duties of managing the Praesidium had fallen by the wayside.

His job—managing the Mythean Guardians and maintaining the balance between earth and the afterworlds—had been a form of atonement. For the last two hundred years, it had been more important than anything else in his life. With Aurora's potential return, it was but an afterthought, and he despised that.

Footsteps charged down the hall, followed by the patter of smaller feet. He strode toward the door and swung it open.

Esha pushed through without slowing down. "Do you have any idea what you sent me to do?"

The cat hissed.

He wanted to growl back. "Your job. Why the hell are you so angry?"

Her eyes blazed, their amber ignited to fire, and her chest rose erratically with her heaving breaths. He dragged his eyes away to focus on her face.

"You sent me to bind another soulceress to eternal prison. Using magic that would forever forfeit some of my power."

"Did you?"

"No!"

His head spun as he watched her fling herself into the chair across from his desk and bow her head into her hands. He took a step toward her, then stopped himself abruptly. She'd screwed him and hadn't completed her assignment. Why was he walking toward her in comfort?

But the magic would steal some of her power? Shite. He hadn't known that. "You can regenerate."

"Yeah, unless I give it away freely through a blood ritual. Then I regenerate less." She shook her head and dragged her hands through her hair. "But that's not the point! You sent me to hurt another soulceress, Warren."

"She's a monster. You should be distancing yourself from her, if anything."

She lifted her head from her hands and looked up at him, dawning horror on her face. "I've never met another one. I'm the only freak like me. Why would I do something to keep her locked up? Why would I want to stay away from her?"

Blood pounded in his head, and his fists clenched uncontrollably. "Because she's fucking evil!"

Esha didn't flinch, but her face paled.

"What the hell does that even mean? People say I'm evil too. How am I supposed to believe that in this case, she is super evil and not just like me?" Her hair began to float around her head, eerily juxtaposed against her pale, shocked face. Her anger and disappointment were so deep that they manifested themselves through magic.

"I've never said you're evil. And despite the way I've put my foot in my mouth, I doona think it either," he said.

Skepticism flashed in her eyes.

"I gave you this assignment for the greater good, Esha. If it were up to me, I'd kill her. You've got to trust me on this."

"Trust you? That's what I did when I went to help the witches. They've treated me like I'm nothing for ten years, but I went to help them because I thought you needed me as part of the team. Instead, you sent me to hurt my own kind—and myself! I trusted that you had the guts to get over what I am. I know you're attracted to me, but you treat me like I'm some awful, untrustworthy jerk when all I've ever done is help you. Gods, I panted after you like a bitch in heat, thinking you were something different, something better than all the other Mytheans who reject me based on what I am." She surged out of her chair. In her rage, she was a tempest.

"Helping the witches is your damn job!" He ignored everything else she'd said, knowing that she was right, that he'd put his foot in his mouth too many times and been an arse. But he couldn't deal with such personal issues right now in the face of Aurora's release.

Her face twisted. "You know what? Forget it. And forget you. I don't know why I ever thought it would be a good idea to work for the university. You're a bunch of bigots and I'm through with you." She spun around and headed for the door, her cat hot on her heels. It looked back and hissed at him, citrine eyes all but shooting sparks.

"Where are you going?" After what she'd done—failed to do—could he stop her? Would he? Letting her run might be the kindest thing to do.

"Away. I'm done with the university. Fuck your world peace, fuck your departments and teams. Fuck all of it. I'm done."

Leaving for good? She couldn't. He charged after her, reaching out to grab her. He needed her to stop Aurora. He needed her... for himself. He ruthlessly crushed the errant thought.

Esha glanced back over her shoulder, then reached out for her cat. When she made contact, they disappeared. He thought he heard the words *fuck this* echo as she departed.

Eyes blurred with tears, Esha stumbled through the door of her tower flat.

"Pathetic," she muttered. What kind of badass was she if she was crying over that stupid asshole and this stupid place. Gods, *she* was the stupid one. She hadn't cried in years, not since she'd run away from school. She'd made herself tough, someone not to be fucked with.

And look at her now.

Esha's heart clutched as she looked around at the flat that had been her home for a decade. The windows that she'd loved when she'd first seen her new home looked out on Scotland's Lowlands. The hills and green forests had reminded her of her old life. They'd been her bail-out option.

Joining the university permanently had been a huge change from her solitary life as a mercenary, most of which she'd spent out in the Highlands, hunting the creepiest of crawly rogue Mytheans. The sight of the green hills out her window had initially reminded her that she could leave whenever she wanted to, return to her roots as a solo mercenary who didn't need anyone.

Hell, that was what she'd been here all along. Mistakenly, she'd thought she was joining a team when she'd signed up ten years ago, but nothing about her lifestyle or work had really changed. She should have known something was up when they'd given her the tower at the farthest edge of campus, as far as possible from the other Mytheans.

She scrubbed the tears from her face again as she walked to the middle of the floor and sat. Her face was leaking, and it was embarrassing.

I'm not a freaking wimp. I'm a badass. The Chairman curled up next to her, so she sank her fingers into his warm fur, sighing at the comfort that rushed over her. It wasn't much, but it was enough to stop the tears. *He* was her family. Her familiar was the only one who'd been at her side this entire time. She loved Ana too, but she could escape Otherworld so rarely.

Esha lay back on the wooden floor and stared up at the beam-supported ceiling. She'd loved this place at first, but all the shit that had happened recently made her realize that it had become a prison. A prison in which she accepted her outcast status. She'd thought it didn't bother her, that she was above it.

But she wasn't. All the little bad things—the glares, snide comments, loneliness amongst a sea of other Mytheans—were piling up until they became too much to bear. This last event pushed her over the edge. This place was breaking her apart.

As the fog of exhaustion crept across her mind, a glorious idea came with it. Esha didn't have to stay at the university in hopes of finding a place to fit in. Another soulceress was about to arrive in Scotland.

Esha had been alive for more than three hundred years, and for the first time in her long life, she had a chance to meet another of her kind. Another soulceress wouldn't cringe at the sight of her. She might even know things that Esha didn't about being a soulceress. Maybe she could even teach her to control her power collection. If she could do that, then she could have a more normal life.

Best of all, she would know someone who would accept her for who she was.

CHAPTER NINE

Warren stared, slack-jawed, at the space that Esha had only recently inhabited.

She was gone. Totally out of reach. He'd been a bastard and had driven her away because he was so fucked up. Regret for the pain he'd seen in her eyes was a physical ache in his chest, but he pushed it aside for the bigger problems that loomed on the horizon.

There was no way to convince her to help keep Aurora imprisoned. He'd done everything he could, tried to follow the rules of the university, but she'd be getting out no matter what.

Sick joy dawned within him. His extremities tingled with it. He'd done everything he could, but Aurora was going to escape.

Which meant he could hunt her, his conscience clear. His mind spun with the possibilities, a tornado within his head.

Focus, you bastard. He began to breathe deeply, counting back from one hundred. By the time he reached the thirties, his breathing had calmed. By the tens, he'd gained control of his rampant mind.

First step, he had to go to the witches to learn the details of Aurora's release. Afterward, he'd find Esha and apologize. But this had to come first.

Thirty minutes later, Warren strode into the witches' part of campus. He reached the door, but the sound of arguing stilled his fist. Raised voices and sparks flew out the window, nearly singeing his cheek. Curious, and ever cautious of witches in an uproar, he sidled along the cottage wall until he reached a window.

What he saw within made his brows draw down. A dozen witches stood in varying states of disarray around the room, yelling at each other. One pulled at her hair in frustration, while another yanked books off the shelf so fast that they flew to the floor when she decided they weren't what she was looking for.

Familiars in all shapes and sizes—cats, rabbits, wolves, snakes—prowled anxiously throughout the room, avoiding an area near the ceremonial table that glimmered like heat over the desert.

"Shut it, ladies! We need to get our shit together!" Cora's voice broke out over the din. The fat marmot on her shoulder tried to hide under her pink hair but was too big.

"We're screwed, Cora, she's going to be here any minute!" A dark-haired witch gestured toward the shimmering area over the table.

"Do you think I don't know that? Damn it! I never thought she'd be strong enough to break out this early. I swear all this mortal technology makes the aether thinner. We're lucky she didn't get out earlier."

"Do you think..." a timid witch began. "Um, do you think she's coming for vengeance?"

Cora groaned at the question. "I don't know, Luca. Probably. Aurora didn't exactly want to be imprisoned. But we only did what we had to do. We were right under the law."

A flash of light. Howling wind so fierce that Warren was blown back a few steps. He leaped to the window again in a heartbeat once it died down. His heart plummeted and his fists clenched. *Shite.*

Aurora stood within the room, right where the shimmering air had been. Her short golden hair whipped about her face, set aloft by an unholy and unnatural wind. As Esha's had done when she'd been angry. A sleek black cat sat at her heels, emerald eyes fierce.

Aurora's eyes blazed black as they stared—straight at him.

"Well, well, well. What have we here?" Her voice echoed with evil, but Warren barely had time to process it.

He charged into the cottage, straight for the unholy bitch. *Mine.* Her death would be his, and with it, his soul. Rage propelled him forward faster than he'd ever moved.

Pain. He slammed into a force field and his body was thrown back, the shock of her power still echoing through his veins. The sounds of the other witches hurrying away from Aurora were drowned out by her laughter. It scratched over his nerves and plucked at his sanity. All the peace and control he'd worked so hard to gain slipped from him as his blood roared in his ears.

Kill her. Take back what's yours.

"Stupid man. Do you think I'd actually come here?" she asked.

He surged to his feet to face her. Her form hovered off the ground, slightly translucent. The gray robes she wore floated unnaturally about her slender frame, a color so dense it sucked the light out of the room. It was dull as slate against her glowing golden skin.

"Where are you?" His breath came short with his rage, strangling his lungs like briars wrapped around a fence.

"Please. I won't be telling you that. However, I will say that I'm glad to see you here. You'll do just fine for my purposes."

"You knew I'd be here?" There was no way.

"Nay. I came to ask these cowards for what I wanted." She gestured to the cowering witches. "But your passion will ensure that I get what I want."

Pride propelled Cora forward, but only a few steps. "You broke the law. We did only what was required when we locked you up for abusing your powers."

"What do you know of my powers? You're but an animus witch. Go talk to your marmot." Aurora waved a dismissive hand.

"Bite me, Cruella. There are enough of us to stop you again if you pull a repeat of your past," Cora said.

"You're wasting my time," Aurora snapped. She waved her hand and the witches were forced to their knees, struggling fiercely against her hold, their faces contorted with rage and their shouts echoing about the room.

Still on his feet, the strength leached out of Warren's muscles and his stomach lurched. What the hell? He was never ill, and this wasn't the same as what the witches were experiencing.

He swallowed hard, forcing the bile back, and said, "Where the hell are you?"

"What, you want to kill me to get your soul back?" She laughed.

"Aye."

She rolled her eyes and his muscles bunched, prepared to launch himself at her even though it would be pointless.

"I knew that's what you'd say. But you canna find me," she said. "No' where I'm going. The only one who can find me is another soulceress. And there's one here at the university. I can feel her. Bring her to me."

"Why?"

"I want a friend, that's all." Something swirled in her eyes, something dark and unreadable that took him back to the awful night when he'd traded her his soul. Her power seethed around her, so strong that he could almost feel it, though she wasn't even truly in the room. She looked nothing like Esha, but the power was there. That similarity was impossible to deny.

"That's no' all you want," he said. Bring Esha to her? Risk her like that?

"Either way, bring her to me. Then you can have your soul back."

Nay. It was too good to be true. "That's all? Why no' just come get her yourself?"

"And let the university hunt me down? I'm no' stupid. I want to meet her on my terms, where I make the rules and remain safe. Why would I give you the advantage by coming there?"

"How are we supposed to find you if you won't tell me where you are?"

"She can find me. Bring her to me and your soul is yours."

It was clearly a lie. And there was so much beneath the surface of her demands and her plans that he couldn't identify.

"You've got one chance, Warren." She waved her hand again and released the witches from their enforced submission.

As they stood, his muscles turned to jelly and his stomach revolted. What the hell?

"Bring her to me, Warren," Aurora said. The air around her shimmered again, then collapsed in on itself until she disappeared with a pop.

He almost went to his knees with the sickness that surged through him. What the hell was wrong with him?

Once his stomach had settled a bit, he spun toward the witches and demanded, "That's it? That's all we fucking get?"

"Just a moment," Cora said. She and the other witches were moving about the room, chanting spells and righting chairs that had overturned in the first rush of wind that had come with Aurora's appearance.

Warren stumbled over to the area where Aurora had been floating but could feel no difference in the air. He breathed deeply as the sickness began to fade and some of the strength returned to his muscles.

Eventually, Cora approached him and said, "Are you okay? You don't look so good."

"Aye."

Cora shook her head. "No, there's something wrong with you. I can sense it."

"I'll be fine." But it hit him again, a wave of nausea so intense that he almost stumbled.

"What the hell is wrong with you?" she whispered. "It's like Aurora had some kind of effect on you."

"Nay. Of course no'."

The confusion that creased her brow turned to shock. "Oh, shit. Of course. Hang on a second."

Warren put a hand on the table to steady himself and watched her run over to a bookshelf in the corner. She plucked a volume from the top and leafed through it as she returned to him.

"Here it is," she said, peering at the pages. "It says that every time she uses the power that your soul provides, it takes some of the strength from your body as well. It makes you sick."

"Then why has this never happened before?"

"She was neutralized in the aether, so she couldn't use your soul."

Warren dragged a hand across his sweating face, the cramps in his gut like squirrels run amok in his intestines. How the fuck was he going to face her like this? "Is there any kind of spell that could cure this?"

"Cure? No."

"What about neutralize it?" he asked.

Cora frowned, a thoughtful light in her eyes. "I'll ask my sisters. Some of them work for the infirmary. There might be something you can take. Wait over there."

"Thanks." Warren stumbled to the chair that she indicated under the window. How the hell would he defeat Aurora if she had him crippled by illness?

Twenty minutes later—during which time he watched the witches put their cottage to rights while Cora and two of her sisters went to the infirmary—Cora returned.

"Here." She handed him a clear plastic bottle full of neon-green pills. "These should keep the symptoms at bay. But you can't take them forever. They'll eventually become ineffective. Then they'll kill you."

Shite. "How long can I take them?"

She shrugged. "Two weeks, maybe? It's different for everyone. One every twelve hours."

He fumbled one out of the bottle and swallowed it dry. "How the hell did she get out so soon?"

"Too powerful, I think. She's stronger than we thought. Stronger than any soulceress before her."

"What the hell does she want with Esha?"

Cora looked away, hesitating. "I don't know. But I'd guess that she wants her power."

"Her power?"

"Yeah, they can steal each other's power. Or their ability to absorb power, that is. It's one reason that soulceresses can be so strong—they have a potentially infinite well of ability. And why we stay the hell away from them."

Damn. He hadn't known that. Esha could permanently steal another's power, not just siphon it off temporarily? "Can they steal yours?"

"We don't know. None have tried in our written history, but that doesn't mean they can't. It's why we wanted Esha put on the other side of campus when she joined."

"Does Esha know soulceresses can steal power?"

Cora shrugged. "Doubt it. She'd probably have taken ours if she knew, right?"

Warren wasn't so sure. "How many soulceresses are left, if they've been stealing each other's powers all these years?"

"I don't know how often they do it. They used to be very loyal to each other, since no one else wanted to be around them. Aurora is one of the few who rampantly stole souls and power. The Burnings killed most of them. I think that Esha and Aurora are the only two left in Britain. She must want Esha's to complete her collection."

The idea of Esha's power being in Aurora's *collection* made his chest hurt. But if she didn't have her power, then she'd be normal. The idea wasn't wholly unappealing when he thought of it that way. Though he wasn't a big enough arse to wish her power away. But how would he ever convince her to help him, especially after his first blown attempt?

CHAPTER TEN

"Come on, Chairman, we're blowing this Popsicle stand."

Esha swung her bag onto her shoulder and headed for the door of her tower apartment. This was it—she was leaving. It hadn't taken but a moment to throw her valuables in a bag. A couple of goofy T-shirts from Ana, the Chairman's fluffy green squeaky toy that was the only thing he deigned to play with, her journal, and a necklace that was supposedly from her dad, though she'd never met him, so she couldn't be sure.

Her first stop would be to see the witches and check on where the soulceress might go when she was released. If they didn't know anything, the second would be to the historian Lea's office. She might know. Either way, the other soulceress would leave the university right away. Hence the packed bag.

She skipped down the spiral staircase, her dire mood improved by the possibility of what was to come. The brisk November air hit her face as she ran out the door at the base of her tower. Nearly all of the leaves were off the trees now. Snow would be here any day.

"New adventure, Chairman."

He meowed, low and deep, as he trotted at her side.

As she was pushing her car keys into the door lock, a hand landed on her shoulder. Shocked, she spun around and threw a blast of power that put the assailant on his ass.

"Warren?"

He coughed and rose, shaking the dirt from himself. "Aye. Damn, lassie, what'd you pack in that punch?"

"You're lucky that's all it was. Only an idiot would sneak up on me." She looked him up and down, letting the insinuation hang in the air. He might be an idiot, but not a bigger one than she. And he was a hot idiot. Golden hair that was such a contrast to the shadows at his feet whipped in the wind. "Why the hell are you sneaking up on me, anyway? I thought you'd be smart enough to leave me the hell alone."

"Never been too smart."

A lie, but she played along. "Yeah, I guess that's true."

"I need your help."

A little thrill skittered over Esha's skin. *Ignore it.* "Not interested. Last time you needed my help, you set me up. Oh, and that was last night. Not nearly long enough to forget."

He stepped toward her. The breath caught in her throat, and she backed up until the cold metal of the car pressed against her back. She despised herself for backing away, but she couldn't trust her control where he was concerned. She was determined to have a little more self-respect this time around.

"No' intentionally," he said.

"You're saying you didn't know I'd be locking up another soulceress?"

"Nay. But I dinna know the extent of the spell or what it would mean to you."

"Why me?"

"I need your help to find another of your kind. Soulceresses can find one another. You're the fastest way for me to get to her."

Really? "Why are you looking for her?"

"Her power outplayed that of the imprisonment spell. She's out, and she's gone rogue." He paused. "We want to make sure she's on our side."

"Like you did with me." *And see how well that worked out.*

"Basically." He looked away, swallowed hard.

He's lying. Warren was a terrible liar. A disgusted laugh burst from her lips. He expected her to trust him. But how could she when he made it so clear that he didn't trust her?

"If you insist on having this conversation, don't lie to me. You aren't planning to ask the other soulceress to join the university."

His jaw clenched.

"What," she said, "not used to being caught in your lies?"

"I doona lie—"

"Often. I know. You're too bloody honorable to stoop so low. But you did this time. Why?"

"Because I need your help, damn it!"

Esha had to work to suppress a shiver of delight at his words. On the surface they were what she wanted to hear. To be needed was a lovely thing. But beneath, the reasons for his lies writhed. "You think that the reason you want the soulceress will keep me from helping you, don't you?"

A tic began in his jaw.

"You're going to imprison her again. Or kill her. Aren't you?"

His eyes flickered at the word *kill*. She had him. She laughed, the sound dark and bitter. "You were going to try to trick me again—into helping you hurt another of my kind."

"She's evil, gods damn it!"

"So am I, according to you! There's no way in hell I'm helping you with this. All you've done is fucking lie to me when you *need* me." There was that word again. That lovely, lovely, dangerous word. "And inevitably, you need me to do something that I absolutely refuse to do. I'm not leading you to her so you can hurt her."

Warren dragged a hand through his hair, frustration evident on his face. "Honestly, Esha. I doona think you're evil. I've been an arse to you. Unforgivably so. It's just... You tie up my mind and my tongue until I say the worst possible things. And I'm no' trying to shift the blame. It's my own damn fault that I get screwed in the head around you. And I'm sorry."

Shock almost put her on her ass. A genuine apology... for her? An apology that confirmed she wasn't crazy for what she believed was happening between them?

Huh. "Well, don't do it again."

"I mean it. I am sorry. And I really do need your help with this. This soulceress actually is evil. If you knew the things she's done..." He slashed the air with his hand, frustration welling out of him.

"Well, why don't you tell me?"

"I canna."

"No, you *willna*." She mimicked his accent and kicked the gravel at her feet. "I'm getting sick of being used, sick of being lied to, and sick of being left out of the important information."

"It's... personal."

The soulceress had done something to him, then? Had they been... lovers? Her stomach pitched. No, that wasn't possible. She wanted to kick herself for even caring. Of course she didn't care. "She meant something to you?"

"No!" His eyes were fierce, the storm within them raging at the thought of the other soulceress.

He really did intend to kill her. Once again, he'd come to her for help to destroy her own kind, but he wouldn't even tell her the truth of why. Was she really so abhorrent? Was her kind so terrible that he was bent on destroying them? Would she have to go with him to protect the other soulceress?

"Help me. I can make it worth your while."

"How?"

"Money."

"Do I look like I need money? My skills are worth a fortune." She conjured a fireball, then made it whiz around his head. "I won't sell them to hurt another soulceress."

"A department of your own at the university. With assistants."

"Do I look like I need help?" *Though it would be nice to have a team.* "Anyway, who are you going to get to work with an evil bitch like me?"

"You aren't evil. I know that everyone treats you that way. But you aren't."

He hadn't answered her questions, though they were nice words. But she wanted action.

"We've determined that you have nothing I want," she said.

But he did have something she wanted. She didn't want him finding and killing the other soulceress before she could find her. Esha might be able to find her the fastest, but only if everything went right. She had no idea how or where to start. If she left Warren to find her on his own, there was always a chance he'd beat her there.

He'd hurt her and lied to her. But she was pretty used to that. She didn't particularly want to be around him anymore, but if it meant improving her chances of finding and saving the other soulceress, she was all for it.

"What's her name?" Esha asked.

"Aurora."

"Aurora." She liked that name. "Say I help you find Aurora. You can't kill her. That's not an option if I help you. And I get to talk to her first."

His nostrils flared. "Seriously?"

She nodded.

"No' a chance," he said.

"Give me a break. I know I'm your only option. You wouldn't have asked for my help otherwise. Promise not to kill her, let me talk to her, and I'll help you."

When he scowled at her, she grinned, knowing that she had him.

"Fine."

He'd agreed not to kill Aurora. He might be lying, but from the granite in his gaze, this was the best she could hope for.

And he was honorable. Most of the time. She'd need to be there when he found her, that was certain.

She shivered at the strange sensation that quivered along her nerves at the idea of actively trying to protect another Mythean. All her life, her job had been to kill rogues. It was a solitary existence. The only beings she'd ever considered risking her life for were Andrasta and the Chairman. Now she'd aligned herself with some other unknown soulceress?

Yes. For the chance to meet another Mythean, one who wouldn't judge her for something she couldn't control? To have her questions about her power answered? Absolutely.

Resolutely, she stuck out a hand. "Deal."

Relief coursed through Warren when Esha offered to shake on the deal. He gripped her hand, trying to ignore the goose bumps that rose on his skin. Electric.

"Thank you." He released her hand and stepped back, then cursed when he nearly tripped over the damn cat, who'd moved from his post beside the car.

"Watch it," said Esha. "You don't want to get on his bad side."

"What, or he won't use the litter box?"

"Please, that's my punishment. You, he'd wait until you were asleep, put a spell on you, and then eat your face."

His head snapped to the side to look at her. "The hell you say." When he saw the gleam in her eyes, a short burst of laughter escaped him.

"Seriously, though," she said, "he's got his ways."

Warren looked down at the soot-black cat at his feet. The beast turned its head to glare at him, white fangs gleaming in the light. He growled back.

Esha laughed. "Get over it, alpha dog."

Warren looked away from the cat. He'd just had a pissing contest with a house cat. Fucking embarrassing.

"So now what, boss?" She looked him up and down, her face daring him to contradict the title the way he had the other night in the pub.

He didn't. He liked the idea of having control over her. The setting sun gleamed on her rich black hair, a striking contrast to her pale skin. Aye, this was a woman he wouldn't mind telling what to do. She wouldn't listen, of course. But he liked that too. "You're supposed to be able to find her."

"Sure, but how?"

"You doona know?"

She shrugged.

"Well, think, damn it."

"I thought you'd have some inside info on how this soulceress tracking is supposed to go."

"I doona."

Esha rolled her eyes. "What do you think, Chairman?"

No response. Did she expect it to answer?

He searched his mind, turning away from Esha because she did nothing but cloud his thoughts with images of her, ideas of what he might do to her if she weren't a soulceress and didn't hate him. He stared out at the grove of oaks in the distance and caught sight of a rabbit bounding between the trees. An idea sparked to life.

"Packs of shifters can sense each other when they're nearby. Sometimes they can even find each other from far away. Now that Aurora has escaped, maybe she'll pop up in your subconscious."

"What, like radar?"

"Just try."

"Fine." She leaned back against her car and closed her eyes. Eventually her breathing calmed. Movement behind her eyelids gave him hope. This was working. It had to be.

Suddenly, she snored. Then laughed.

"Damn it, Esha, you need to take this seriously."

"Whatever, you have to admit that was funny."

When he said nothing, she shrugged again and said, "Fine. But I don't have a damn radar like our furry friends. That's not going to work. Give me a minute to think."

Tension thrummed beneath his skin as he waited. Of course this wasn't going to be easy, but even if he could get her to cooperate, he'd be in close proximity to her for the duration of their search. He'd been so obsessed with getting Esha's help in finding Aurora that he hadn't thought of the logistics of actually being near her for so long. In the past, he'd avoided her for a reason. His control, something he'd always prized in himself, was shot around her.

Even now, just standing near her lightened something within him. He'd never met anyone like her, someone who *saw* him. Hiding the darkness within, the lives he'd taken, had become second nature to him. Mytheans killed all the time, but he wasn't one of them. Death didn't come so easy. Yet she knew that he'd done evil things, could see it on him, when no one else could. Esha could see the shadow of his past, and she didn't hold it against him. It unsettled him. Intrigued him.

"I can't sense her," she said. "If I can't sense her, then it has to be something we have in common that will allow me to find her. What do we share?"

"The way you reap power."

She glared at him. "What, we're supposed to track all the poor, temporarily weakened Mytheans and find her that way? It's a needle in a haystack, and you could do that without me."

"Good point."

"Anyway," Esha said. "If she has her familiar, she can aetherwalk. Does she have her familiar?"

"Aye, a black cat like yours. Sleeker looking, though."

The Chairman hissed.

"Right, needle in a haystack plan is out."

"What kind of mythology do soulceresses have? Maybe it's related to that."

Every species had stories about its origin, books that contained its history, bards that recorded its songs. The soulceresses would too.

"I don't know much. There was never anyone to teach me about soulceresses specifically." She looked away. He swore he caught a glimmer of sadness, but then it was gone. No, that was ridiculous. Esha was tough, one of the toughest Mytheans at the university. "I don't know a lot about it. I've never tried to learn. But there's a place that was once vaguely mentioned in history class. The *howf*."

"Isn't that a pub?" He hadn't heard the word in ages.

"Can be, but *howf* also meant *meeting place*. For debates and that kind of thing. Ours was enchanted, and since we were the only ones who could enter, it was also used to store the documents and books that we didn't want falling into the wrong hands."

"That's got to be it. She said that only you can find her, and if you're the only one who can enter the *howf*, that's got to be it." Aurora was smart. It was a surefire way to make sure he brought Esha. "Let's go there."

She laughed. "Yeah, right. It sounds totally badass, so don't you think I would have gone there before?"

"You doona know where it is?"

"Not exactly, I've got a pretty good idea. Wouldn't take too long to find. But it's not the location that's the problem. It's the guard. If you don't know how to get in, or the rules once you're there, it's as dangerous as trying to get out of hell. Soulceresses won't have anyone stealing our secrets, so they enchanted the place. Older soulceresses taught younger ones how to get in."

Damn it. "This is our only lead, and you're telling me you canna get in?"

"Basically."

"What kind of cut-rate soulceress are you?"

She merely raised an eyebrow. The cat didn't even bother to hiss at the insult. "Please. I'm an awesome soulceress. You aren't going to goad me into this."

Damn it, she was always going to be one step ahead of him. He liked it. Though it was proving to be a pain in the arse.

"Is this really our only lead, then?" he asked.

Esha looked away. Minutes passed before she spoke again, during which time the first snow of the season began to fall lightly around them.

"Yeah," she said. "It's the only thing I can think of."

She'd racked her brain, but the truth of it was, she knew little about her own kind. There hadn't been any parents to teach her, and her school had stayed the hell away from teaching about soulceresses except for a brief mention. But what little she'd heard of the *howf* had been riveting.

It still was. A place that held the secrets of her kind? She'd never tried to find it before. Not only was it dangerous, but she wasn't sure she wanted to know. What if her kind were as evil as everyone said? Did she really want to face that?

But she'd already set out on this path, and she finished what she started. "Do you even think she'll be at the *howf*?" she asked.

"Doona know. Do you?"

She frowned and mulled it over. "No, I don't think she will be. Too dangerous to risk meeting us at a place with so many unknowns that she couldn't account for. If I were Aurora, I'd want to meet on my home turf. But I'd make you work for it by sending you someplace dangerous for the clues." That decided it for her. The other soulceress probably thought like she did. "I'll try to take you there."

As much as it made her skin cold to think of it, the idea of learning the secrets of the *howf* was tantalizing. She'd had centuries of ignorance about her own kind.

"Excellent. Where is it?"

"Fingal's Cave."

"Fingal's Cave? That odd rock formation off the Isle of Mull?"

"Yeah, the one on Staffa."

She'd never been to the small, uninhabited island located off the west coast of Scotland. The cave, made of towering octagonal rock formations, sat at the base of a vertical cliff and opened right into the sea.

"The soulceress *howf* is in a cave that is well known to mortals? The Giant's Cave is famous," Warren said.

"Fingal's Cave is just the entrance. The geological formations that draw mortal attention are an unavoidable manifestation of our power. But back when we used it, mortals weren't taking tour boat rides. And Fingal wasn't a giant. That's just a myth, meant to scare away the few mortals who might want to visit. His name was Finn. Finn MacCummhail, and he was a soulcerer. Not the first of our kind, but the most powerful."

"What happened to him, if he was so powerful?"

"Some say he was killed in the Burnings. Others say he sacrificed himself for the remaining soulceresses with magic meant to hide them from other Mytheans. Those few who survived believed that it was Finn MacCummhail who crafted the magic that calmed some of the hysteria. As for the *howf*, the entrance is at the back of the cave. It's only visible to Mytheans, not mortals, and it's submerged at high tide. If we miss the tide, we could be crushed by the waves."

"Can we aetherwalk? It would save time."

"To Mull, yes. Not to the cave, because the *howf* will be protected by magic that won't allow us to just appear inside. Any other species who can aetherwalk could gain access that way."

"We'll take a boat, then. Tourist boats won't be running this time of year, which helps us avoid people. When can we depart?"

"I need to refuel my power." She watched his face for any sign of a grimace, so used to seeing it on the faces of Mytheans was she.

Nothing. Not even a flinch. Did he really not care that she was a soulceress? She wanted to believe that.

"All right. I'll give Cadan a call. He has a house on Mull. He might know where to get a boat. I'll come get you in a few hours, and we'll head over there, all right?"

"Fine. I'll check the tides. We might have to wait until tomorrow to approach the cave."

Which meant they might be spending the night together on Mull. Esha swallowed hard.

CHAPTER ELEVEN

"We're screwed, Chairman," Esha said to her familiar as she trudged up the spiral staircase to her tower. "There isn't enough power in the world for us to beat what's coming at us."

He meowed his agreement, and she held the door open for him at the top of the stairs. He sauntered in and settled in front of the fireplace. Meowed again.

Absentmindedly, she waved a hand at the fireplace and flames burst into existence. Within seconds, he began to snore. She felt a smile almost stretch across her face, but it faded as she went into her bedroom.

When she reached the far wall, she pulled the dagger from the sheath in her boot. She grimaced as she made a small incision in her palm and placed her bloody hand against one of the stones that looked like all the rest. The stone disappeared and she reached into an enchanted space and withdrew a wooden arrow.

Please work. Andrasta had only given her one arrow, and Esha had never used it before. With a deep breath and a prayer for luck, she snapped it in half.

One second. Two. They were agonizing.

Then her friend stood before her. Naked and dripping wet, with a scowl that would rival a wet cat's. A glorious laugh burst out of Esha's chest, as if the tension and disappointment of the day refused to be held any longer.

"Why the hell are you laughing? What's wrong?" her friend demanded.

The arrow was for emergency use only. It dragged her friend out of Otherworld no matter what she was doing there.

Esha tried to stop, even clapped a hand over her mouth, but her laugh had become one of those uncontrollable freak-out laughs that was more about panic and less about humor. The glorious power that seeped into her from Andrasta only emphasized it.

"Ah, I'm sorry," she said, finally catching her breath. "Let me get you a towel."

She tossed her friend a towel and then found a T-shirt and jeans. They wouldn't fit the much shorter Ana, but they'd have to do.

"I didn't even know if that arrow would work," she said, watching Ana dry off and tug on the clothes.

"Me either."

"What'd I do? Pull you out of some humpathon with Adonis?"

"Wrong afterworld. He's Greek, not Celtic. I've never even met him. I was taking a bath."

"Sorry." Esha tried to grin, but her laughing binge had sucked any levity right out of her. Her previous happiness was as gone as tuna in the Chairman's bowl. She headed into the living room and curled up on the couch, knowing that Ana would follow.

"Thanks for coming," she said when Ana entered the room. "I'm sorry I had to use the arrow."

"It's fine. I gave it to you so you could call me if you needed to." With no phones or email in Otherworld—what with it being the ancient Celtic afterworld and all—there was no way to get in touch with Ana. Normally she just showed up when she could get away for a visit. "What's wrong? Why did you need to see me?"

"For your power," Esha said, guilt twisting something inside her until she swore it was a physical pain.

"Oh fates, don't worry about that. You can have it all!" Ana could read her so well, but she meant what she said. Ana hated the power that made her a god.

"Thanks. That's not how everyone else feels." *Whiner.*

Esha rarely moped, but Ana was the only friend she had who didn't speak Cat and just having someone to talk to made her want to spill her guts sometimes.

"You really need to get over that. Worrying what those assholes think isn't going to do you any good."

"I know. And I don't really care. Not normally." Beating herself up over something she couldn't control was the height of stupidity, and Esha made a point to limit any conscious stupidity.

"Is it that asshole Warren again?"

"No. He actually apologized for being a jerk. I know he still has a deep-seated problem with what I am, but I think it's mostly my own issue. Every other Mythean is an asshole about it, so I guess I'm just sensitive. Maybe too much so."

Ana just shrugged. What else could you do in the face of truth? "Why do you need so much power all at once?"

"I don't have time to find a big enough group of Mytheans before I have to go with Warren tomorrow to find the soulceress *howf*."

"Why the hell are you going there? Isn't it super dangerous?"

Esha told Ana all about Aurora and Warren and the hunt for one of her own kind.

Ana frowned. "But he's been such a jerk to you. You're helping him?"

Esha shrugged. "It was a good apology, but mostly I want to meet her. I've never tried to learn anything about my people. When I ran away from school, I was just trying to survive. By the time I got here, I guess I'd just turned into a big wimp who only wanted people to like her, and I figured that if I stayed away from anything related to other soulceresses, it would help."

"Wow, I had no idea. You're always such a badass, hunting rogues and spitting in the eye of anyone who looks at you wrong." Her friend paused. "Which is basically everyone."

"Yeah, well, my plan was crap. I know that now. I want more. I want to meet someone like me. Someone who won't judge me on sight."

"I don't judge you."

Esha smiled. "I know. And it means the world to me. It does. But I want to find this other soulceress. Maybe learn to control my power collection better."

They talked for another hour, mostly about Otherworld, since Esha wanted to take her mind off things. Eventually, Ana left, but not before repairing the arrow in case Esha ever needed it again. Her power coursed through Esha's veins as she checked out the tide charts and packed a small overnight bag. She was just closing her laptop when a knock sounded at her door.

"Hang on!"

She tugged on her coat and grabbed her bag. The Chairman was hissing at the door when she headed over to open it.

Warren stood outside, clad in a beat-up leather jacket and jeans. She told herself not to think about how good he looked. He made her act like a spaz, so the smart thing would be to ignore him.

"Ready?" he asked.

"Yeah. Come on in."

He nodded and stepped inside. Absentmindedly, she twisted the lock in the door while following him into the room with her eyes.

"What did you find for a boat?" she asked.

"Cadan has one at his house that we can borrow. It's got a trailer that we can use to get it to a better place to launch. We can stay at his place, too, if need be."

"All right. Since the boat is at his place on the south side and we need to tow it north, we're going to miss low tide this afternoon. The next low tide during daylight is at three o'clock tomorrow afternoon."

"That's less than an hour before sunset. We'll need to hit it right on the nose or we'll be in the dark. Let's go tonight, stay at Cadan's, and use the time to see to the boat. He said he hasn't used it in a while, so we'll need to make sure everything works."

"Okay," she said, but her mind went straight to the idea of spending the night in Cadan's house with Warren. The place was big, but still. "Do you have everything you need?"

He held up a duffel.

"Good. We'll leave from here. You're going to have to wrap your arm around my waist," she said as she stepped closer.

He stared down at her, his eyes intense, then wrapped a hard arm gently around her waist.

Her eyes snapped back to his face when he spoke. "I wanted to say thank you again for helping me with this. It's... really important."

Struck by the sincerity in his voice, she nodded, unable to break eye contact. Finally, she looked away. "I'll take us to Cadan's house. I've been there before, so it won't be a problem."

When she could feel the Chairman twining himself about her legs, she focused on his energy and her destination. Moments later, they stood in the front hall of Cadan's home on the Isle of Mull. Sunlight streamed through the windows to illuminate a wooden floor and gray walls decorated with paintings of faraway landscapes.

"You can open your eyes now," she said. The Chairman unwound himself from her legs and stalked off, presumably to find the kitchen.

Warren removed his arm from her waist and she mentally kicked herself for mourning the loss of him. She tossed her bag onto a bench, then turned to him. "Shall we go check out the boat?"

Later that night, after inspecting the boat and hitching the trailer to the Land Rover in Cadan's garage, Warren wandered downstairs for dinner. Dealing with the boat had taken hours, then a shower and calls from work had kept him busy. He'd tried to keep his mind off Esha and he'd failed. Of course.

The kitchen was dim when he stepped inside, but the glimmer of light from the other room provided enough illumination that he ignored the light switch in favor of heading straight to the fridge. A quick glance revealed beer in the refrigerator and TV dinners in the freezer. He snagged a beer and put it on the counter, then wandered toward the walk-in pantry.

"Warr—"

He stumbled straight into Esha, who'd apparently been in the pantry hunting down some dinner as well. A box of crackers was clutched in her hand.

"Sorry." But he didn't step back to give her any space. He couldn't. His mind was too wrapped up in how she looked.

Her hair was wet from a shower, and she wore loose cotton trousers and a threadbare tank top that molded to her breasts. No bra. The sight made his brain short-circuit and any thought of his long-enforced celibacy flee like a coward from a dragon.

"You're looking for dinner too?"

He could barely hear her through the buzzing in his head. Without her usual armor of jeans and a leather jacket, the sight of her, so different from what he was used to, made him realize how much he wanted her. Made him realize how damn long it had been since he'd been with a woman.

Now, when he needed his iron will more than ever, it fled. The scent of her banished it from his being. They were a mere foot from each other, so close that it was easy to reach out with a trembling hand and cup the back of her head. Her raven hair felt like silk against his fingers. How long had it been since he'd touched something so soft?

Her lips parted and her amber eyes took on a wary sheen. "What are you doing?"

The words were but a whisper that bounced ineffectually against the force of his desire. He pulled her closer until he could feel her breath against his lips, hot and sweet.

"This is a bad idea," she whispered, but she didn't push him away.

Aye, it was a bad idea. Celibacy had been working really well for him. It kept his mind clear and focused, which he sure as hell needed. The responsible Warren who worked tirelessly for the university would have stiffened his shoulders and walked out. The Warren who'd decided to fuck the university and hunt for the soulceress who had stolen his soul didn't care. The pressure of the last few days was breaking him.

Breaking him down into the components of his basest self: Need. Lust. Instinct.

He pulled her to him, groaning low in his throat when her body pressed against his. As his mouth closed over hers, she moaned, parting her lips. She stroked her tongue against his, inviting him in. He followed, desperate to taste her, to see if she was as sweet as he suspected.

"Warren." She dropped the crackers and ran her hands up his chest and into his hair, gripping his head and holding him tightly to her, as if she never wanted to let go.

His surroundings faded. She was hot and warm and wet in a way that shot a bolt of lust straight to his cock. He wanted to touch her, to taste her, to tear her clothes off her and know every inch of her. The celibacy that had allowed him control over his life and peace in his mind suddenly seemed ridiculous.

Desperate, he yanked her up into his arms and pressed her back against the wall just outside the pantry, cupping the back of her head to protect it from the hard wood.

Her long legs closed around his waist and she rolled her hips. His cock surged at the feel of her, hot and soft against him. Only a few layers of fabric separated them. Too much.

"Gods, I want you," he muttered, and gripped the curve of her ass.

Her mouth dragged down the side of his neck and he moaned, gripping her hips and grinding his cock against her softness.

"There." She gasped. "Right there."

She moved against him, gracefully at first, but soon devolved into mindlessness in pursuit of pleasure.

Could she come like this? The idea spurred him on, made him thrust and capture her mouth in hopes it would push her over the edge.

"Yes." Her hands fisted in his hair as her hips grew frantic.

She was close, he was sure of it.

A great boom of thunder shook the house, and darkness crashed around them as the power cut out. Esha stiffened in his arms, her trance broken. She shuddered.

"Bad idea." She scrambled out of his arms and away. "This has only ever ended terribly with you."

"I—"

"No, we're a bad idea, Warren. You don't like me. Once, I wouldn't have cared. But I do now. I want more than this." She ignored the crackers she'd dropped and turned to leave, snagging his beer on her way out. "I'll see you tomorrow morning."

Warren squeezed his eyes shut and leaned back against the pantry wall. A heavy breath heaved through his lungs. *Damn it.*

Suddenly, a wave of nausea replaced the desire, almost bringing him to his knees. Sweat broke out on his brow and he swallowed hard, trying to force the nausea down. His muscles weakened until he had to grip the door frame and will himself to stand.

Time for more pills.

CHAPTER TWELVE

Getting to the island was going to be a bitch. Warren surveyed the crashing waves that pounded the pebble beach, then looked over at Esha, who stood with her hands on her hips and serenity on her face. Afraid of nothing.

They'd avoided each other this morning and hadn't spoken much while driving out to Bunnessan, the little town where they were going to put the boat into the water. Early afternoon sun struggled to illuminate the turbulent sea.

"Putting the boat in is going to be wet," she said, nodding at the waves. "Once we're out to sea, I can dry us. I'm not too keen on speeding through November winds on the Celtic Sea in wet clothes."

Warren wasn't as worried about that, or even about getting the boat into the water. It was landing at Fingal's Cave that concerned him. If the winds were as strong there, the waves would be crashing into the vertical rock face. Navigating out of the cave would be a bitch too, since it would be dark by that time. He glanced at Esha again. Was he willing to risk her safety?

He didn't have a choice. Not if he wanted to get his soul back. Memories of last night's debilitating cramps hardened him. If he didn't get his soul back before the medicine stopped working, he'd be completely nonfunctional.

And it wasn't like he was going to turn Esha over to Aurora. Once Esha led him to Aurora, he'd have her safely away before he confronted the other soulceress. Though how he was going to manage that, he still wasn't sure.

"Let's put the boat in," he said.

Within twenty minutes, they had the boat launched. Waves crashed over the bow of the sleek powerboat as they sped through the water. Turbulent gray clouds crawled over the horizon, threatening an early dusk if they kept up through the day. Just what they needed.

Though the air was brisk and the wind fierce, Warren could feel the heat of Esha, who stood right next to him, hanging onto the support bar attached to the steering console. He forced his attention to the wide gray ocean.

"Shite," he said, thirty minutes later when he caught sight of Staffa. The small island rose vertically out of the sea, waves crashing against its steep sides.

"That's it." Excitement and fear thrummed in Esha's voice as she pointed to the dark space at the waterline of the cliff.

Warren steered the boat closer, slowing as he caught sight of the waves. The sound of them crashing against the stone carried even over the wind. He glanced at his watch, then caught Esha's eye.

"It's almost exactly low tide. It's now or never, but those waves are still pretty fierce," he said.

"No problem. We're entering a soulceress space. I can guide us in. I don't have a lot of control over elements, but enough that I can get us in safely. I think."

Gods, she was brave. The prospect of piloting a small boat into the churning water of a cave made solely of vertical surfaces perfect to crash your boat against would have lesser Mytheans running with their tails tucked.

Esha walked to the bow for a better view. Her midnight hair whipped in the wind and spray splashed her. The entrance to the cave loomed ahead, dwarfing her tall frame. Regret that he was putting her in danger crept under his skin with little claws, an itchy feeling he couldn't shake. He was supposed to be in control of the situation, to be able to protect her, but already things were getting out of hand.

Warren piloted the boat inside, gritting his teeth at the narrowness of the waterway and the sight of the waves crashing into the vertical walls. When he'd been mortal so many years ago, it would have been considered a fairy cave, its octagonal pillars of basalt a gate to their lair. Inside, it was narrow, the cathedral-like pillars soaring high above the waterline. There was no entrance to the howf that he could see. Nothing but stone walls.

"There's no place to tie off," he shouted over the echoing sound of crashing waves. "We should retreat outside the cave and hike in."

No sooner had he said the words than the water surged up, crashing over the bow of the boat and throwing him to the stern. He choked on the saltwater that burned his throat and eyes and heaved himself to his feet.

"Esha!" he roared.

"Here!" She coughed and stumbled upright from where she'd been thrown to the floor at the bow.

Behind her, the water rose again, unnaturally high and shaped like a long-armed beast. It reached out with unnatural arms and threw their boat against the cave wall. Fiberglass crunched and the boat crashed back into the water, listing dangerously to the side. He held his feet, but Esha was thrown to the floor once again. He started toward her, only to stumble when the boat was thrown into the other wall. Fiberglass crunched again.

Shite. They would sink. Their boat was no match for the unnatural magic that haunted this place.

With a glance at Esha to determine that she was alright, he yelled, "We're getting out of here!"

"No!" Esha screamed and threw a bolt of flame at the water beast. It shrieked and steam rose off its surface. Esha cast a bigger flash of fire at it. It evaporated, vapor sizzling and filling the cave with a steam that burned his lungs.

To hell with this. With the waves crashing and the steam filling the cave, this place was nearly as dangerous as it had been. He yanked the lever to reverse the engine, but before he could back out, a huge wave picked up the small vessel and threw it at the cave wall. Fear for Esha nearly sent his heart through his chest. He charged at her. Just as the boat was about to crash into the great stone wall, he dragged her to the deck and curved his body around hers to protect her.

He braced himself, praying to the god he no longer worshiped to protect them. But instead of the thundering crash he expected, the boat sailed gracefully down upon the wave.

"Get off me." Esha pushed at him. She was soaked and still choking on seawater, but she stumbled to her feet.

What the hell? Frowning, he released her and stood. He spun in a three-sixty, taking in the giant cavern they'd entered. The boat floated in a small pond in the center, phosphorescence in the water illuminating the walls made of octagonal pillars. If he squinted back the way they'd come, he could just make out a shadow of light from the entrance to Fingal's Cave. The steam was gone, along with the water beast. A quick survey of the boat revealed that the rails and part of the sides were nearly crushed, but it was still seaworthy. Barely.

"What the hell was that?" he asked.

"Protective magic." She scraped her wet hair off her face, then leaned over and coughed, no doubt trying to get the seawater out of her lungs. After a few heaving breaths, she stood. "It activated when we neared the entrance. I didn't think I'd manage to stop it."

"You were quick, though." They'd have been dead if she hadn't been. "Good work."

"No. Good luck. I didn't know what would defeat it. But it sure as hell confirmed we're in the right place."

"Aye. But doona scare me like that again. I thought you were going to crash into the stone wall."

"I can take care of myself." She spun to take in the cave, a look of awe and apprehension on her face. The cat was leaning out of the boat, batting at the phosphorescence and no longer concerned about threats.

"Is this the *howf?*"

"No, it's the entrance. It was once part of Fingal's Cave, but it was enchanted to keep it hidden. It gives us the time and secrecy we need to find the *howf.*"

"Why the hell did you no' tell me we'd be crashing through an imaginary wall on a giant wave you'd be conjuring?"

"I figured you'd be able to see through the illusion, since you're a Mythean. I guess you're not the right kind of Mythean."

He frowned. But it was true. There was nothing right about him. He caught her looking at him and shook the thoughts away. Carefully, he steered the boat toward the shore that looked the best for landing. When they ran up onto the pebble beach, the Chairman was the first to hop out, followed by Esha. While she explored the huge cavern, Warren tied the boat off to one of the rock pillars.

"Start looking for anything out of the ordinary," Esha called, her voice echoing off the soaring stone walls.

Warren glanced around at the phosphorescent pool and the octagonal pillars. The whole bloody place was out of the ordinary.

After twenty minutes of climbing over the pillars and searching the walls, something finally seemed odder than the place itself.

"Esha, come here," he said, not bothering to speak up since sound traveled so easily here. He heard her approaching, could even hear the padding footsteps of the cat, but he kept his eyes on the faint letters etched into the wall, afraid that if he looked away he wouldn't find them again.

"What'd you find?" Esha stopped next to him. He gestured to the writing. "Wow."

"Can you read it?" He couldn't tell what language it was.

"No. But what's below it?"

His eyes flicked down, and he noticed a hand-shaped carving in the stone. It was rust colored. "That's blood."

"Damn." Esha reached for her tall boot and withdrew a slender dagger. "It's got to be part of the magic that allows one to read the writing. A sacrifice."

"Wait." He grabbed her hand, pulled the dagger free. "Let me."

"No."

"I'll do it. You've done enough."

She frowned, her eyes darkening with something like worry, then nodded. He sliced his palm, a long incision that stung like hell, then pressed his hand to the wall. The ground beneath his feet rumbled ominously, then began to crack apart, the stone heaving toward the ceiling.

"Shit!" Esha cried, and stumbled backward.

He grabbed her before she fell off the pillar upon which they stood, but it continued to rise as the ground around them cracked and rumbled.

"Give me the dagger!" Esha grabbed it from his hand and sliced her palm, then trust her hand against the stone wall. The shifting stone beneath their feet ground to a halt, then slowly returned to normal. The Chairman hissed, then returned to batting at the water of the pool.

"Why did it start? Hell, why did it stop?" Warren asked.

"Because you aren't a soulceress. Your blood was all wrong. I should have seen it coming. Stupid."

"It's fine now." She'd saved their asses twice now.

"For now." She glanced at the letters carved in the stone. "Good news is, I can read the writing."

"And?" He glanced around at the stone, confirming that it was no longer moving.

"It's a riddle. *There be more of we upon these walls, too hard to find once darkness falls. Light from magic will reveal, the secrets that we do conceal.*"

"More of *we*?" Warren asked.

"Yeah. And, *darkness falls*? It's always dark here, except for the phosphorescence in the water that lights the place up a bit."

"Are you sure you got the translation right?"

She punched him on the arm. "Yeah. It wasn't like I had to work at it. I just knew it. That's definitely what it says. Is *we* more soulceresses?"

"Or more letters. Another message."

"There's no way we'll find them, especially if they're high up." She craned her neck back to search the ceiling and higher walls. "Is that what the light is for?"

Warren shrugged. "Give one of those fireballs you like so much a try."

They were her signature, after all. He rubbed his cheek, recalling the wound she'd given him a few weeks ago by flinging a fireball in his direction when he'd snuck up on her in the underground.

Esha held out her right hand, palm up, and a small ball of fire ignited from thin air. She flung it up into the cavern and it flew slowly about the room, illuminating the walls and ceiling where the light of the glowing pond didn't reach. For the first few minutes, he only saw more pillars. Esha's scowl confirmed that she was having as little luck.

"There," he said, pointing to a far corner of the room, about halfway up the wall. It was still a good dozen meters off the ground, however.

"I see it," Esha said. "But I can't read it. Even if I got below it, I think it would be too small." A sound of frustration escaped her as she smashed the fireball into the wall.

"Hey! Doona hurt the image."

But the letters briefly glowed, their lines distinct from the dark wall into which they were carved.

CHAPTER THIRTEEN

"Whoa," Esha said, her eyes riveted to the glowing letters. But before she could make out what they said, the light disappeared. She frowned, then conjured a second, larger fireball and immediately threw it into the wall. She watched, her breath caught in her lungs.

"Damn it," Warren said when the light faded from the letters again.

"It glowed longer that time, though."

"Is it the wrong kind of light?"

Esha heaved out a sigh and leaned against the wall. "You could be right. The riddle talks about darkness falling. Maybe it means night. Has it gotten dark outside?"

Warren looked at his watch. "It's past four, so yes."

Sunlight. The opposite of night. Energized by the new tactic, Esha pushed herself off the wall and turned to face the letters closest to her. They were just at her eye level.

"Come here, Chairman," she said, gesturing to the cat, who still splashed in the pond, searching for fish or crabs or whatever lived in there. Apparently he only disliked water that didn't contain snacks.

When she felt the cat twine his body about her legs, she closed her eyes and focused on the connection with him that would enhance her power. She pressed all ten fingers against the engraved letters, focusing on the sharp feel of them beneath her fingertips.

"What are you—" Warren broke off when she shushed him.

Vivid images of a summer day played through her mind as she imagined the heat and warmth of the sun. Channeling that thought from her mind and out through her fingers, she pushed sunlight into the letters etched on the cave wall. When she felt like she'd forced enough light into the wall, she opened her eyes.

Nothing. Just a vague glow.

"Damn it! That's all the magical light I've got," she said.

When she turned to face Warren, she caught sight of a trail of glowing paw prints that led from the pond. She glanced down at the Chairman. His front paws glowed from the phosphorescent water. "Look at that...."

She met Warren's eyes, startled to see a grin stretch across his face. "Clever," he said.

Esha leaned down and swiped a finger across the Chairman's front paw. When she raised her finger, the water clinging to the tip made it glow. With a deep breath, she pressed the tip of her finger to the first letter of the riddle, the *T*. When she removed it, a small spot glittered with the enchanted water. Suddenly, the glittering light streaked along the letters, from the *T* to the *h* of the first word *There* all the way through to the end of the phrase.

"Look over there," Warren said, pointing to the letters she'd found higher up on the other wall. They'd begun to light up too, as had three other inscriptions scattered about the cave.

"Whoa."

The letters floated off the wall, swirling about each other until they formed another riddle that hung over what now appeared to be an entrance. It was still closed off by a wall of rock, but from where she stood now, with the glowing words hanging above it and pillars of stone arranged as if to frame it, it was definitely an entrance.

"What does it say?" Warren asked.

Esha squinted at the letters. The words were just as easy to understand this time, but it wasn't a riddle. "It says that the body cannot enter, only the soul."

Warren's gaze whipped away from the words and toward her. "Only your soul?"

"Yeah. Makes sense, I guess. It's not an easy thing to do. Takes a hell of a lot of power, and hurts like a bitch, but a soulceress can separate her soul and send it forth to another place with the help of her familiar. Anyone else would need the help of a soulceress to do so." Esha looked at the letters again, a language that she'd never seen in her life. "Not to mention the hidden language and the water beast. Those protections are an ideal safeguard for the cave."

"Makes sense. But do you even have enough power?"

"After the water beast? Maybe. Only one way to find out, though. Want to come?"

The question hit Warren in the gut.

Aye.

She'd be tearing her soul from her body to help him. The idea made his stomach pitch in a way that had nothing to do with Aurora's sickness. He didn't want Esha going in there alone, to face gods knew what. What if she needed him? She could be trapped there, hurt forever.

"I canna," he said. He didn't even try to hide the regret in his voice.

"Scared?"

"Nay. I canna." He had no soul to send. "And you won't either."

The words were a revelation to him, escaped from his mouth before he had a chance to even process them. Give up this lead? So as not to risk her?

Aye. Not even to find Aurora.

When had he gone from not worrying about using Esha to find Aurora to refusing to put her in danger? But hadn't protecting her been his plan all along? He'd planned to have Aurora's head before Esha ever met her. He'd caused too much death in his life. He wouldn't be the cause of Esha's.

"Did you seriously just tell me what I can't do?" Her eyebrows arched.

"There's got to be another way."

"There isn't, and I'm going. The light-up letters are pretty clear."

"Doona go. She could be in there. If I canna go, I will no' be able to protect you."

She laughed lightly. "Not knowing what's in there is precisely the reason I want to go. And she isn't in there. I'm sure. Mostly. Thanks for the offer, but I'll be fine."

He stepped toward her, his hand outstretched. She didn't step back but she raised her brow again. His hand dropped.

She was right. She could take care of herself. And she wasn't his to command. His fist clenched to the point of pain. "How will you do this?"

"I leave my body in a safe place—with you, in this case—and the Chairman takes my soul through the portal."

"Will he leave his body too?"

"No, he'll turn to smoke."

Warren had seen the cat perform that eerie trick. Witches' familiars not only enhanced the witches' power, but had their own as well. Soulceresses' familiars were likely the same. "How long will you be gone?"

"I don't know."

"You'll have to come back with at least a little power, or we won't be able to get the boat back out through that magical stone wall."

She looked toward the boat and frowned. "You're right. It took magic just to get in the entrance. I wasn't expecting that. Well, I'll just have to not get hurt then."

"*Doona* get hurt. I can swim out of here, but if you're too hurt to get yourself out, my dragging you across the Celtic Sea could kill you."

"I'm tougher than I look."

"That you are."

Esha sauntered toward the gate, her tall form dwarfed by the pillars that surrounded the two-meter-wide expanse of otherwise unimpressive stone. When she reached it, she turned to slide down against the wall and sit with her back to it.

"It's now or never. When my soul leaves my body, it will go with the Chairman through the gate." She glanced at it.

"Which, apparently, is just a wall. If I can't get through, I'll just come back. If it works, my body will stay here."

"Will your body be alive?" He didn't know if he could deal with standing guard over her dead body.

"Yeah, but it'll look like I'm in a coma. Just ignore me, I'll be fine."

Ignore her? Not bloody likely. He'd be watching her and the gate like a soldier waiting for news from the front.

"Well, here goes nothing."

"Wait—"

She looked at him, curiosity in her eyes.

"Doona. There's got to be another way."

"I'll be fine." She closed her eyes and reached out to touch her cat's back. The two of them shimmered, the cat changing first to a shadowy form of his scruffy black self. Esha followed, a ghostly version of herself separating from her body and joining the cat.

With a wave to him that glimmered in the dark cave, she followed the cat's shadow until they disappeared through the wall.

A great gust of breath escaped Warren, one that he hadn't realized he'd been holding. What the hell was he doing, dragging others into this web of misery that had begun when Aurora had stolen his soul? He'd thought he'd do anything to get it back, but the sight of Esha slumped against the wall of the dark cave made him as sick as Aurora using his power.

He strode over to her body and sank down onto the floor next to her. Gently, he tested her pulse, his breath stuck until he felt it beating steady and true beneath his fingers. His heart clutched as he looked down at her. Though she drove him crazy, he'd been drawn by her bravery and willingness to help over the last several weeks.

He leaned his head back against the wall and stared up at the ceiling. The cold slide of sweat dripped down his temple.

Fear. Something he hadn't felt for another in centuries.

CHAPTER FOURTEEN

Esha hated the feeling of having her soul sucked from her body. She had barely enough power to complete the task, and once the excruciating process of tearing each bit of her soul from her mind and limbs was over, she just felt weightless, which was vastly superior to the tearing part of the operation. The Chairman stayed close by her side as they passed through the gate that led to the *howf*. Without him, she'd be stuck without a body. If she ran out of power, she'd be stuck like this forever. It'd be the worst way to go. Unable to feel or talk, she'd be worse than a ghost.

"Thanks, dude," she said, not surprised that the words had no sound. She no longer had actual vocal cords, after all.

With a deep breath and a wave to Warren, she nodded to the Chairman and they passed through the gate. It felt no different to pass through rock than it did air, which was strange in itself. But when they entered the *howf*, the feeling of abandonment struck her hard. She'd have gasped if she'd had a body, but instead she just felt lost. Dead, almost.

She squinted in the darkness, but was unable to see anything, so she focused on forming a ball of fire in her hand.

Its unnatural brightness illuminated the space with a dim orange glow that reached all corners of the medium-sized space.

It was a meeting space, but one that had been constructed and decorated hundreds of years ago. A fireplace with no flue that would have been lit with magical smokeless fire, plush chairs, and small tables. Bookshelves and paintings covered all of the walls. And a fine layer of dust covered everything in sight.

With the Chairman following at her heels, Esha explored the room for clues. This was the only place she could think of that would tie her to another soulceress. There had to be something, but she needed to look quickly. She hadn't mentioned to Warren that she couldn't stay separated from her body for long without making it permanent. Only as long as her power lasted, and she barely had enough to say so.

She skimmed the titles of the books, but nothing stood out. They were primarily histories of her kind, along with histories of other types of Mytheans. Knowledge was power. The soulceresses agreed with the university on that one.

Noticeably absent were spell books, which Esha hadn't expected to find. Those were used by the hacks who worked in covens. Soulceresses manifested their desires with a thought and power.

"Well, Chairman, I've got nothing," she said soundlessly as she continued to look around. A few books were left open on the tables, along with scattered papers and a few wine glasses, as if the place had been in use and then suddenly deserted.

The air of abandonment and death that permeated the howf was probably left over from the Burnings. The few who had survived had lain low until the hysteria was over. Now, there were so few left and the threat so distant that they could move about without too much fear, as Esha did.

If they'd visited, they hadn't moved anything. Wise, considering the fact that Esha could feel an imprisonment charm on the place. Anything removed would result in consequences. Was that one of the reasons it was supposed to be difficult to leave here?

With the bookshelves and paintings all inspected, Esha wound her way around the tables and chairs, inspecting the things laid out upon the tables. She reached out to touch a piece of paper, but when she did so, she swore she saw her hand disappear. So quickly she couldn't be sure, but her time was drawing to a close.

Nothing on this table, so she moved on. A square of white on another table caught her eye. She gasped soundlessly. On the largest table in the middle of the room sat an envelope.

With her name on it.

With a trembling hand, she picked it up. Though she had no body, the items in the room had obviously been enchanted to be manipulated by souls.

Who could have written to her? *Stupid question.*

Before her eyes, the hand that held the letter flickered in and out of existence. Damn it.

She was running out of time. Esha glanced nervously at the Chairman. He flickered too, and she swore she saw annoyance in his eyes. Biting her lip, she began to tear the letter open. She just had to glance at it long enough to get an idea of the message. But her flickering hand wouldn't work properly. One second, she felt the letter's seal beneath her fingertips—the next, nothing.

Swallowing hard, she debated the pros and cons of trying to remove the letter from the room. Determining that it was worth chancing the unknown penalty and unwilling to risk losing her body, Esha dashed for the entrance with the Chairman at her heels. Her arms flickered as she skirted a chair. So close—the entrance was just ahead.

She would make it in time. She had to.

With a deep breath, she plunged through. As soon as she landed on the other side, a harsh wail echoed through the cavern. It tore at her eardrums and howled through her mind. To preserve her sanity, she focused on finding Warren.

Near where she'd left him, he surged to his feet, her limp body cradled in his arms. Esha hurtled toward her body. She gasped as she opened her eyes and met Warren's. Strong arms held her tight to a broad chest, heat radiating through every inch of her.

"We need to go," she said, struggling to escape his arms.

The shrieking turned to howling, a sound so harsh it threatened to make her black out. She gestured to the boat that was their only hope of safety.

As soon as Warren put her down, she grabbed his arm and turned toward the boat. A glance behind her showed that the stone entrance to the *howf* was bulging outward, some areas more than others. Stone should *not* be able to move like that.

"Come on." With the letter gripped tightly in her hand, she sprinted for the boat.

After only a few steps, an agonizing pain tore across her back. She stumbled, a scream caught in her throat, and lost her grip on Warren's hand. The pain began to paralyze her and she fell to her knees.

Before she could fall any farther, Warren swept her up and charged forward. Out of the corner of her eye, she caught sight of a great stone claw reaching out from the entrance, growing longer as they ran. She could no longer feel her legs.

"Hurry." Her fist clenched around the letter that had caused so much trouble.

Warren leapt into the boat, the Chairman behind him, and she cried out at the pain that streaked across her back as he jostled her. Darkness crept into the corners of her vision, but she fought it, desperate to not lose consciousness with certain death chasing them.

"Hold on for me, damn it. I'm going to get you to safety, I promise." He wiped wetness from her cheeks, and only then did she realize that she was crying. "But first, can you get us out of this damn cave?"

"Can summon a wave... but can't... aetherwalk."

She had to get them out of here. She was the only one who could.

He nodded at her, then wrapped his jacket around her before returning to the wheel. Cold crept along her skin as he started up the engine. It was going to be close. Closing her eyes, she focused her remaining energy on calling forth a wave big enough to carry them out of the cave.

"We're nearing the wall," Warren shouted over the otherworldly shrieking that still bounced off the stone walls.

She reached for the Chairman, pathetically grateful to feel his fur against her palm. The effort to dredge up enough power to create the wave had her head spinning, but soon she felt the surge of water beneath the boat. It roared in her ears. Or was that the pain?

She managed to crack her eyes open long enough to see them rise closer to the ceiling of the cave and fall on the other side.

The boat crashed down and blackness took her.

CHAPTER FIFTEEN

The bitter taste of fear flooded Warren's mouth as he piloted the barely functional boat out of the cavern. Gods, this thing had better make it to shore. He could barely keep his eyes off Esha's collapsed form, though every time he looked at her, something inside him twisted painfully. Dragging his gaze from her, he forced himself to focus on the water. Getting her back to Mull was the only way to ensure her safety.

When he cranked the engine up to full speed, the bow rose in the water. A growl escaped his chest when he saw seawater tinged red trickle from beneath Esha's prone form.

Faster. He pushed the boat to its limits, flinching every time a large wave smacked the bow, and with it, Esha.

A mile from shore, with the boat failing due to the damage to the hull, he checked his phone. Finally, cell service.

"Cadan," he said when his second-in-command picked up. "I need you to send a healer to the village of Dunessan. Esha is wounded. We'll land in ten minutes."

"Aye. No' a problem."

"The best, Cadan."

"Aye, I know."

Despite the cold air, sweat trickled down his back as he piloted the boat toward shore. Blood still seeped from beneath Esha. Her face was stark, whiter than he'd ever seen it, and even her red lips were chalky.

As he beached the boat, he squinted through the starless night, looking for the healer sent by the university. There was no one. No one there to save Esha. She was immortal, but that only meant *stronger*. Age and disease wouldn't kill her, but grievous injury could, especially if it was magical.

He couldn't lose her. He wouldn't. He rushed to the front of the boat and swept Esha up into his arms. A crumpled envelope was still clutched in her fist. He pried it out of her hand and stuffed it into his pocket.

There had to be a mortal hospital somewhere on this island. Though it went against the laws of their kind to alert mortals to their presence—and taking an immortal with freakish healing abilities to a mortal hospital would definitely do so—he didn't care.

She was cold in his arms as he cradled her, shielding her against the whipping sea wind. Though he tried not to jostle her as he stepped upon the shore, a weak moan filtered through her lips. When he looked up from her face, he caught sight of a shimmering patch of air that marked a portal about to open. Thank gods.

Within seconds, a healer stepped through. Gods damn it, she was young—didn't look to be any older than a teenager. This was the being to whom he was supposed to entrust Esha's life?

"Are you Warren?" she yelled in a lilting voice.

"Aye," he said as he strode toward the Range Rover with Esha in his arms. The girl met him at the back door. "Open it."

She did. With her help, he carefully laid Esha upon the back seat, shifting her so her wounded back didn't press against it. The sight of the angry red gashes made his stomach lurch. He'd seen far worse, but it was the fact that they marred her flesh that bothered him.

"What happened to her?" asked the healer as she laid her palm gently on Esha's side.

"Attacked by an enchanted stone wall. It formed a great claw and swiped at her. Are you old enough to be doing this?"

The healer slanted him a glance and said, "I'd bet I'm older than you are. Appearances are deceiving."

The healer climbed into the back with Esha, wedging her small form in the gap between the backseat and the front. "We need to get her somewhere warm and dry."

"Aye," Warren said, and within moments, he had the Range Rover back on the main road.

"What about the boat? Isn't it Cadan's?"

"I'll buy him a new one. How's she doing?"

"Poorly. How far to shelter?"

"About thirty minutes to Cadan's house. There's no decent shelter between here and there."

He tried his damnedest to avoid potholes and bumps in the road, but every time Esha moaned, it cut through him like a blade of fire. A deer jumped into the road. When he swerved to avoid it, Esha's damned feline yowled as if it could feel her pain.

"Do something for her, damn it," he said.

"I am. Just get us there."

The miles to Cadan's house were the longest he'd ever traveled. He was a bastard for dragging Esha into this. Though it had seemed necessary at the time, every sound of pain stabbed him with regret.

Finally, after half an hour of cold fear, they arrived. Warren carefully carried Esha's limp body into the house, desperate not to hurt her any more.

"What'd you do to her?" he asked the healer as he climbed the stairs to one of the bedrooms. A faint blue glow surrounded Esha, and though she was pale, her face was no longer twisted with pain.

"The blue glow is a halting spell. There's poison in the wound. Now it won't travel any farther. But she's in less pain because of her familiar."

"The cat?"

"Yeah, he can lend some of his strength to her. All familiars can."

Warren looked down at the cat, who ignored him. Maybe the beast wasn't so bad after all. In fact, he'd be thawing a tuna filet for him at the first opportunity.

"But you've stopped the poison. You'll be able to heal her." It was more a statement than a question as he laid her upon the bed. Esha would get better. She had to.

"I don't know."

Somebody was torturing her, and all she wanted to do was sleep. Esha tried to lift an arm to push away the person who was dragging sandpaper across her cheek, but the arm weighed a million pounds.

Or had someone tied her down? A chill crept along her skin, and her breath grew short. She couldn't move. Someone had tied her up. *No.* Her muscles burned as she tried to struggle, but she could barely move her limbs. Though it hurt like a bitch, she dragged her eyes open.

And stared into the furry face of the Chairman. She exhaled.

"Go away, tuna breath," she gasped.

When the cat settled by her side, her heart rate slowed, and her breathing calmed. If the Chairman was corporeal and sleeping next to her, they were safe. Had they been in danger, he'd have turned to smoke to protect himself until he could help her. Still, being weakened like this, unable to protect herself, made a cold sweat break out on her skin.

Soft sheets were smooth against her palms, the light in the room pleasantly dim. Enough to see by, but not enough to irritate her pounding head. It was warm as well, and contrary to her previous fear, she was held down only by a light blanket. *Safe.*

Relatively.

She turned her head and caught sight of the door to the room just as a large figure walked through it.

"Esha." Relief was strong in Warren's voice. "How do you feel?"

He knelt by the bed, his eyes searching her face. He looked... tired. Handsomely rumpled. Golden hair, normally at least somewhat neat, stuck out and a frown seemed permanently etched on his face.

"Water." Her voice scratched in her throat as though she were trying to swallow a burr.

He nodded, his lips tight. When he returned to the bed with a small glass of water, he lifted her head gently and held the glass up to her lips.

"What... happened?" she asked when she finished.

Her eyes drifted closed as he recounted the attack at the cave, memories of which came to her in hazy bits and pieces, and the healer who had fixed her up. "You should be back on your feet within a few days. Whatever poison was in those claws is out of your system, but it weakened you. The healer had never seen the like."

"Not poison. Magic."

It had been her penance for removing the letter from the cave. But she'd lived, hadn't she? Had she been alone, she would have died. Warren had saved her life. It put a bitter taste in her mouth. That was *her* job.

"My letter?" Just saying the words sapped what little strength she had.

"Later. Rest," he said.

She wanted to argue, but was too weak to speak. She swore she felt his hand brush her hair away from her face, but she didn't have the strength to open her eyes to look. He'd saved her, she thought, as she drifted off to sleep. And now he was taking care of her. Though she hated relying on anyone, it was... nice... to have someone take care of her.

Unusual, but nice.

CHAPTER SIXTEEN

Warren stared blindly into the refrigerator. He'd come down to the kitchen for something, but he had no idea what.

Gods, he was tired. In the two days since Esha had been wounded, he'd done nothing but sit by her bed and stare at her—unusual behavior for someone who didn't care. He dragged a hand through his hair, disgusted with himself. For getting her into this situation. For being unable to leave her side.

What if he had lost her? He stared blindly into the refrigerator as memories of her bravery flashed across his mind. She'd never let anyone take the hard job from her. Wouldn't trust them enough to do so. He'd never met anyone as mistrusting yet fearlessly brave as Esha. And he'd nearly gotten her killed.

A demanding meow caught his attention. He looked down to see Esha's cat at his feet. Normally, he'd think that the cat wanted to be fed. But after walking downstairs last night and seeing the cat devouring a piece of salmon he'd dragged out of the newly stocked refrigerator—courtesy of the healer, since Warren wouldn't leave Esha's side—it was clear that the cat could take care of food for himself.

That meant he was now doing a Lassie for Esha.

At least, he wanted to assume that the cat was here to tell him that Esha had awakened. Unless something was wrong.

Forgetting all about lunch, he took the stairs two at a time to her room. The iron bands around his heart eased just slightly at the sight of her in bed. The glow had returned to her ivory skin, as had the red to her lips. She was on the mend.

"How are you feeling?"

"Starving."

Thank gods, she was feeling better. He nodded. "I'll be back."

Down in the kitchen, he threw together some sandwiches and tea, along with a bit of broth in case she wasn't feeling up to a heartier meal, and returned to her room.

"Here." The awkwardness in his voice was painful to hear as he set the tray down on her lap. She'd managed to scoot herself up in bed until she was almost sitting upright. "Do you need help?"

"I've got it." She dug into the sandwiches with gusto, then sighed with pleasure over the tea. When she finished eating, she looked up at him. "How long have I been out?"

"It's been a couple of days since you woke last."

When she stretched, his eyes followed her movements like those of a wolf. He looked away quickly, embarrassed. She was sick, damn it. He wasn't an animal.

"Is that all?"

"Aye. Do you need to, ah..." he gestured toward the door leading to the bathroom.

She shook her head.

He nodded. Maybe she was well enough now to answer the question that had been burning in his mind. "Why did everything go wrong back at the cave?"

She looked away, reaching out for her cat. Once she'd sunk her fingers into its fur, she looked back at him, guilt etched on her face. "I broke the rules. I spent so much of my time searching for a clue that by the time I found it, I didn't have time to read it. When I removed something from the *howf*, the magic activated to stop me. If you hadn't been there, I never would have made it out with what I'd taken. I'd have... died." She glared at him, her fine black brows drawn over gleaming eyes.

"Hey. Doona be mad at me. I was just trying to help."

"I know. But protecting myself is my job and I failed. I did something stupid and nearly died for it." She looked down at her cat, but the fierceness of her disappointment radiated from her. "I've always been smarter than that."

He had a feeling that this might be the first time someone had ever stepped in and saved her ass. But if he asked, she'd bite his head off.

"Thanks for saving me." She looked up. She'd managed to swallow most of her disappointment and gratitude showed through.

He felt his chest swell, but he just nodded, then looked away from her. Toward the window, the door. Anywhere but at her.

She sighed dejectedly, then leaned back on the pillow. "I lost our only clue. And I don't even know what it said."

"The letter?"

Her eyes brightened, and she sat up a bit straighter. "You have it? I thought I lost it."

"Aye, you had a death grip on it when you collapsed in the boat. I saved it. Figured it was important."

"Thank gods." She collapsed back on the bed, relief evident in her face. Then she lifted her head, looking at him suspiciously. "Did you read it?"

He shook his head. He'd wanted to. Gods, how he'd wanted to know what was within the crumpled envelope bearing her name. But guilt over getting her into this situation had hounded him, and he'd been unable to open it. His desire to do right by Esha now warred with his rage against Aurora.

He still had to kill Aurora, there was no choice in that. Who was to say that she wouldn't repeat her past, threatening mortals and Mytheans alike? There was more at stake here than just his soul or the soulceress who had started to work her way into his head.

"You should rest," he said.

"I want my letter."

"After you rest. There's nothing that can be done now, with you in this state."

"Might I remind you that you owe me? The least you can do is give me that letter, since I'm in this state because I'm trying to help you."

"I know that. But you need to rest."

"You don't know what I need." Her eyes flashed at him, stronger than the rest of her body—an eerie reminder that she didn't need to be physically strong to fuck with him. Her magic would do that just fine.

"Aye, I do. The healer told me. Nothing that will set back your progress. And how do you know the letter isn't enchanted to cause problems when it's opened?"

She frowned. He could tell from her face that what he'd said had hit home.

She pursed her lips, and her brows drew together over her eyes. "Fine. Tomorrow. But what am I supposed to do until then?"

"Rest. Get your strength up."

"By staring at the wall? I've been sleeping for more than a day. I'm getting out of bed." With a determined look on her face, she heaved herself up off the pillows.

"Doona!" He stepped forward, arms outstretched to stop her.

"Ow!" Grimacing, she lowered herself gingerly back onto the pillows. "Damn, that creepy stone claw did a number on me, didn't it?"

"Aye. You'll be out for at least another day. Should be able to walk by tomorrow morning."

She frowned at him. "I should be healed by now. What kind of cut-rate healer did you hire, anyway?"

How could she think he wouldn't make sure she had the best? But the sight of her laid out in bed, still pale and drawn from the pain, nearly made him bark out a cynical laugh. Of course she didn't trust him to take care of her. He'd gotten her into this mess. Hounded her until she'd given in and put her life in danger to help him.

"I'm sorry, lassie. She was one of the best, but your injuries are unusual. You won't heal as fast as you normally would, but she did the best she could."

"Oh, that just sucks." Her eyes rolled back in her head. It was obvious she hated being confined like this. Inactivity was as familiar to her as the moon.

"I'll bring you some books. Or a TV," he said.

"What, you don't think I like to read?"

"Doona know. I'm just trying to help."

She looked at him strangely, eyes roving over his face as she thought about his words. "Really?"

"Aye."

"Well then, how about a game of cards later?"

She wanted to play a game with him? "For stakes?"

"Maybe. Why not?"

"Um, aye. That's fine." How high could the stakes be, after all?

CHAPTER SEVENTEEN

Two hours later, Esha lay in her damned prison of a bed waiting for Warren to come back for their card game. Waking up almost totally incapacitated had been a real mind fuck. Sure, she got dinged up when out hunting rogues, but never to the point of becoming bedridden. Then again, she'd never come up against another soulceress before, even one who had long since disappeared after casting her magic.

Idiot. She was aware that she sometimes took stupid risks, but when they always worked out, could they really be considered that stupid? Until this last one. This task with Warren had turned out to be more than she'd bargained for. Apparently there *were* some things that she couldn't do alone.

But with Warren as a partner? It was an idea that initially would have thrilled her. Now it made her wary.

What she really needed was more information. Warren wasn't telling her the full truth about why he was looking for Aurora, and Esha wasn't about to let her lack of knowledge become a liability.

Hence the card game. While it would be nice to take her mind off her helplessness, what she really wanted was to pry some secrets out of Warren. What better way than by distracting him with cards?

"Esha?" Warren's deep voice sounded through the door and made shivers run down her spine.

"Come on in." She pushed her hair back and sat up straighter in the bed. Not that she cared what she looked like. 'Course not.

The Chairman glanced up from cleaning his manliness at the foot of the bed and gave her a look that said, *yeah right.*

"Oh, put your turkey leg down," she told him, nodding at the back leg he'd stuck up in the air.

He just glared at her. She scowled back, then looked up from the cat to see Warren striding toward her, confident and sexy as hell. *He's a jerk*, she reminded herself. *Don't forget that.*

But was he, really?

"So, what are we playing?" he asked, holding up a deck of cards and a sack of pistachios. The corner of his mouth kicked up in a half-smile, and she felt her heart skip a beat.

"Pistachios?"

"Sure. Keeps the stakes low. Since I chose the stakes, you can choose the game."

Esha frowned. She wanted info, not pistachios. "Why do you care if they're low? Scared I'll make you play strip poker?"

Warren's gaze heated as his eyes traveled from her face down her body. Heat crept along her nerve endings, and she realized she'd invited the look that set her mind ablaze.

"Is that really an option?" he asked.

She swallowed. Was she ready to deal with a naked Warren? To play a game of chance that could end with him on top of her?

Yes.

Inwardly, she shook her head. No way was she going to let that happen. She'd thrown herself at him enough in the past, and all it had netted her was rejection and mean comments. Even if he was being nicer to her now, it didn't negate the way he'd tricked her in the past or the fact that he wanted to kill Aurora.

She was turning over a new leaf.

"Pistachios it is." She'd find a way to up the stakes later. And she'd keep her clothes on, damn it. "How about Texas Hold 'Em?"

Warren's grin widened, and he nodded as he walked toward the bed.

"Hang on, I'm dying to get out of bed," she said. If her traitorous body was going to keep up with her resolve, she couldn't be anywhere near Warren and a bed. Gingerly, she rose and walked to the little sitting area under the windows.

"How do you feel?" Warren asked as he rushed over to help her into a chair.

She swatted his hands away. "Fine. A lot better, honestly."

Most of the pain had faded, leaving only muscle aches and exhaustion. She'd walked some laps around the room today, just to prove she could, and even managed a short shower. The exercise had actually improved her strength some.

She stretched her arms over her head, carefully working her sore muscles to see if she could loosen them up. Warren's eyes followed her movements, his gaze hot and his jaw tight. Slowly, she lowered her arms, looking away at the last second. This was going to be hard.

She reached for the bag of pistachios to dole out their lots and nodded at the deck. "You can deal this hand."

"Are you any good at this game?"

"Not bad. I liked cards at school, though that was long before poker. Poker's much better than what we played." But she was a natural, considering that she could magically manipulate the cards in the deck. But she wouldn't tell him that.

"School?"

"The North American Academy for Immortal Magics." She said it in the tone that the headmaster had always used, official and staid.

"I take it you dinna like it there."

"How do you figure?"

"Did you no' run away before you graduated?"

"None of your business. How did you know that, anyway?"

"Before we invited you to join the university, we did some research on you. Got to know your background, your leanings."

Meaning, did she lean rogue or with the university? "Hmm. Well then, I guess you know all about me. So why are you asking?"

"Because I don't know as much as I'd like to. And I'd like to hear the details from you."

Startled, she met his eyes. He looked almost as surprised as she was to have admitted to such a thing. Had Warren had a change of heart about her? Accepted that he was attracted to her, despite the fact that she was a soulceress?

If the kiss the other night was any indication, then yes.

She wasn't sure how she felt about that.

"You know what we need? A drink." She nodded toward the door. "How about you go fetch us something? I'll deal."

He looked down at the cards, obviously wondering if he could trust her to deal when he was out of the room. Like it mattered. But she just smiled in what she hoped was a winning fashion.

"Don't worry about those. I'll play fair." *As fair as you've played with me.*

Her smile faltered only slightly when he met her eyes, but whatever he saw in her face had him nodding and rising to go find something to drink. She couldn't help but follow him with her gaze. His stride was powerful, matched by his rugged build and suited to the masculine bedroom in which he'd placed her.

Her heart clutched a little, reminding her of all the times she'd wished she had his undivided attention. Now that she had it, she wasn't sure what to do with it.

Quickly, she dealt a hand, not bothering to fuss with loading the deck. Playing a few honest rounds would allay any suspicions he might have. The cards had only been laid out on the table a moment before he returned with a dusty old bottle of whiskey and two tumblers.

"A man after my own heart," she said, eying the bottle with appreciation.

"I thought you'd like this. Found it in Cadan's stash in the basement. He makes his own."

She nodded, remembering hearing something about that. Cadan had one of the oldest and most famous distilleries in the country, from what she recalled. With his immortal life and exceptional memory, he had an advantage when it came to running a long-term business in which age acted as a sign of quality. Mytheans all had that going for them, if they chose to utilize it.

Her eyes followed Warren's big hands as he uncorked the bottle. Scars ran across the backs from when he'd still been mortal. He'd been a warrior, but what kind she wasn't sure. His hands were gentle as he worked the cork free, and images of what they could do to her flitted across her mind.

She tore her gaze away from his hands, only to meet his eyes. Her own darted away and she cursed herself silently. She needed to calm down. Somewhere between departing for Staffa and sitting here, she'd lost some of the shell she'd cultivated to protect herself.

Now she was just a chick with a crush, and it was pathetic. She accepted the glass that Warren handed her and inhaled.

"Thanks," she said, then nodded at his cards and the pile of nuts she'd laid out for him.

When he'd picked them up, she dealt the flop. The three cards stared up at her from the middle of the table, and she frowned at her shitty hand.

"No' what you'd hoped for?" Warren asked.

"You never know, it could turn around."

It didn't. After he'd swept the small pile of pistachios he'd won toward his side of the table, she handed over the cards. He dealt and they played several hands while the howling wind outside added atmosphere to the low hum of their conversation. She kept it superficial—gossip about the university—and with the dim light from the table lamps, it felt like they were in their own little world. It was nice to sit across from him and just play cards. Though tension was thick in the air and accentuated by covert glances, it felt good to spend time with him when she wasn't yelling, having to act tough, or trying to seduce him.

Lulled by the coziness of their surroundings and distracted by Warren's warm presence, she didn't bother to introduce more complex conversation that would get her the answers that she wanted. She didn't even bother to stack the deck in her favor, and as a result, she lost three hands out of five. Not bad, considering that she was playing fair, but it reminded her that she'd suggested the game for a reason.

With the warm hum of whiskey in her blood, Esha figured that it was time to up the ante with a question or two. She met his eyes over her hand of cards. "Why do you want to catch her so badly? Your commitment seems... personal."

"What do you mean?"

"You're handling this one personally. In the ten years I've been with the university, I don't think I've ever seen you go out on an assignment."

He shrugged, and she took it as an assent.

"Why is it that you don't? You're relatively young to lead the Praesidium. Warriors your age would normally be raring to fight." Hell, in their world, anyone who wasn't bedridden liked the occasional scuffle.

"Three hundred and eighty-four is young?"

"Compared to Cadan and the rest."

He nodded. Most Mythean Guardians were older than he was. "I killed enough people in my mortal life."

"Who?" From the darkness in his voice, he wasn't talking about just any casualty of war.

"I'm done killing," he said, ignoring her questions. "I doona want to anymore. I haven't in over three hundred years."

"Not even rogues?"

He shook his head. This battle-hardened warrior, covered in scars from his past life, didn't even want to kill rogues? Killing rogues was a good thing. Mythean survival depended upon their living under the radar of mortals. Rogues were so selfish, or so crazy, that they didn't care about revealing their presence. Some were Mytheans who lived on earth, others were demons escaped from one of the hells, but either way, consensus had it that they were best disposed of quickly if they refused or were incapable of mending their ways.

Who had he killed in his past that had traumatized him to the point that he wouldn't even kill rogues?

"Anyway," he said, "the Praesidium isn't about killing. It's about protecting."

"Those important to humanity, I know. But sometimes there's fighting and killing. And you don't want any part of it. Were you ever a Mythean Guardian, out on the front lines protecting those who hold our fate in their hands?"

"That's a romantic way to look at it. But no, I wasn't."

"You were made the boss without ever serving with the troops?"

He shrugged.

"You must be a good leader."

"I read people's strengths well, which is important when assigning Mythean Guardians to a case. I'd lived at the university for about fifty years before I met Aerten, and she decided that I'd be a good candidate for the job when she couldn't be on earth."

Esha had only met Aerten, the Celtic goddess of fate, once, when Warren had invited her to be a consultant for the

Praesidium. Aerten had met with her to approve it. Esha had to agree that the goddess had an uncommon insight. If she thought Warren read people well, then he did.

"So, about Aurora, then ..."

Warren handed her the deck of cards to deal and said nothing. She gave him a loaded look, not wanting to let him off the hook. Still, he said nothing, just nodded at the cards.

"Fine. At least tell me why you couldn't go into the *howf*." When she'd asked if he'd wanted to come, he'd said he *couldn't*, and with real regret in his voice, not that he didn't *want* to.

"No' going to happen," Warren said. There was no way he'd be telling her about his soul.

Though the card game had been pleasant—hell, more than pleasant, sitting across from the soulceress with her gleaming golden eyes concentrated on the cards and her throaty voice filling the room—it would be a bad idea to share the real reason he was hunting Aurora.

"Come on, I'll just keep asking," she said, and dealt the cards. "Or maybe I'll ask around the university."

"The hell you will."

She raised her eyebrows. "I'm not above it. My life's at risk in this search, and I want to know why it's so important."

He stayed silent.

"How about we play for it. If I win, you tell me. If you win, you can keep your secret."

Warren eyed the cards she'd laid out.

"You know I won't hesitate to ask around."

He could probably beat her if she played fair. There was no guarantee she wouldn't manipulate the cards with her magic, but there was also no guarantee that she wouldn't ask around at the university. Part of him even wanted to lose, if he was honest with himself. He'd never told another what had happened to him, had carried the burden himself.

As he should.

But still.

"All right, lassie. I win, you drop it. You win, I'll tell you why I couldn't go into the *howf*. Best two out of three."

She smiled, then dealt the flop.

Damn it. His hand was shit and had little chance of improving when the next cards were revealed. He looked up to see her smiling at the cards, lush red lips parted in a grin that caught his breath. Silken black hair swept over her shoulder and hung down in waves, making him wonder what the strands would feel like between his fingers.

H stifled a frustrated groan and dragged his gaze away from her lips and his mind away from thoughts of throwing her on the bed and finding out just how good she tasted.

But he wasn't able to get his mind back on the game. Within minutes, she'd won that hand with cards that would have beaten his no matter how good his focus. "That's the best hand you've had all night," he said.

"Lucky me." She handed him the cards.

He accepted them and dealt out their hands, glancing up once to see her peering hard at the cards. Didn't she trust him to deal fairly? He scowled.

He glanced at his cards, cursing silently when he saw a two and a nine against a flop that did him no favors. The next two cards laid upon the table didn't help.

He'd lost.

Esha confirmed it by laying her hand upon the table and grinning at him. Her cat slinked around the feet of her big chair, peering up at him and flicking its tail.

"Well," she said, letting the word hang in the air as she refilled his glass and her own with the bright amber liquid that so perfectly matched her eyes.

Carefully, he placed his cards on the table and leaned back in his chair. He focused on breathing in, then breathing out as a chill ran over his arms with little mouse feet. Was he really going to reveal to another how he had become what he was? To her?

She sat across from him silently, her eyes searching his as she waited for his tale. He'd made a deal, and he never went back on his word.

"I'm happy to wait all night," she said. Instead of being challenging as he'd expected, her voice held an undercurrent of understanding. Patience. Considering what he'd put her through, she deserved to know.

"I doona have a soul." The weight of a secret held hundreds of years too long lifted off his shoulders even as his breath stuck in his lungs and his head buzzed. What could she possibly think of him now?

There was nothing more important in their world than souls. They were the core of a person, the part that gave a Mythean immortality on earth or allowed mortals to pass on to their afterworld. Without it, he was a... thing. Not really a Mythean, not really a mortal.

When he caught her gaze, he saw surprise. Shock, even. Her lips parted on a wordless question as she searched his face, no doubt looking for the joke.

"You're... serious?" she asked.

He nodded.

"How? How is that even possible?"

Possible? How could she not know it was possible? She was a soulceress. Souls were her stock in trade.

She scooted forward in her chair and reached out a trembling hand to touch him. He shuddered when he felt the warmth of her hand against the side of his neck. It radiated through him, a brand that felt as though it would last forever. Unable to help himself, he reached up and pressed her hand against his unnaturally cold skin, reveling in the warmth of her.

He watched warily as her gaze searched his face and then traveled down his body to settle at his feet.

"So that's why," she murmured.

Cold returned to him when she withdrew her hand. He wanted to reach out and snatch it back, but resisted. He was stronger than that. He'd borne this alone for centuries, as he deserved to. Just because she now knew didn't mean that he needed her any more than he had before he'd told her.

"Why, what?" he asked, grateful when her gaze returned to his. Maybe she'd see more than he wanted her to, but the connection he'd formed with her by revealing his true self provided desperately needed oxygen in an airless world. He could breathe better just by catching her gaze with his own.

"Your shadows don't stick to you. They're from the people you've killed, aren't they?"

He nodded once, a sharp jerk of his head that connected to his heart and pulled at it the way it did every time he thought of that long-ago night. His cousins hadn't deserved the death he'd delivered with a joyful heart, and now, because he'd sold his soul, the evil deed didn't even have a way to haunt him properly.

"You have no soul for them to cling to, so they hover around your feet. I always wondered why that was."

Not knowing what to say, he downed the rest of his whiskey. He met her eyes as he lowered his glass, surprised to see no judgment in their depths.

Damn her. He should be judged, gods damn it, and found wanting. But in her eyes there was only curiosity. He shifted in his seat, poured another glass of whiskey, then completely ignored it in favor of staring at the complex woman sitting across from him.

"How did you lose your soul?"

The whiskey in his blood urged him to tell her, but more than that, it urged him to kiss her. Sitting across from her all night had made his blood hum. Even telling her his secrets hadn't dimmed that. The opposite, really. It made him want to be closer to her—the only one who saw him for what he was. With every truth he told her, she saw him more clearly. First with her innate ability, then with the truths that spilled from his lips.

Her ability to see the truth of him had once unsettled him. It still did, but in a different way.

"How about another hand of cards?" He needed to change the subject before she changed too much of him. Being alone, presenting his facade to the world, was the way he'd learned to cope. She slowly peeled his facade away, but what would she find when she finished? What would he find?

She looked askance at him, obviously questioning his tactics in changing the subject, but agreeing nonetheless. "I don't know. What are the stakes?"

"They ought to be higher, aye?"

She nodded warily, obviously still wanting to pry more information out of him.

"You win, I answer a question. I win, I get a kiss." Had he just said that?

Aye, a kiss would distract her from her questions, and him from his painful musings. With bated breath, he watched her, wondering what she would say.

"Seriously?" Esha said, thrill and shock competing within her, each eager to be the victor.

He was trying to distract her. That was it. And it was working. With a shaking hand, she added her cards to the pile and shuffled them, embarrassed to see the deck falter in her hands.

She looked up from the cards, stunned to see the sincerity in his face. He'd had a couple of glasses of whiskey, sure, but not enough to affect a man as big as he.

He actually wanted to kiss her. But then, he had in the past as well. It was her species that repelled him. He objected to what she was, not what she could do to him with a kiss.

"I don't know if I want a kiss from you anymore." *I definitely do.*

He made her crazy. Made her cry and be all weird and emotional and feel too much. It sucked and inevitably led to dangerous places where hearts were broken. Except, he had bared his soul to her. Told her truths that she doubted he'd ever told anybody. That had to count for something.

"I can make you want it." His voice rumbled low, sending a shiver through her.

She reached down and sank her fingers into the Chairman's fur, desperate to ground herself and steel her heart against Warren's eyes, which tracked her movements with a heat that burned her to the core.

Slowly, he reached for the cards held loosely in her hand, his fingers brushing hers as he took the deck. She stifled a gasp at the spark that traveled up her arm. The Chairman stalked out of the room, clearly wanting no part of what he sensed was coming.

She watched Warren deal the cards, his big hands deft on the little rectangles of paper. He took her silence as assent, and by the time she had her cards in front of her and the flop laid out, she realized he'd distracted her from magically stacking the deck.

So this would be a true game of chance. Did she want to win, or lose? A glance at her cards revealed that it could go either way.

Warren's golden brows drew together as he looked at the cards, but she couldn't tell whether it was from worry or concentration.

Here goes nothing. She nodded at him to lay down the next card, and when it still didn't reveal her fate, she nodded again. When he laid down a jack, a shiver of anticipation crept along her nerve endings. She had a good hand, but not a sure thing.

With a bracing breath, she laid down her hand, looking up to see the light of triumph flash across Warren's face as he laid down his own.

"Damn it," she said, knowing from his look alone that she'd lost. Lost because she'd forgotten to use her magic to turn the tide, even after seeing the dismal flop. What had she really wanted if she was becoming so careless? Nervously, she rose and backed away from him. Only when her back hit the wall did she realize that she was making the situation worse. Nowhere to run now.

"So, tomorrow then?" she asked.

"No, lassie, I'll be taking my prize now."

CHAPTER EIGHTEEN

Esha's eyes widened as Warren advanced on her with a prowling gait. He was huge, looming above her and stacked with muscle and masculinity that made her heart pound with nerves and desire.

For tonight, he was hers. Despite all the things he'd said to her in the past, she still wanted him. And it terrified her.

She couldn't lose her heart to him. That would lead to the same place it had with Brian. With all the other Mytheans with whom she'd ever tried to start something. Warren wanted her now because he'd never had her, but once the novelty wore off, he'd remember what she was. There was no way she could bear it if he turned from her once this was over.

But she'd made the bet. And she wanted this. She'd just keep her heart separate. Esha straightened to meet him, wincing slightly at the pull in her back. But she didn't cower, especially from the man she wanted so badly.

She looked up at him when he stopped in front of her and met the heat of his gaze. His strong hands gently gripped her upper arms. Heat flared within her from that simple touch and her breath caught when he bent his head to hers.

She rose up on her toes and pressed her lips to his. The heat of his mouth and body threatened to go to her head, so before she lost her senses, she dragged her mouth away. "There. A kiss."

He looked down at her with a grin, then stepped closer until she was pressed against the wall by the steel strength of his muscles. "I doona think so, lassie. I want a proper kiss."

"A proper kiss?"

"Aye. I know you're capable of it. I want a kiss like the one the other night. You wanted me then, and I'd bet a fortune you want me now."

"I don't." She looked away.

"Aye, lassie. Is that why you're trembling?"

I'm not. But she was. He wanted to kiss her. Knowing what she was, he still wanted her. But for how long?

She repeated her vow not to fall for him again, then rose up on her tiptoes with a sense that this was something different, something new and very possibly stupid, and pressed her lips to his.

Warren held himself stock still when he felt her breath feather across his lips. Then connection. A groan tore from his chest when her lips met his. Such a light touch, but it was the most delicious thing he'd ever felt.

She might be a damn soulceress, but she was his.

He moaned and drew her against him, fitting her sleek curves against the harder planes of muscle that ached for her.

"That's it, lassie," he muttered as her tongue traced his lips. He ran his hands up the curve of her waist, wanting to tear the clothes from her and lick every inch of her flesh.

Be easy with her. Though she'd shown no sign of pain this evening, she was injured and he'd be damned before he'd hurt her any more.

Gently, he cupped the back of her head and thrust his tongue between her lips, the honey of her kiss making his head swim.

Must stop.

He broke away and leaned his forehead against hers. Tension thrummed along all his muscles, his cock so hard it nearly pained him. The scent of her hair clouded his mind, and all he could hear were his breaths sawing in and out of his lungs. But then the sight of her glistening lips nearly stole his good intentions.

"We have to stop. Your back is injured..."

"My back is fine. I swear." She yanked his mouth back to hers and arched her back until her breasts pressed against his chest. At the feel of her softness, his resistance broke. He plunged his tongue between her lips and moaned when she returned his kiss. Such fierceness.

Desperate to feel more of her, he stroked the skin at the small of her back where her shirt rode up. She gasped, and the delicious sound sent a shiver across his skin.

"You like that, do you?" he said at her ear.

Gently, he ran his hands up her back, cripplingly grateful that her wounds had healed and she would mend. She was so soft. Too soft, too precious, to be torn so gruesomely. He wanted to kiss every inch of her back, to make it all go away.

From his mind, from hers, so that neither of them had to relive these painful and terrifying last days.

He dragged his mouth from hers and ran his lips along the side of her neck, inhaling her scent while savoring the feel of her beneath his lips and hands. Soft and curved against his hardness, but with muscle and strength that protected her. Cleverness that protected her.

He loved her strength, her daring and courage—the traits that made her put her life in danger every day. As she'd done for him. After every terrible thing he'd said to her. He hadn't meant them, not truly. But she believed he had.

She deserved better than he, something he'd been too stupid to realize when he'd been bothered by her species. When he'd been avoiding her because of what she was. Now he couldn't care less.

She was all he wanted. *This.*

Esha shivered at the feel of his big fingers skimming across the sensitive skin of her back. Goose bumps broke out on her arms as he dragged his tongue along the side of her neck.

"You're so beautiful." His gravelly voice at her ear made it so she could barely think straight. She should stop this. When they finished, he'd eventually look at her with derision again. Today or tomorrow, it didn't matter. She couldn't bear it. This was different from the one-night stands she used to keep the loneliness at bay.

This would hurt her. This was *something.*

He dropped to his knees in front of her. All thought of self-preservation flew from her mind.

"Wh-what?" she stuttered, her hands flying immediately to his strong shoulders.

She looked down at him. When she met his eyes, she gasped at the intensity of the desire within them. His big hands ran up her sides, supporting her and raising her shirt all at once.

"What are you—" She gasped when she felt the heat of his tongue against her stomach. Her head dropped back against the wall, her eyes sliding closed at the delicious feeling of his rough hands against her sides, his hot tongue tracing its way along the waistband of her pajama pants.

He was so close to her sex that she ached with anticipation. For something she'd never had, not when sex had always been about racing to the end and leaving. But with Warren...

His mouth pressed lower, dragging her soft pants down until she felt the heat of his tongue through the lace of her underwear. When his hands ran down her sides to the edge of her pants, her eyes jerked open. Startled, she looked down at him and met his gaze.

"Let me. Please." His fingers curled beneath the waistband of her pants, awaiting her permission. She'd never seen anything like him, this golden god kneeling at her feet as if to worship her. With his hands. His mouth.

"I want to feel you. To taste you." There was such need in his voice, such desire.

Her mind buzzed. No one had ever said anything like this to her before. No one had ever looked at her like this.

Her mind raced. A kiss was one thing, but this... If he did this and rejected her, it would break her.

"I—I—" She couldn't think straight with his big, hard body pressed against hers and his gentle hands poised to bare her to him.

"Let me do this for you. For me." His eyes were hot on hers. "Trust me."

Did she? Could she? She wanted this so badly. With the same fierceness that she saw in his eyes. Wordlessly, she nodded, unable to turn away from what he offered. Even if it was only for tonight—even if it broke her.

She bit her lip as she watched him bend his head to her. How had it come to this? Sex had always been on her terms. But now, Warren had her pressed up against the wall while he stole her mind and her self-control. It made her vulnerable to him in a way that terrified her.

But not enough to stop.

She dropped her head back against the wall once more and closed her eyes, the anticipation so unbearable that she couldn't look.

Cool air brushed against her thighs, her calves, as he lowered her pants. With a press of his mouth to the front of her underwear, he looped his fingers through the sides and dragged them down as well.

"Beautiful." The word, so singular, yet so evocative, made her snap open her tightly closed eyes.

Soon, his strong hands were supporting her hips, his mouth back on her stomach, teasing her with proximity and promises. He leaned back to look at her, and using his knee, nudged her legs apart. She felt so exposed, so vulnerable. Yet so powerful, with him on his knees looking at her as though she was the most beautiful thing he'd ever seen. Her heart threatened to pound out of her chest.

She cried out when he blew a puff of breath against the curls at her sex and her hands shot down to sink into his hair, whether to stop him or press him against her, she wasn't sure.

The first stroke of his tongue against her flesh made a cry break from her throat. The second parted her sex and dragged a groan from Warren.

"I'll make you forget every man before me," he said, his voice fierce, as he lifted one of her legs and draped it over his shoulder.

Her fingers tightened reflexively in his hair as he bent his head back to her sex. She jerked at the feeling of his tongue on her clitoris.

"This. I've never—" She broke off, unable to continue, yet wanting to tell him that for her, this was more than just physical.

Warren groaned against her soft flesh, his hands tightening reflexively on her hips. That she'd let him, when she'd let no other? He stroked his tongue over her sex, savoring her taste, one that only he knew. No other would.

Determined to make sure she wouldn't regret her decision, he laved the tight little bud of nerves that was the center of her pleasure. She'd begun to pant, sharp cries escaping her throat as he sucked on her clitoris.

He never wanted this to end, but he'd lose control long before. Though he wanted to yank his trousers off and thrust himself inside her until she screamed his name at her orgasm, she was too delicate from her injury. This would have to be enough.

And it was. More than. With her swollen flesh beneath his mouth and her ass gripped tightly in his palms, there was nowhere else he'd rather be.

Wanting to taste more of her, he thrust his tongue into her tight entrance. She cried out, the sound making his cock jerk against the confines of his trousers.

"You'll come for me, lassie," he said against her pussy. She moaned in response, arching her hips against his mouth.

"Warren." She gasped. "I want you—" She cried out when he sucked gently on her clitoris. "—inside me!"

He groaned. His cock ached for it, throbbing for want of her. But this wasn't about him. And she felt so damn good against his mouth that there was no loss.

He stroked her entrance with his fingertips, the feel of her a drug against the sensitive tips. Gently, he pushed a finger inside of her.

"So... perfect." He groaned as her flesh clasped him. She rocked against him, her hands tightening deliciously in his hair.

"Warren!" Her voice was breathless, caught on a tide of need. She was close, so close, and he wanted to feel her pleasure.

"Aye, lassie. I know what you need," he said against her flesh. He added another finger and fucked her with them, marveling at the silken wetness of her. She'd grip his shaft so perfectly, her wet heat clenching around him until his seed burst from him. The mere thought had him bucking his hips, desperate for release.

Control it. This was about her.

Her thighs trembled as her orgasm approached. He reached up to support her, pressing a hand against her chest. He could sense the need building within her, coiling and tightening as it was within him. She was close, he knew it as well as he knew how much she needed it. How much *he* needed it.

He needed to feel the orgasm wash over her. The one that he gave her.

"You're going to come for me, lassie, so hard you'll forget your own name."

She cried out when his mouth closed over her pussy again, his tongue stroking her clitoris. He glanced up, mouth still on her, to see her lithe form arch off the wall as she clenched around his fingers.

The sight of her, the feel of her, the closeness, tore the orgasm from him, so hard and shocking that his mind went blank. He dropped his head and shuddered at her feet as a vortex of pleasure racked him, so unexpected, *so perfect.*

When his body calmed, and hers did too, he sat back gasping, staring at his knees. He'd lost himself in her, grown too close. Dangerously so. Terrifyingly so. He'd thought he could play this game, that he could give her pleasure and hold himself back. How wrong he'd been. He'd been so damn close to breaking his vow of celibacy—and hadn't cared at all.

He surged to his feet. Panic clawed at him, made him back away from Esha. On the wave of panic came a bout of nausea so fierce that he felt his face twist, and his knees almost buckled. His muscles spasmed.

Damn Aurora.

CHAPTER NINETEEN

Esha sagged against the wall, her breath heaving in and out of her lungs. That had been amazing. Warren had been amazing. After everything he'd said to her, he actually liked her enough to...

She caught sight of his face. He'd backed away from her and stood in the center of the room, wearing a look of such disgust that it hit her in the gut like a fist. He looked at her as though she held a cobra.

No, as though she *was* the cobra. What they'd just done made her soul feel raw and open and defenseless. As though all her protective layers had been peeled back.

And now this? He felt regret so soon? It scraped at the tender, newly revealed parts of her soul.

Idiot. I am such an idiot.

With painful precision, Esha straightened against the wall. It felt as delicate as her heart, as if one wrong move would shatter both to pieces and the house would crumble around her.

"Get out," she said, horrified to hear her voice break on the last word.

How had everything gone from wonderful to horrifying in the space of an instant? He could be with her until he remembered what she was. And that hurt more than it ever had before.

"Out!" She gestured to the door, which swung open with a bang. She couldn't bear to look at him right now, but more than that, anger with herself seethed beneath her skin like a living thing. She was falling for him, and this was the obvious consequence. She'd been *such* an idiot. No longer.

"No." Warren's voice was as hard as granite.

"What do you mean, no?"

"I mean, I'm no' leaving. I—"

"Yes, you are. Do you think me so spineless that I'd want to be near you when you look at me like I'm a monster? After... after..."

She couldn't believe he wanted to talk. *Now?* He'd just had his mouth on her, making her feel things she'd never felt before. Then, *that* look. The one that defined her life, that told her where she fit in his estimation and everyone else's. It tore at her heart like little claws made of glass shards, and reminded her how desperate and stupid she'd been.

She didn't blame him for how he felt—how could she? Everyone else felt that way. She should expect it. But she'd been stupid enough to fall for him anyway, to let something like that happen. She was just going to get hurt again. Like with Brian.

To make matters worse, his expression had now changed from blank to almost caring, as though he could see through her to the writhing mess of insecurity and pain beneath her facade. Like he gave a damn how she felt. It was all so quick, her head almost spun with the changes that flashed across his face.

Her eyes burned for how pathetic she'd been, immediately accepting the affection he offered at the expense of her own pride. It was all she had. Now she stood before him, about to cry, with her pants at her feet.

The idea so horrified her that she flung her arm out and commanded, "Go!"

The force of her power propelled him backward, out the door and into the hallway. The look of shock on his face as the door slammed in front of him only made her angrier at them both. If he couldn't accept her when she was bared before him, as vulnerable and powerless as she'd ever be, then he'd never be able to accept her when she was at her strongest, and to him, most horrifying.

Warren stared at the door that had slammed in his face, the sight of Esha burned into his retinas. She'd glowed with power, her amber eyes an eerie beacon shining with rage and pain while her onyx hair floated about her head. She hadn't seemed aware of her body's changes—or she hadn't cared.

Neither did he. What once would have disgusted him— because gods, she'd looked like Aurora in her anger all those years ago—no longer bothered him.

He was an arse. Panic had made him flee from her, push back from her as though she were poison. He was losing control of himself, giving in to his baser instincts and chucking his celibacy out the window. It freaked him the hell out. He knew what she'd seen in his face: panic and regret.

Then came the wave of sickness that even now twisted his guts into a mess. Gods knew what she'd seen on his face when that had come.

The medicine was becoming less and less effective. Soon, he'd have to take three pills a day. The witches had been wrong. He had less time than they predicted and it was fucking things up even more. With a disgusted sigh, he shoved a hand through his hair, then clenched his fists and barely resisted punching the wall.

Being with her like that had stripped him bare, forced him to examine himself and his actions. He found himself wanting.

But he had enough problems without adding Esha to the mix. She was damned complicated. And she made his already complex and insane life only more so. His celibacy and rigid lifestyle had kept his demons at bay. And it was becoming all the more apparent that she was the key to his Pandora's box.

CHAPTER TWENTY

The next morning, Esha cracked open her eyes to the sight of her pants crumpled on the floor. She dragged a hand across her face and groaned. She'd been so anxious to get out of them last night, yet here they were today, reminding her of what an idiot she'd been.

She could actually *feel* her cheeks burn. Freaking embarrassing. Not her behavior last night—pathetic is what that had been—but the fact that she was embarrassed this morning. Esha Connor didn't do regret or embarrassment. Enough people didn't like her. She wasn't about to start not liking herself.

Make a bad decision? *Move forward and don't think about it.*

A desire to pretend that everything was normal had her rolling out of bed to search for Warren. Whether or not she actually wanted to see him was a moot point. They had a job to do, and now, more than ever, she wanted to find Aurora.

The Chairman meowed from his spot at the foot of the bed, clearly annoyed by the jostling. He obviously thought that the huge, regal bed suited him.

"Oh, get up, lazy-butt," she said, and walked to the window. She stood there for a moment, absorbing the stunning view of the ocean that crashed into the cliff below the house, hoping as she did that she could absorb some of its immutable strength. If only she could be like the ocean. Constant. Unaffected by change, unable to be hurt.

She frowned. Even the ocean could be hurt. If the ocean wasn't impervious, how could she be?

Esha blew out a disappointed breath and headed to the bathroom. After a quick shower, she found her duffel bag in the corner where she'd put it when she'd first arrived. As she fished out a new pair of jeans and a T-shirt, she realized that her leather jacket had been destroyed by the claw.

A pang shot through her. Her jacket was like her armor. Without it, she felt naked. If she hadn't used up her last little bit of power on Warren last night, she could conjure a new one. As it was, she couldn't produce a hair tie.

She heaved a sigh and dragged her T-shirt over her head. No doubt she'd have to find some abandoned eighties windbreaker in a closet of this house and wear that. What a shitty way to face Warren—in some teal-and-yellow monstrosity.

Her snort of laughter was cut off by the sight of a beam of sunlight shining upon the chair near the window.

A honey-brown leather jacket was draped over it. She frowned and walked over. When she lifted the soft leather and turned it around, she saw that the claw marks in the back had been sewn together.

Inexpertly, for sure, but by someone who had tried.

She swallowed hard as her mind reeled. Warren had done this. But why?

Gingerly, she put it on and sighed at the warm clasp of comfort. But all the comfort in the world couldn't push aside the doubt that crept into her mind.

Warren had mended her jacket. That didn't jive with what she thought she'd seen on his face last night. Had she overreacted?

No. Of course not.

The Chairman meowed, low and deep. He couldn't read her mind, but damn it, whatever he was saying sounded a hell of a lot like *you're a spazzy idiot.*

She kicked the chair leg, then winced at the sting. She just wasn't used to this kind of thing! One-night stands were her game. Dealing with Warren was a whole different matter.

And they had to work together.

She had no idea what she was going to do when she saw him, but better to get it over with. She was grateful to see the Chairman at her heels. He'd like to stay in the big bed all day, but he probably wanted to keep an eye on her more, so she didn't make a fool of herself.

"Good luck, pal," she whispered. "But thanks."

On her way down the stairs, she gave herself a pep talk about how their interactions were going to go from here on out. Professional. Courteous. Reserved. She was going to act like a totally normal Mythean.

Together, they would find Aurora, Esha would keep Warren from killing her, she'd learn more about her past, then figure it out from there. Away from Warren, because she obviously couldn't be trusted around him.

Bright sunlight sparkled through the foyer windows, tempting her with freedom. A short walk wouldn't hurt, and Warren was as likely to be outside as in.

"Outside it is, Chairman," she said to the cat who trotted at her heels. She wasn't avoiding Warren, since she might find him out there. And she needed to stretch her muscles.

As soon as she stepped out into the brisk Highland air, she was grateful for her jacket. The gift. But she wouldn't think of that. A quick yank of the zipper closed out the biting wind.

The rolling mountains at her back kept her company while the sea shone before her. The Chairman chased bugs in the grass. Though the house sat on a small cliff with no beach that she could see, she could hear the waves crashing on the rocks below.

Within a few minutes of her glorious walk, she sighed. She was totally avoiding seeing Warren. "Damn it, Chairman. Let's head inside."

After a quick stop in the kitchen for a granola bar for her and chicken for the Chairman, she said, "Okay, *now* we're going to go look."

The Chairman followed her out of the kitchen, still licking his lips from the chicken and the last bite of her granola bar. *Weirdo cat.*

She'd searched through a half dozen rooms on the first floor of the big house when she finally pulled up short at the door of the workout room. She stopped dead in her tracks and her heart stuttered its last. At least, it felt like it.

Within, Warren was beating the hell out of a punching bag in the corner, viciousness in every strike. Sweat dampened the back of his gray T-shirt, making it cling to the curves and planes of his muscles. He looked like a damned sex buffet.

She closed her eyes and told herself that she didn't care at all. This was work and that was what she would focus on.

With a bracing breath, she opened her eyes and strode forward. Warren turned to face her. His broad chest rose and fell with his heaving breaths and his golden hair was mussed.

"I thought you didn't fight," she said.

Warren looked down at his hands, flexing them. "No' to kill. But I do fight." *Myself, the things I've done, the past I try to outrun.* "There's violence in me, always has been. It's better if I get it out. When there aren't people around."

"Oh." She looked away.

"You're feeling better."

"I am."

"Have you had breakfast?"

"Yes. I want to see the letter."

Warren nodded, not surprised that she'd want to get to the point. "It's in the library. I'll get it."

She followed him out of the room, and as Warren strode along next to her, the clean scent of her caught in his lungs and arrested his thoughts. He hadn't expected to see her so soon, and when he'd caught sight of her standing in the doorway, his brain had overloaded with a dozen thoughts.

Memories of the taste of her, of her cries of pleasure echoing in his ears. The rage in her eyes as she propelled him out the door, the hurt that had edged in at the corners. The past days of working with her and realizing her cleverness and bravery. His confusion over what she wanted from him. *Why* she had ever wanted him.

"I'll need to go somewhere populated with Mytheans to restore my power," she said as they walked down the hall.

"All right. There's a gathering of Mytheans near Loch Buie. A Mythean Highland Games, run by a local laird. It's being held on his land today and tomorrow."

"How do you know that?"

Because when he'd woken up this morning, he'd thought of her needing more power. Something that had bothered him before had become a priority. "I knew you'd need a boost."

"So that I can find Aurora for you." Her voice had a glass-sharp edge.

"No, for you."

"Sure. Let's go get the letter."

Moments later, they walked into the big, book-filled room that served as the library. Warren had spent many an hour here over the last three centuries, poring through Cadan's ancient collection. Most older Mytheans read a lot.

With a deep breath, he withdrew the letter from a secret compartment in the bottom drawer of Cadan's desk. Esha snatched the letter from him as soon as she saw it. She turned from him and walked toward the window.

"Hey," he said, following.

"My letter, Warren." She raised it. "See? My name on the front."

He nodded. He'd know the contents soon enough.

With her full lip bitten between her teeth, Esha squinted as she carefully peeled open the letter's seal. The envelope fluttered to the floor as she opened the folded slip of paper. Her brows drew together as she read.

"What is it?" The tension was killing him, a boa constrictor that wrapped around his chest. As much as Esha could be the best kind of distraction, Aurora's threat hung over his head like a guillotine's blade. Time was running out, and Aurora had proved that she had the strength and the stone heart to make him truly suffer.

"Oh shit," Esha breathed. "She wants us to go to Iceland."

"What the hell? Why there?"

She turned to face him, surprise raising her brows. "There's an abandoned soulceress settlement. I didn't think it still existed, but I guess it does. Soulceresses used to live there before the Vikings came. All I know is that the ancients built a city as far from other Mytheans as they could get so they knew they would be safe. When they needed a power boost, they'd simply aetherwalk to a Mythean settlement, juice up, then return home. But when the Vikings came in the ninth century, they eventually had to leave. I guess the settlement is still there, probably hidden from mortal eyes by magic. But it makes sense that she would hide out there. She said she's in the temple."

"Do you know where it is?"

She shrugged. "Not enough to aetherwalk there, but I've heard it's located in the middle of the biggest glacier. If I got close enough, I'm sure I'd sense the old magic."

"Gods damn it. Why did she no' just tell us to go there in the first place?"

Her eyes narrowed. "For the same reason the letter is addressed to me and hidden in a place that only a soulceress can enter. She wants me to come to her. Only me. But you never mentioned that she knew me. Were you ever planning to tell me?"

Shite. Truth or lie? A lie would be easier. But she already mistrusted him. Another lie could be the one that permanently broke this fragile thing between them, if it hadn't been destroyed already. And he didn't want to lie to her, not anymore. He'd lied to so many. The praise he'd received for his work, his good deeds, was hollow from people who didn't know who he truly was. What he'd done.

The idea of true honesty with anyone, but with her especially, was irresistible. "Aye, she wanted you specifically. And nay, I probably wasn't going to tell you. I wasn't even going to let you get near her, for fear of what she'd do to you."

"So you didn't mean it when you said you wouldn't kill her?"

"She canna be allowed to live."

"You don't know that! Why did she ask for me specifically? Who is she to me?"

"Just another soulceress. She said she wanted a friend. It's ridiculous."

Something like pleasure shone in her eyes. It made him nervous. Esha liked the idea of being Aurora's friend. Something dark and sick welled within him that had nothing to do with Aurora's magic. Over his dead body.

"The witches think she'll try to steal your power," he told her.

She laughed. "Steal it? That's not possible."

"Aye, it is. The witches said so, and she's more than capable of it."

"I don't believe you."

"You doona have to. But it's the reason she wants to meet you, and the reason she never will. I'll no' let her take your power from you."

She shot him a skeptical look. "Whatever. You'd like me better without it. Why are you telling me the truth now?"

"Because I doona want to lie anymore. And I would no' prefer you without it. No longer. It's part of you."

"I'm not even going to pretend I believe what you're saying." She leaned down to pick up the envelope. "We're going to find her. You can't do it without me, that's clear. We'll see who gets to her first, and who gets what they want. And you're wrong."

He'd made a giant fucking mess of this. A month ago, he'd pushed her away because of what she was and the vows that he'd made, all the while she'd been throwing herself at him. Now, as he realized how much she was starting to mean to him, he kept screwing things up and pushing her farther away.

If he could just get Aurora out of the way, everything would be fine.

CHAPTER TWENTY-ONE

Esha climbed out of the passenger seat of the Range Rover and onto a huge green field milling with hundreds of cheering Mytheans. The sun shone as brightly as it had at the house, sparkling on the saltwater loch she could see from the field. Someone had probably called in a favor from a weather witch to keep the rain away for the games.

It was still cold, though, and she yanked up the zipper of the jacket that Warren had repaired for her. She should have thanked him for the jacket, but her initial awkwardness this morning had been replaced by anger at his secrets.

Did knowing the reason for his lies—that he wanted to protect her—outweigh the sin of the lie? She had no idea. She just knew that she was tired of trying to figure it all out.

"Well, now what?" Warren asked as he joined her. They'd parked off to the side of the festivities with the other vehicles. They watched hundreds of Mytheans crowding food and beer stalls and gathered around a group of individuals tossing great logs through the air.

"Ten pounds that girl wins the caber toss." Esha jerked her head toward a small blond woman about to heave a log.

"I won't be taking that bet, lassie."

"Figured I'd give it a try." Taking his money might make her feel better, at least a little.

Esha watched Ana heave the caber nearly 100 meters down the field. She hadn't expected her friend to be here, but Ana had always been competitive. It made sense for her to sneak out of Otherworld for the games. Since she was one of the more ancient goddesses, a normal Mythean would have a hard time beating her unnatural strength.

Esha turned from her friend and walked toward the far end of the field, where a group of spectators milled around a beer stall.

"Do you no' want to head toward the strongest competitors?" Warren asked from her side.

Ouch. "You really think I'd go steal another Mythean's power right as they're about to compete?"

"Of course you would no'."

"Sure I would." What was it about him that made her lie and say things to make him think the worst of her? Even back when she'd wanted him to like her, she'd done it occasionally. Anytime someone thought the worst of her, her porcupine quills went up and she said whatever they were most expecting to hear.

Now, with the mixed signals he kept throwing at her— nice gestures combined with lies and disgusted looks—she wanted to put him neatly into a box that wouldn't hurt her. A closed box.

"You would no'. You're just saying that to throw me off."

She shrugged, but by then they had reached the group of spectators. The glorious rush of power soared through her, like sunlight melting the ice that had filled her body. She closed her eyes to enjoy it. There were so many people here that they wouldn't even notice feeling a bit tired. If a witch tried to perform a huge spell, she might find that she didn't have enough juice, but that was unlikely. And she'd get it back soon enough.

She looked down at the Chairman to find him rubbing himself against Warren's leg. Apparently sometime during the last couple of days, while she'd been out, the Chairman had decided that he didn't hate Warren.

"What the hell have you been feeding my cat?" Had he been nice to the Chairman? He hated the Chairman.

"Nothing." But his face was too innocent.

She tapped her foot, then raised a hand as if she were going to cast a spell at him.

"Fine. I made a fire for him."

The Chairman *did* like fires. "And...?"

"Might have opened a tuna can. He can open the fridge himself and get whatever meat is inside, but the tuna can was giving him trouble."

This big warrior had opened a tuna can for her cat? A cat he used to hate? What the hell was going on here? Lies and manipulation, while mending her jacket and feeding her cat?

Overwhelmed, she spun around and headed over to another group of spectators to fuel up on more power and get some space to try to ground herself after such startling revelations. If the Chairman wanted to be a traitor for a fire and some tuna, he was his own cat. If she were honest with herself, she couldn't blame him.

Warren watched Esha storm off and cursed.

"Why are you such an asshole?" A feminine voice demanded from behind him.

He turned to see the small blonde who'd tossed the caber so far. She was slight and pale, but an angry energy radiated from her and made her appear far larger. Apparently she'd snuck up on him while he'd been watching Esha.

"You're Esha's friend?" Warren asked.

"Yeah. And the Celtic goddess of victory, so you'd best not be messing with my friend or I'll make you regret it."

"You're Andrasta."

"Yeah, you got that right." She stuck out her chin. She was an antagonistic little thing, with speech that was far more modern than most gods'.

"What's your problem?" he asked.

"You. I watched you from the other side of the field. What'd you say to Esha to make her storm off?"

"I probably put my foot in my mouth."

She stepped back, as if surprised by his admission, but recovered quickly. "You do that a lot, from what I hear."

Esha had told her about him? "Aye, I've been known to."

She scowled and tapped her foot, taking his measure.

"So, you know about Esha's past," he said. He didn't understand her, but he wanted to. She wasn't pissed that he'd fed the cat; it ate anything it could get its paws on. Once he'd even heard her tell it they'd order pizza soon and that it could have half Hawaiian.

So why hadn't she liked the fact that he'd been nice to her cat? He'd done it because the beast had grown on him when he realized how important it was to Esha's health and happiness, but she'd been upset by an innocuous deed. As she'd been upset last night, ready to jump to the worst conclusion about him.

A conclusion he deserved. He'd been a lying bastard. But even before she knew the extent of his lies, she'd been ready to write him off. Why was trust so hard for her?

"Why is she so..." He gestured with his hands, trying to explain her.

"Awesome?"

"Nay. I mean, aye, she is. But no' that. Why is she so—ah—difficult?"

"Difficult? You mean, wary? Tough? Prickly like a porcupine?"

"Aye. She doesn't trust easily. At all, really."

Andrasta's eyes lit up. "Because you are all assholes." She gestured wildly with her hands. "Every single one of you at that university is a giant asshole. Except that new girl, Diana. Esha said she doesn't suck."

"What the hell?"

The goddess, who looked more like a pissed-off college student, grabbed an arrow out of thin air and twirled it in her fingers, faster and faster as she scowled at him. She chewed on her lip, clearly thinking of what to say next.

"Esha cherishes her badassery. It's her armor. I'm not going to give anything away that threatens that. But think about this... What if every Mythean in the world treated you like shit because of something you couldn't control? Everywhere you went, you were met with sidelong glances or

175

outright disgust? For her, it started as soon as she came into her power, with some stupid boyfriend who ditched her, and it only got worse. She doesn't even actually hurt anyone."

As he'd suspected. "But her power reaping...?"

"Oh fates, don't call it *reaping*. How creepy is that? Like that guy in the black cape that some mortals believe in. Who is he? The grim reaper? You're comparing her to the freaking death guy when you do that. Anyway, it doesn't actually hurt people. Makes them a little weak for a while. Maybe they won't win their next fight. But if they don't get into one, it doesn't ever matter anyway."

"I never—"

"Yeah, you didn't know, because she doesn't get power off you. She told me. But you still hate her for something she can't control, and it doesn't even affect you."

"I doona hate her." The opposite—more every day. "But she doesn't care that other people doona like her. She relishes it, from the way she acts." But that wasn't true now. He was just fighting it because it made him realize how badly he'd probably hurt her.

And how much she probably wanted Aurora as a friend. Aurora had played her so well. And him. Dangling the one thing Esha truly wanted in front of them both.

Once, he wouldn't have cared whether Esha got what she wanted. Now, he wanted nothing more than to fill her days with friends, to show her that they'd all been wrong about her.

When the hell had he become such a sap? It was threatening his end goals, which truly were a matter of life or death. Not for him, but for her as well.

Andrasta confirmed his suspicions when she said, "Yeah, because she has to. She's pretended that she likes it until it has almost become a reality. She comes off all *I don't care* and badass to protect herself—it's really not that hard to figure out. But deep down, it kills her. And lately, her shell has been cracking. I think it bothers her more than ever. Anyway, the moral of the story is that you're an asshole. Try not to be." With a smile that was more a snarl, she strode off toward Esha. Briefly, she turned around to say, "Oh, and go fuck yourself."

Warren heaved a sigh and rocked back on his heels. What a bitch. With a grin, he realized that he liked her. And that Esha was so much more complex than he'd realized. Beneath her tough exterior, years of rejection had her ready to be disappointed, ready to mistrust, ready to run.

He'd lived down to her poor expectations. Hurt had shone through the anger in her blazing eyes last night. She hated being feared. Being despised for what she was. Decades of rejection had her looking for it at every turn, and he'd obliged. He hadn't meant it. His panic had been about his own fucked-up self. But how was she to know that? And when she was so damaged, how was he to convince her?

Esha frowned at the sight of Ana walking away from Warren. She'd been watching the hill race and absorbing the power of the spectators when she'd caught sight of the pair of them out of the corner of her eye. What had they been talking about? Ana was headed toward her, and she picked up her pace when she got closer.

"Esha!" Ana called, a broad smile stretched across her face. She flung herself into Esha's arms for a hug when she reached her, and Esha grinned broadly. They pulled apart. Damn, it was good to see Ana, even if it had been a short while since she'd seen her last. With her life acting so crazy all of a sudden, the familiar felt even better.

"You wipe the floor with them?" Esha nodded toward the caber field.

"Yeah. Almost didn't, but pulled it out in the end."

"As you do. How long are you out of Otherworld for?"

"Another hour or so."

"Too bad it can't be longer."

Ana shook her head and danced nervously on nimble feet. "No. Things are happening in Otherworld."

Esha frowned at the look on Ana's face. She was scared. "What is it? What can I do?"

"I don't think you can do anything. But I think Camulos might be alive."

"What?" The word came out in a near-screech. "No, that's terrible." Fear made her skin prickle. The god whom Ana had killed was still alive? He'd want vengeance on her friend.

"I don't know what to think. I don't know how he could still be alive. I thought I killed him. But I can feel him, and I couldn't before. I came here to the Games to see if anyone had heard anything, but they haven't. I don't know where he is, but he could be after me. He might want his godhood back." Ana's mouth was pinched in fear.

Esha's stomach dropped. To get his godhood back, he'd have to kill Ana. Nothing could happen to her best friend.

She wouldn't let it. "He won't get to you. He won't. I'll help you."

"You've got stuff to deal with."

"I can fit it in. I can always fit it in for you."

Ana smiled, reached out, and squeezed her hand. "Thanks. I don't think he can aetherwalk. So few can. As long as he can't, I've got a huge advantage. I'm on my guard here, and I'm protected in Otherworld."

"Seriously, Ana, if you need me, I'll be there."

"I know. If I learn more, I'll let you know."

"Swear?"

"Yeah. But more important, what's up with Warren?"

"Things are a mess, of course. What were you two talking about?"

"He wanted to know about you. I gave him hell, but I don't get what your deal is with him."

"No deal. He can't see past what I am, and I'm too smart to deal with that kind of shit." The words sounded false even in her own ears.

"Are you sure? Because he was asking about you. I think he was trying to understand you."

Really? She scowled at the little burst of hope. "It doesn't matter. We're a mess, and we can't seem to meet on equal ground. It's bound to end in disaster."

"Maybe. Or maybe you're just waiting for people to reject you."

"Can you blame me?"

Ana sighed and looked away. "Well, no. But I think Warren might be different."

"I wish." *And I wish I were different.*

She felt like she was drowning in this situation, unable to figure out Warren's motivations and feelings and unable to interpret her own. All she knew was that he made her feel crazy. And she hated that. Worse, he was still determined to kill Aurora. "It doesn't matter anyway. He's been lying about Aurora, the other soulceress. Apparently she wants to see me specifically. And he won't budge on sparing her life, even when he knows how important it is to me. It's a deal breaker, so there's really not much to be done."

"Bastard."

"Yeah. But it's cool. It sets me straight on how this is going to go—all business from here on out. And the first thing on the list is finding Aurora and keeping Warren away from her. I'm not going to worry about him anymore. It was a bad idea in the first place." He made her too freaking melodramatic, crying and yelling and throwing all kinds of fits that weren't normal for her. It was unacceptable, and frankly, it freaked her out.

"Yeah, good idea," Ana said.

Esha could tell from her voice that Ana didn't believe her. Worse, she wasn't sure she believed herself.

CHAPTER TWENTY-TWO

"That puddle jumper is supposed to get us to Iceland?" Esha asked.

"Aye. It'll do fine. The university has been using it for years," Warren said.

The pilot gestured to them from the small set of stairs that led up to the university's private jet, and he started forward across the rain-darkened tarmac of the small Mythean airstrip on the south side of Mull.

"You know, *for years* really isn't the best way to sell this tin can," Esha said from behind him as she and her cat followed him to the plane.

"No' that many years. It'll get us there. And it's better than burning up your power by aetherwalking."

Esha made a noise of assent from behind him. They'd left the Mythean games two hours ago, intent on making their way to Iceland and the soulceress settlement. Because there would be no power to draw from at the settlement, Esha didn't want to burn hers by aetherwalking. She'd need all she could get when they faced Aurora.

They hauled gear bags that they'd packed in the morning across the tarmac. Thank gods Cadan had camping equipment. It had saved them a trip into town. No doubt the location would be remote as hell.

"This isn't so bad," Esha said when they entered the cabin of the plane.

Warren looked around at the cream leather of the eight plush seats. "No' too bad, at all."

Esha took a seat in the middle. Warren joined her. She slanted a glance at him, then reached forward and grabbed a magazine from the back of the seat in front of her.

She was going to ignore him? He supposed he couldn't blame her, but it made guilt spike inside him. It lasted through takeoff and well into the flight, until he couldn't take it anymore. There was no flight attendant, so they had privacy. And Esha couldn't run away.

"Hey, I want to apologize for last night. And everything that happened before," he said.

"Don't worry about it." She didn't look up at him, instead choosing to flip more quickly through the magazine's pages.

"I do, though. You thought I regretted kissing you. I could tell. But I dinna."

"Whatever, Warren. It was a one-time thing. Just a roll in the hay, as they say back in America. Seriously, don't worry about it."

She didn't mean it, not from the way she'd looked at him last night, not from the hitch in her voice now.

"You're afraid of rejection, so you look for it everywhere."

"Ugh. People need to quit telling me that."

"Andrasta told you that too, did she no'?"

"How do you know that?"

"I asked her. I wanted to understand you."

Skepticism flashed across her face. "Asking someone what it's like to be feared and despised your whole life doesn't make you understand it. And why the hell do you want to understand me, anyway? So you can get me to do what you want more easily?"

"No, lassie. Because I care for you."

"No. At best, you want to sleep with me. But care for me? No. Don't say that, because you don't."

"You doona know that."

"Please. I am what I am. And Mytheans don't like what I am. But I'm used to it. I don't hold you to any higher standard than I do them. Maybe once I thought you were different, but I was wrong and it's fine. I agreed to help you find Aurora and I'm not going back on my word, so don't worry about that. Let's just do this job and go on our way."

She'd erected a mental wall against him. More than that, she expected so little of him. Of any of them. It made his chest hurt.

"I'm no' saying these things because I want to ensure that you'll help me. I do care for you. You're brave and smart. You've had adversity in life that few can understand, yet you've risen above it and become one of the strongest Mytheans in Scotland. But you're compassionate. You helped Diana, and you're helping me. I was stupid no' to see past what you are."

Her eyes widened. "Good words. Some guys have a knack for good words."

Like the boy who'd ditched her when she was young and coming into her power? "I mean them. They're no' just words."

She frowned doubtfully. "My whole life, only Ana has ever been unreservedly nice to me and not turned on me. But you expect me to trust you when you need my help and might say anything to get it?"

"I already told you, I trust you not to go back on your word."

"You trust *me*? Really?" Disbelief and sarcasm tinged her tone, but desire edged beneath. She wanted his trust, even if she didn't want to admit it. "Maybe so, though I've no idea how I'm supposed to believe that. Or you, when you're so hellbent on killing Aurora."

Tell her. His initial prejudice against her was born of his past and what Aurora had done. His unwillingness to compromise on Aurora's fate was directly linked to her evil deeds. Esha needed to know what was at stake before she could ever possibly trust him. All he had to do was tell her.

But he couldn't. Not when it would reveal the horror of his past. Keeping this secret had become his identity. Atoning for it even more so. And now he was going to reveal it? Face the censure and disgusted looks he'd avoided for centuries?

Esha shook her head and said, "Forget it. You're right. I'll help you find her, though there's no way I'll let you hurt her. As for whether or not you trust me and don't hate what I am, it doesn't matter, does it? I came onto you first and started this mess, so it's right that I finish it." She turned back to her magazine and began flipping the pages.

Damn it. She was shutting him out. He wanted her to believe him. Not just because they needed to have the same goals when it came to Aurora, but because he really was starting to care for her.

"Wait. I've got to tell you something."

She slanted a skeptical glance at him.

"It's about Aurora. And me. I've been acting like an arse because my mind is a mess right now. Aurora's release is… a huge problem for me."

She arched a brow.

"You know that I doona have a soul."

Skepticism faded from her face as understanding bloomed. "Oh, shit."

"Aye. I sold it to Aurora. In exchange for the lives of my fellow clansmen. That was after I'd killed my four cousins— men I loved like brothers." He could feel her gaze boring into him, and though he met it briefly, his gaze was drawn to the window behind her shoulder. He couldn't bear to look at her when she wrote him off for good.

"How?" she whispered.

He started at the beginning, with the witch burnings and his time as a mortal. When he got to the part about Aurora's mother coming to him for help, he saw Esha's hand tighten on the armrest of her seat. The murder of his cousins made her gasp, as did the scene of Avera's death and the rescue of the child.

"When the fire was raging through the forest and getting closer to my village, I offered her anything to stop. She was driven mad by the death of her mother, and she wanted my soul. I sold it to her in exchange for her mercy for my village. It's the last thing I remember. I came to in the forest, which was blackened by fire and destroyed. Eventually I learned that she'd been arrested by the university for stealing many more souls all across Europe. She was overwhelmingly powerful, or they'd have killed her. I want to kill her for making me a soulless monster."

"Not a monster," Esha said, concern for Warren suppressing all the hurt and confusion of the past days.

Worry radiated from him, and disgust as well. The shadows at his feet writhed and she wondered again about them. Was it possible to have shadows because you believed so truly that you'd committed evil? But he hadn't. Not really.

"I'm sorry for your loss, and for your cousins' deaths, but it was a mistake. Not some great big evil crime. Mytheans kill people all the time."

"But that's just it. I'm no' a Mythean. I was young and cocky and self-righteous and violent and I enjoyed taking their lives. While I was killing them, I loved every second."

Esha shrugged. "Sure. They were evil. I love killing rogues."

"No, they were my family, and they were afraid and confused. That's what had them out there hunting witches. And I killed them. Worse, I loved doing it. I was a different man then, as zealous as they, but with a different goal. It blinded me to the fact that they were being drawn in by the witch hunters." Tortured memories flashed in his eyes.

Understanding dawned. So that's why he didn't fight anymore. He didn't like the person he was when he had a sword in his hand. "You didn't do anything wrong. They used their superior strength and the power of a mob to kill innocent people."

"Maybe. But I'm no' so different than they. Worse, now that I've sold my soul. I'd do it again to save the village, but I've no humanity left. That's what I'm fighting for."

No humanity? She couldn't imagine what it would be like to believe you'd sold your humanity. To live without your soul, with the threat of it being used against you. Wouldn't she do anything to get her soul back if it were in the hands of another?

"Gods, Warren. You're as fucked up as I am. No wonder you back away from me. We're a terrible pair."

A chuff of dark laughter escaped him. "Aye, perhaps. But I doona back away from you because I doona want you. I back away because I've used abstinence to keep my mind off the past."

"Wait, what?"

"Celibacy. About a hundred years ago, I stopped doing anything that made me feel too much—sex, drink, hell, even betting on horses. High emotions remind me of everything I felt in the past and cutting it out made me a hell of a lot more sane. Once I noticed how much calmer my mind was, it was easy to cut out the good stuff."

Shock blanked out all the thoughts in Esha's mind. No sex in a *century?* "Wow."

Warren looked away, the barest hint of red at his cheekbones. "Until you, that is."

The overhead speaker emitted a dinging noise and the melodious voice of the captain interrupted the jumble of thoughts fighting for real estate in Esha's brain. "We're about to start our descent into Höfn. The local time is six-fifteen in the evening, and the weather is a balmy thirty-one degrees Fahrenheit."

Esha used the distraction to break the conversation, and Warren seemed okay with it. She had a hell of a lot to process, and maybe he did too.

Thirty minutes later, they descended the roll-away stairs onto the tarmac at the tiny Mythean airport in the southern Icelandic town of Höfn. Cold wind whipped through the dark night, the only illumination from a half-full moon and the landing strip's lights.

Warren gestured to an SUV pulled up to the side of the only building. "That'll be Felix."

Esha nodded and followed him over to their contact from the university. Felix had apparently worked at the university in the eighteenth century, before moving to Iceland to get away from the crowds. Esha had never met him before, but when he stepped out of the SUV she thought he looked familiar.

He was big and hard-looking, with dark hair and eerie silver eyes. He held out his hand and said, "Felix."

She shook. "Esha. Thanks for meeting us."

The drive to the southeastern edge of the glacier was quiet. Felix wasn't much of a talker, but with everything running through her head, Esha didn't mind. He dropped them off at a small house on his property, told them the fridge had food, and that he'd be back in the morning with snowmobiles that they could take up onto the glacier to find what they were looking for. They hadn't mentioned exactly what it was and he hadn't asked.

"Not much for conversation, is he?" Esha asked as Felix's SUV lights disappeared up the drive to the nearby house he'd said was his. She turned from the doorway and shut out the cold night air.

"Nor company. Felix helps out the university staff now and again, but for the most part he keeps to himself." Warren turned and opened the fridge, then pulled out the minimal contents for dinner.

Esha looked around the small space. It was a two-room wooden cabin. One room for a tiny living room, kitchen, and dining area, with a bedroom and bath in the back. A little loft over the bedroom served as a second sleeping area. The Chairman had already set up camp on the sofa.

"How do you feel about pork chops with a side of zucchini?" Warren asked.

"Fine."

"Good. That's all that's in here. Looks like Felix stocked us up for the night. And tomorrow. There's eggs and milk."

"Nice guy. You cook?" she asked. It was too awkward to keep silent.

"Aye. Canna live as long as I have and no' learn." He set a skillet on the stove and started to chop the zucchini. When he finished, he searched the three cabinets and pulled down salt and pepper and oil. "But doona expect anything fancy. No' much in the way of spices here."

"As long as I'm not cooking, I'll be happy." She went to the fridge to grab a beer she'd spotted there. "Want a beer? Oh—but you don't—"

He smiled. "I drink. Just in moderation."

"So, moderation for beer, but abstinence for everything else?"

CHAPTER TWENTY-THREE

Warren felt his cheekbones heat. "Aye, except with you. Give me a beer."

She held out the bottle and their fingers touched. A thrill crept up his arm. He wanted to yank her to him. Instead, he turned toward the stove. As much as he wanted her, it was a terrible idea. And he wanted to prove that he wanted her for more than her body.

He tossed the pork chops in the heated pan. Out of the corner of his eye, he saw the Chairman perk up from the couch and then hop down to stalk into the kitchen. He stared up demandingly at the stove, his bullish little face intent on the sizzling meat.

"Chairman, leave him alone."

The cat ignored her.

"He wants pork," he said.

"He wants everything."

"Aye, and he'll have it. There are three in here." He'd planned to eat two, but with the Chairman looking at him like this, there was no way he wasn't sharing. And he doubted the

Chairman would settle for the tinned cat food they'd brought for the trip.

After a few minutes, the pork was done and the zucchini nearly there. He slid the chops onto a plate, then plucked one off and put it on a smaller plate for the cat.

"Watch your hand! That's got to be hot."

He shrugged. Though he wasn't a true Mythean, he had their healing ability. He felt pain less than mortals and wounds healed quickly, especially small ones. Considering that without his soul, nothing on heaven or earth could kill him, a little burn from a pork chop was nothing.

"It's fine," he said, lowering the now cooling chop to the floor for the cat. If the Chairman had been a normal cat, he'd have cut it up. But he'd seen the Chairman with a steak he'd pulled out of the fridge back at Cadan's house on Mull. The cat liked the challenge of tearing into a whole piece of meat.

"You're feeding my cat again?" she asked, something unidentifiable in her voice.

"Aye. I like him."

He caught her appraising look as she raised her beer bottle to her mouth. He had to force himself to drag his gaze away from her lips. He shifted and turned back to the stove, hiding the fact that his cock was growing obnoxiously hard just from looking at her. It took only a second to serve up the simple meal and he and Esha sat at the small table pressed against the wall.

"Thanks," she said when he placed the dish in front of her.

He watched her take a bite. There was a primal satisfaction in feeding her. He hadn't had anyone to take care of in centuries.

"This is really good. Do you do a lot of cooking back home?"

"Some. I've a nice kitchen that I remodeled a while back. I actually used to live in your tower flat before you arrived at the university."

She did a double take. "Oh? I thought it was just for outcasts."

Guilt stabbed at him, an icepick straight to the gut. "Ah, well."

"You know it's true. It's a beautiful place, but it's at the far edge of campus, as far from everything else as a building could be."

He sighed. "Aye. When you came, we weren't sure where to put you. I liked it when I lived there. A fine place."

"I guess it is, if you don't mind being a pariah."

"You're no'."

"Yes, I am." Her voice was fierce, the amber in her eyes darker than usual.

"You shouldn't be."

"Sure." She stabbed another piece of zucchini, clearly wanting to change the subject. "So, why were you placed in the pariah tower?"

He shrugged, not wanting to answer. But he owed her the truth. "You once called me a mystery monster."

She flinched. "Sorry about that."

"Doona worry about it, you were right. When I sold my soul, I became something *other*. Deathless in a way that no other immortal is, since I have no soul to take my consciousness to an afterworld."

Esha put down her fork and stared at him. "So you mean that decapitation or immolation or magic can't kill you like it will the rest of us?"

"Aye. Without my soul as my ticket to an afterworld, my body will reform with my consciousness. As a result of the change, I popped up on the university's radar. I couldn't stay with my clan. It would reveal the existence of Mytheans."

"Maybe not."

"Well, it would reveal that immortality is possible, since I'd never die. That's close enough. The university knew they had to do something with me. They gave me a place to live— the tower, since they dinna know what I was or what I was capable of—until they figured out a place for me."

"With the Praesidium."

"Aye."

She nodded, then laughed bitterly. "So maybe if I stayed another hundred years, I'd make it out of pariah status."

"You're no' a pariah to me."

The smallest smile pulled at the edge of her mouth, but she changed the subject. "So, your kitchen. Did you do the renovation yourself?"

"Aye. I like to build things."

"I know." He raised an eyebrow, and she flushed. "I saw you go into the Veterans' League once, to do woodworking with the soldiers. Why do you do that?"

He shrugged. "I like it."

She nodded encouragingly, brows raised, as if she knew there was more that he wasn't saying. But he'd said enough today.

"You finished?" He nodded at her plate.

"Um, yeah."

He grabbed it and his own and put them on the counter, then leaned over the sink and closed his eyes. Opening up to someone was fucking hard. It came in fits and starts. He'd held his darkest secret for so long that releasing it made him feel empty. It had defined him, but in the worst way.

Now, when it came time to share more, it felt like pulling the words from his heart, but they were tangled around the veins and muscle.

Gradually, he realized that the heat he felt at his back was Esha standing so close to him that he could feel the warmth of her body.

Hesitantly, Esha laid a hand on the tense muscles of Warren's back. She'd followed him over here, unable to help herself even though she knew he sought distance from her. From sharing more.

That, she could understand. Trust and change weren't easy. She swallowed hard, acknowledging that where she had trouble trusting, so did he. But she was so close now, desperate to know more about him. She was throwing herself into this, but couldn't seem to help herself. "You go to the Veterans' League as a way to atone, don't you?"

He stiffened, but turned to look down at her. He stood so close that she could feel his heat. She had to stifle a shiver that rushed over her. When his eyes met hers, intense and hot, she felt the heat of a flush creep up her cheeks.

"Aye. And it helps me, no' just them. I'm no' a good man. No' what everyone thinks I am."

She raised a hand to his chest, laying it against his pounding heart. "Why is it such a secret? You've done it for years and no one knows about it."

He shrugged, but his gaze dropped to her mouth. The hunger in his eyes sent a streak of heat straight to her pussy. Now that he'd had a taste of what ditching celibacy was like, he wanted more, it seemed.

But she'd told herself she was going to be smart about this. Not get involved, especially not after everything he'd told her. She could fall for a man like him. But falling for someone had never ended well in the past, and it wouldn't end well this time either.

She pulled away, but was stopped short when he reached out and wrapped a strong arm around her waist.

A small gasp escaped her. "I should—"

The heat of his lips cut her off. One of his big hands cupped the back of her head, pulling her closer to him until the full length of her body pressed against his. Unable to help herself, she moaned at the hardness of him. His muscles, his hands, his cock. It was like being pressed up against warm, living steel.

His mouth was ravenous on hers, hot and skilled and desperate. She could feel the years he'd been denying himself, and against her own best instincts, wanted to be the one he chose to be with for the first time in so long.

When his big hand spread across her lower back and yanked her closer to him, all thought of objection fled. She ran her hands up the hard muscles of his chest until she could wrap her arms around his neck and sink her hands into the soft hair at his nape.

"Fuck, I want you." The words were harsh against her lips.

Yes.

Still kissing her, he spun her around until the countertop pressed cold and hard at her back. She cried out when she felt his hands grip her ass and lift her up onto the counter. His hips pushed her legs wide until his cock was pressed hard against her sex.

Warren groaned at the feel of her heat against him. It was all he could do not to yank the clothes off her and plunge himself deep. He wanted nothing more than to feel her hot flesh close around his aching shaft, pulling him inside.

He'd start slow, thrusting gently until she was begging him to move harder, faster. Anything to make her come. Only when she begged him would he pound into her until the pleasure made her squeeze his cock and he followed her over the edge.

The fantasy only served to stoke his arousal to a fever pitch. He wrapped an arm around her back and pulled her closer until her soft curves were pressed up against him. He grinned when he felt her shiver. "You like that, do you?"

She moaned and kissed him harder. Her hands reached around his back and slid up his shirt, the heat of them a brand on his flesh. When she dragged her sweet mouth away from his lips, he reached up to pull her head back. Before he could, her lips brushed against his neck. Soft licks and sharp bites made his cock jump. He'd never survive this. Celibacy had worked so well in the past, but it was a ridiculous idea now.

"You taste so good," she whispered.

He shuddered and let his head drop back as her hot mouth worked on him. One day soon, she'd be on her knees before him, gripping his hips while he fed the length of his cock between her lips. The idea of her red lips closing over the tip of his shaft made it pulse in his jeans. He'd spill again from the thought of her if he wasn't careful.

He wanted her hands on him, hot and soft on his shaft as he thrust against her. But he wouldn't ask. Wouldn't pressure her into that. Instead, he ran his hands up inside the back of her shirt until he reached her bra. With a flick of his finger, it came undone.

"What are you—"

His mouth cut off her words. "I want to touch you, lassie. Feel your soft breasts in my hands. I ache for you."

She pulled away. "I—um. This isn't a good idea."

His head jerked back, and he looked down at her. She was serious. Though her eyes were hazy with desire and her lips red from his kisses, her jaw was set.

"Really. This... It's just a bad idea. I'm not strong enough for this." She pushed at his chest, and he stepped back. She hopped off the counter and retreated to the first-floor bedroom. Just before she went through the door, she said, "Um, thanks for dinner. See you in the morning."

The door shut behind her and he stood in the kitchen, stunned. One second she'd been moaning in his arms, the next she'd retreated. And what the hell did she mean, she wasn't strong enough for this?

CHAPTER TWENTY-FOUR

The entire world was white. The ground covered in snow, the sky blanketed in clouds, and the snowmobile between her thighs. Esha was just grateful that the snow had stopped falling and hitting her cheeks like tiny daggers whenever she pushed up the clear face-guard on her helmet.

Warren was about a dozen yards away on her right, speeding over the vast snowy expanse of the Vatnajökull glacier. Felix had picked them up right before sunrise and brought them up onto the glacier in his super-Jeep, a great monstrosity of a vehicle on giant tires meant for the remote Icelandic terrain. Though tourists occasionally visited the edges of the glacier, once you got toward the middle of huge expanse, it was miles upon miles of uninhabited snowy terrain.

Warren drove his snowmobile closer to hers and yelled, "Sense anything yet?"

She read his lips more than heard his words and shook her head. Felix had pointed them northwest, telling them that it was the most remote part of the glacier. They'd been driving for hours—thank gods for the spare fuel they'd brought—but she'd yet to feel anything that indicated they neared the city.

"Chairman okay?" Warren shouted.

She looked down at the Chairman, who sat in front of her, secured to the seat in a ridiculous little harness and fluffy egg-like thing. Felix said he'd made it for his dog, and though the Chairman looked ridiculous, he did look happy to be zipping across the snow. The Chairman had always had a thing for speed.

"He's fine," Esha yelled back, and as soon as the words left her mouth, a zip of energy hit her in the chest. She gasped and her hand loosened on the throttle. The snowmobile slowed. Once she caught her breath, she tightened her grip again and caught up with Warren, who'd slowed his pace ahead of her.

"We're close," she yelled. The feeling in her chest—that felt like energy ping-ponging off her ribs—grew stronger as they headed farther into the most desolate part of the glacier.

A spot of shadow on the vast expanse of white grew into a great stone monstrosity that took her breath away. It rose like a great stone castle, sprawling across the ice and defying all logic of city construction. There was no way to survive on the glacier except through magic, which clearly hadn't been spared while constructing the soulceresses' greatest city.

"There it is!" she yelled at Warren.

"Where?"

So he couldn't see it. "Stop your snowmobile."

They pulled to a stop, still half a mile away. Esha climbed off hers and clomped across the snow toward Warren, her huge borrowed snow boots slowing her to a trudge.

"Come here," she said, and pulled off one of her gloves. When he climbed off his machine and leaned close, she pushed up the clear faceguard of his helmet to lay her hand against his cheek. She closed her eyes and willed her ability to see the city to him.

"Oh, fuck," Warren breathed.

She withdrew her hand and climbed back onto her snowmobile. "Let's go."

They set off again. What had initially looked like a great stone wall surrounding the city was actually formed by the backs of the buildings themselves. They rose tall, pressed cheek by jowl, with glinting glass windows that reflected the sun. Every hundred feet or so, a road or path led into the city. Apparently hiding was enough for the soulceresses of old. They hadn't been afraid anyone would find them way out here, not in the ninth century at least.

Warren climbed off his snowmobile and joined her. "Do you think we can leave the machines here?"

"Yes. I think they're hidden within the city's magic now."

He nodded and unstrapped a big duffel from the back of the snowmobile. She unhooked the Chairman from his fluffy space pod, and he leapt down into the snow, immediately sinking in a puff of white. He yowled indignantly, and she leaned down to pull him out. "We've learned our lesson now, haven't we?"

He hissed at her. She laughed, but made a vow to remember to watch out for him around the deeper snow in the future.

Warren tromped through the snow over to her machine, unhooked her duffel and swung it over his shoulder. "Are there any magics we should be concerned about?"

She looked up at the looming gray stone and twinkling glass. Technically, the buildings were too old to have such huge plate-glass windows. Magic had been used to create them, and magic had kept them from breaking over the last millennium. "I assume so. Magic, or something else entirely, is holding this place together. It's too old to be in such good condition. Whether or not there are protective spells in place, I don't know."

"We'll tread cautiously, then."

They set off for the nearest street that spilled out onto the glacier. The gray cobblestone was completely free of snow.

"It's like they left yesterday," Esha said as she poked the stone with the toe of her clunky boot. She wasn't getting any negative vibes, but then, because she was a soulceress, she probably wouldn't. She glanced at Warren and he looked fine, so she stepped onto the street, where gray stone walls rose high on either side of her. "All clear."

She put the Chairman on the cobblestones and the three of them walked down the narrow street. None of the buildings had doors, and it was so eerily quiet and perfect that it made her nervous.

"Wait, where the hell are we?" Warren asked.

"What? We've only been on this street for a minute."

Warren turned in a circle, brow scrunched. Gods, he was handsome, with his gleaming hair and green eyes. Even when he was confused. "Aye. I should be able to see back onto the glacier at the end of the street. I canna. I doona even know which way we've come from. It all looks the same."

"Oh. Wow. There must be a disorientation spell. Only soulceresses can navigate through the city." They'd reached a crossroads of five streets, two of which led upward via stone stairs. It was like a labyrinth of gray stone and glittering glass. "We'll have to stay together."

"Aye, no kidding. Any sense of where the temple might be?"

She looked around. "No. I'm pulled in four directions—the compass points—where important buildings might be. Or something that is important to me. I don't know which."

"All right. We should find a base camp first. Night is going to fall soon. Damn northern sunset."

She nodded and turned left, down the widest and most inviting road. Everything was so monochromatic: gray stone upon gray stone, broken only by the sheen of glass windows. There were doors on this street, though, and she picked one that she guessed was a residence.

"Here goes nothing," she said, and pushed the door open.

Light filtered in to reveal the front room of a shop. Fabric in hundreds of hues spilled from the shelves and the forms of faceless mannequins. She swallowed hard. Fabric shouldn't last a thousand years in these conditions without disintegrating. There was some kind of magic at work here, and it was strong.

"Wrong place," she said, and backed out.

They walked down the street until they reached another crossroads, this one with six streets. She chose right this time, and when she pushed open another door, it led to the foyer of a home. Again, a bright profusion of color gleamed from every surface. Carpet, paint, draperies, all in shades of green and yellow and blue.

"Looks good," Warren said over her shoulder.

The Chairman hurtled across the threshold and out of the cold like he'd been ejected from a slingshot. He was as sensitive to threats as she was, and if he deemed it safe, she assumed she could too. After all, the soulceresses had never fought to protect this place. They'd lived here peacefully and in secret, then abandoned it as soon as the Vikings had landed on their shores in their longboats. So there was nothing to be afraid of, right?

"Strange place," Warren said.

"Yes." Strange to think that hundreds of soulceresses and soulcerers had lived here. Esha had never met even one, yet there had been a time when there were enough of them to create this great city.

They stripped off their snowsuits and snow boots and explored the house in silence. The bottom floor, with its opulent living areas and ancient kitchen, the upper floor with four bedrooms and no internal plumbing, and finally, the basement. Torches mounted to the wall along the stairs were ready to be lit. With a flick of her hand, they burst into light.

"Holy shit," Esha breathed when they reached the bottom of the stairs. They'd descended into a stone grotto. The torches illuminated three steaming pools of clear blue water, natural hot springs that heated the air with humid warmth.

"This is how the rest of the house is heated," Warren said. "But how the hell is it here, in the middle of a damned glacier?"

"Magic, like the rest of this place. Iceland has loads of hot springs. It looks like the soulceresses diverted some and built their houses over them." She walked over and dipped a hand in. "It's nice. Not too hot. I doubt it does much to melt the ice, and magic can help with what little harm it might cause."

The Chairman was batting at the water, no doubt looking for the phosphorescence that he'd found back at the *howf*.

"My ability to navigate works in the house," Warren said. "I've still got no idea how to get out of the city, but I doona have a problem here."

"Good. Maybe because—" She jerked and stared at a shadow that had appeared on the stairs. A soul shadow. It was very roughly human shaped, but made of nothing but black smoke.

"What the fuck?" Warren whipped his head to the left, where another soul shadow had crept out from behind a ledge of rock.

"You see them too?" Esha asked. The shadow on the stairs began to solidify. Her eyes widened. *That* wasn't normal. "Who are you?"

Esha stepped forward. It drifted back up the stairs, and the shadow from the corner zipped out to follow it.

"Wait!" She raced up the stairs after them, Warren and the Chairman at her heels. When she reached the now dim foyer, she waved a hand to light the wall lamps and caught sight of three more soul shadows of varying opacity. They drifted toward the door and then straight through it and out to the street.

She ran to the door and swung it open. Full dark had fallen and the street was nearly pitch black. The soul shadows had blended into the night, but she could still sense them, hovering just outside the door, watching.

A blast of cold hit her, more than just the night air and the snow. Evil—and it was coming from some of the shadows.

"The dark hides them. Can you see them?" Warren asked from behind her. He loomed over her shoulder, peering out into the night.

"No. But I feel them."

"Me too."

That was bad. He wasn't a soulcerer, so he shouldn't feel them. With her skin crawling, she raised a hand and cast protective magic around the house. "They can't come in now. I think they live in the city, and they came out to investigate us."

"Do you know what they are?"

"Maybe. They're not like the shadows of evil deeds that I normally see. They're more solid. Some more so than others. I think they're actually souls." She shut the door and backed into the dim foyer.

"Whose?"

"I don't know. I don't think we should be out in the dark since they're so much harder to see. They're not all friendly, and I've no idea what they're capable of."

"Shite."

CHAPTER TWENTY-FIVE

"Come on, I'll make dinner." Warren turned and started toward the back of the house.

She had to suppress a smile at the familiarity of him cooking for her without asking. Was this what it was like to be in a relationship? Just doing the little day-to-day tasks and looking out for one another?

Except that they were in a haunted city.

Even so, she could get used to it. *Don't.* Self-preservation edged its way in on her sugary feelings. Hope beat back at it. Sanity won out.

She followed him to the weird old kitchen and said, "Actually, I'm beat. I think I'll just have a granola bar in my room. Don't worry about me." She could conjure something decent for the Chairman. It wouldn't take too much power.

"The hell you are. Set up this camp stove." He pushed it toward her. "Please."

Out of the corner of her eye, she saw the Chairman glaring at her from in front of the fire. He wanted some of whatever Warren planned to make. Truth was, so did she, even though it would just be some instant camping meal.

She'd tried to leave, hadn't she? That counted as at least trying to preserve her heart.

"Okay," she said, trying to keep the smile out of her voice. She looked around the kitchen, which looked nothing like a modern kitchen. Long tables butted up against the walls and a huge hearth took up one side of the room. Pots and pans hung from the ceiling, but there was no sink or oven or refrigerator. As ancient as the place looked, she had a feeling it was still far more advanced than what mortals had been using at the time.

The long table under the window was probably best for the camp stove. She set it down and bent over it, fiddling until the flame burst into life. She looked up to see Warren pulling a gallon of water and a few packets of some kind of camp food out of the huge duffel bag.

"Stove's ready," she said.

"Thanks." He got to work, mixing and pouring, until dehydrated beef lo mein came back to life. "So. Why'd you leave America?"

She stilled. He wanted to know more about her. No one except Ana had ever wanted to know about her. And even Ana was primarily concerned with what it was like to be a mortal on earth, not what it was like to be Esha, specifically.

Still, she didn't want to answer. "You don't need any more help?"

"Nay, just wanted to get you to stay."

She grinned, then scowled, and leaned against the table.

"Come on, why'd you leave America?"

She sighed. "There was nothing there for me anymore."

"Does that have anything to do with the fact that you ran away from school?"

She put down her drink. "What is this? An interrogation?"

"Nay." He leaned back against his table, sighing in frustration. "I just want to get to know you."

Her heart thumped a bit harder. She was in for it now. Telling someone about herself, her past, was as foreign to her as the Arctic, but her mouth opened all the same. "Yeah, I ran away from school. I shouldn't have been there—I'm not a witch. But someone dropped me off when I was a child. They didn't know what else to do with me."

"You doona know who it was?"

"No. I heard it was a man, though. Maybe my father."

"Do you know what happened to him?"

"I was told he died shortly after. Some type of terrible curse, but they never explained who placed it on him."

"I'm sorry."

She shrugged. "I never knew him. I'm just happy he tried to put me in the best place, even if that place wasn't so great."

"What was it like to grow up a Mythean?"

"Pretty normal, I suppose." She frowned at the memories. "Until I came into my power. I was a bit like Harry Potter, except I wasn't a hero."

"Well, that's no' so bad. Everyone likes Harry Potter."

"You need to reread the series. Harry had a tough run for a while. But comparing myself to Harry Potter probably makes me a bit full of myself, especially since I never saved the day. I just ran away."

"Why?"

She shrugged. "Being able to manifest my magic without practice and fueling it with the power of the other students didn't make me homecoming queen. My friends and my boyfriend dropped me." No amount of magic could make people care for you. And they'd been more than just friends. They'd been together since they were toddling around in diapers. They had been her family. Until they'd dropped her.

So she'd learned to be a hardass until it didn't bother her anymore.

"Bastard. You couldn't control your power collection?"

"No, never could. Still can't. That's one of the reasons I want to find Aurora. Maybe I can learn how. Then I can have a normal life." She almost smacked herself. Why had she admitted that? Out loud, even. She'd resisted admitting it to herself. Admitting that she wanted more was to admit that she thought her life wasn't all that. Forcing herself to think that everything was perfect almost worked.

If he was giving her a pitying look, she'd kill him.

When she glanced up, she saw that he'd turned back to the stove, as if he knew how much she'd hate him to see her like this.

"How about some lo mein? It's done." He scooped up three big bowls, put one on the floor, and brought the others to the table.

"Thanks."

They ate in silence for the next few minutes, the Chairman's joyful purrs as he scarfed down his bowl of lo mein the only sound punctuating the quiet. Thank gods he was magical or there'd be hell to pay after a meal like that.

The weight of all she'd revealed began to bear down upon her. Had she said too much? Probably. Sharing felt weird and reminded her that things between them were weird.

She fought the darker voice that hid in the corner of her soul. The one that said he was being nice to her because he needed her to find Aurora—whom he wanted to kill despite what it would do to Esha—and because he was totally lost in this city. That when it was all over, they'd be on opposite sides of the fence again. He could have anyone. He didn't need an outcast like her. Getting used to his cooking, his kindness, his kisses would only make her life more barren once it was all over.

No. She wouldn't sabotage this with dark thoughts and insecurity. She'd take him at his word, the way she wanted him to take her at hers.

But she needed to get out of here now. Just to remind herself that she was fine alone. "Thanks for dinner. I should get going."

"Doona go yet."

"No, really, I should get out of here. But thanks." She used a quick burst of magic—not much, of course—to clean her bowl and the Chairman's, then jetted for the door. Out of the corner of her eye, she saw him rising and threw out a frantic little wave and dashed into the hall like a crazy person, a disgruntled Chairman behind her.

CHAPTER TWENTY-SIX

"Ready?" Warren asked Esha.

They stood in the foyer, the first early rays of sunlight illuminating the dim space. He hadn't seen her since last night, though he'd heard her rustling around in the kitchen for breakfast. By the time he'd gotten down there, she'd slipped back up to her room.

"Yes. I think we should be able to see the shadows well enough if they try anything tricky."

"Brilliant." He opened the foyer door and yanked up the zipper of his jacket. It was cold, but the lack of snow within the city meant that they didn't need the damn snowsuits or boots, thank gods.

Esha joined him on the doorstep. "Okay, I think we should head east. I feel the energy of four important places in this city, and I think the temple will be one of them."

He nodded and followed her out the door and up the winding street, where gray buildings rose high on either side. The disorientation that had hit him last night returned now that he was out of the house, so he stuck close to Esha. The morning was perfectly and eerily silent, with no birds to chirp or trees to rustle in the wind.

Within a hundred yards, he became aware that soul shadows lurked behind some of the glinting glass windows. Watching them. "Esha."

"I see them. Just keep walking." Her posture was stiff.

They turned left onto a wider street, one built of octagonal stone slabs that seemed to be a main thoroughfare through the city. Grand buildings lined the street, much wider than the houses on the residential street where they'd set up their base camp. The architectural styles varied, from whimsical to elegant to imposing, but all built of that same gray stone. It was the strangest city he'd ever seen.

Warren glanced behind him to get a feel for the expanse of the street and caught sight of a shadow dipping behind the corner of a building ten yards back. A chill pricked at his skin. It was the first he'd seen outside of a building.

"There's a soul shadow behind us," he said.

"I know. I don't get a feeling of evil off it, though. Or good, for that matter."

"Right." They'd just have to stay sharp.

They walked a few hundred yards down the expansive street until they came to a great open space that looked like a town square.

"I think that's it." Esha pointed to a wide building that sat on the north side of the square. A great portico with four long steps led up to enormous front doors. There were very few windows, far fewer than any other building in the city.

"Do you know what it is?"

"No. Just that it pulls at me."

"We'll check it out, then." He glanced back and saw the shadow advance with them. Following them.

They walked across the too-silent square as the sun finally rose over the tops of the buildings. Bright rays of light fell onto the stone street. The Chairman slowed as he reached the portico, his confident stride replaced with wariness. Esha slowed too.

"He's got a better sense for danger than I do. Especially of the soul variety," she said.

Warren nodded, no longer concerned that he was taking his cues from a cat. As soon as they stepped up onto the first of the four wide steps, soul shadows appeared on the portico.

"Keep going," Esha said. "Act like they aren't there."

Warren put his hand on his sword anyway. Just because he didn't like to fight didn't mean he wouldn't, and the shadows were creeping forward with every step they took. When they took the last step under the portico, the shadows surged forward, an unbroken mass of black smoke.

Sickening chills broke out over Warren's skin when the shadows touched him. The sickness that had haunted him surged, nearly buckling his knees. He drew his sword and swiped at the nearest one, but it sliced ineffectually through it. They became solid when they pressed against him, forcing him back down the stairs, but became smoke when his sword touched them.

"I think they're trying to keep us out!" Esha yelled as she shot a blast of power from her hand that buffeted them back, but only for a moment. They surged forward harder than before, black smoke that flowed and ebbed in the barely-there form of the Mytheans they'd once been.

Warren shuddered again as the surge of shadows sent a chill and a wave of sickness through him. He swiped and thrust with his sword to no avail. "I can do nothing against them!"

Neither could Esha, whose blasts of power couldn't clear the way long enough for them to reach the door at the top of the stairs. They didn't seem to be bothering her as much as him, however. The majority of the shadows plowed against Warren, trying to keep him out.

When something touched his back that didn't feel as sickening as the press of souls, Warren glanced behind him. It was another soul shadow, this one more corporeal than the rest. It was the one that had followed them from their base camp.

It waved an amorphous, shadowy arm and drifted toward the side of the building.

"Esha! The shadow that was following us is trying to lead us around the building." He had no idea if he should trust it or not, but by then the mass of shadows had pressed them down off the stairs entirely.

Esha glanced at the shadow and her brow furrowed. "Follow it!"

The Chairman ran after the shadow, and they followed. It might be a trap, and he'd be prepared if it was, but he doubted it. The shadow led them to the edge of the stairs and around the corner of the building into a small alley. A glance behind him showed that the shadows had stayed behind on the portico, as if trapped. The illness that had tied up his guts in knots and weakened his muscles had faded as well.

"Look, it's led us to a door." Esha pointed to the small wooden door. The shadow hovered just in front of it.

"Let's try it."

The door stuck when Esha tried it, and a heave of Warren's shoulders did nothing as well.

"Here, let me try this." Esha stepped up and laid her hand on the handle. It glowed briefly, then popped open.

"How?"

Esha shrugged as she crept through the small door. "I'm a soulceress, and I asked it to open. I think it's guarded against outsiders but not my kind."

Made sense, given what had happened up on the portico. The mysterious shade, as Warren had begun to think of the shadow that had aided them, followed them into the building. The room was pitch black, a problem that he alleviated with the flashlight he pulled out of the pocket of his jacket.

"Smart thinking," Esha said as the beam of light revealed the contents of the room. Boxes piled upon boxes, all the way to the ceiling. "I have no idea what this place is, though."

"We're in the basement. Let's try those stairs." He shone the beam on the stairs on the other side of the room. "Do you sense any of the shadows?"

"Not in here. I think they were just trying to protect the front entrance."

"Good."

They climbed the stairs in silence, their steps soundless on the stone beneath their feet. The door at the top swung open silently, and they stepped out into an enormous cavern-like room. Light from the few windows beamed down upon a brightly colored marble floor, and the walls were hung with tapestries stitched with explosions of color. It, like the house, was unnaturally well preserved.

"It's a museum," Esha said.

Only then did Warren notice the low tables scattered throughout the expansive room. The soaring ceiling dwarfed them, making one want to look up rather than down. They walked slowly through the room, glancing at the tables and stands upon which precious artifacts sat.

"This must be the oldest museum in the world," Warren said as he glanced around for the shadows that hovered just outside of the great doors on the other side of the room. "Museums dinna exist back then, did they?"

"Among soulceresses, they did. But I don't think this is a museum in the traditional sense, where you display artifacts for the public. I think it is a holding place of our most precious cultural objects and art."

"This isn't the temple, then."

"No. But I'd like to look, all the same." The dim light revealed the wistfulness and sorrow etched on Esha's face. This was the last evidence of her race. Family and friends of her own kind that she'd never have.

"All right. We won't get separated in here. I doona have the same problem navigating within the buildings that I do on the outside."

She nodded and wandered off, her gaze intent upon the tables bearing jewelry, weapons, dishes, and other unidentifiable objects. Warren watched as she reached out now and again to brush her fingertips over shining metal and gleaming, polished wood. The Chairman stuck close to her side, as if he knew she needed the comfort.

Warren shook his head and turned away. He wandered as well, his gaze drawn especially to the weapons. One, a long dagger with an artfully decorated hilt, caught his eye. It looked sharp and deadly and reminded him that his sword hadn't affected the soul shadows. Perhaps only a soulceress weapon would work within the city walls. Feeling slightly guilty but vowing he'd return it when this was all over, he slid the dagger into his boot and turned to find Esha.

She stood on the other side of the room, staring at a huge painting on the wall. She shook her head, then turned and walked across the room. He met her near the basement doors, his steps faltering slightly when the familiar surge of Aurora's sickness weakened his muscles and churned his stomach. Shite. Time for more pills.

"Ready to go?" he asked.

"Yeah. Let's keep working our way around the compass until we find the right building." Her gaze wouldn't meet his and her voice was distant. She'd been closed off all day, ever since she'd retreated last night.

They made it through the basement and out of the building without incident. He popped a pill in his mouth and swallowed it dry, hoping it would work. He couldn't be weakened when he faced Aurora or he'd never get his soul back. He'd have to live like this, a deteriorating mess of weakened muscles and worthless stomach. And he'd thought not having his soul was bad.

The street was silent once again as they made their way east, though the sun had moved across the sky and was on its way down over the tops of the buildings. Warren kept his gaze glued to Esha's back.

After a while, he noticed that the mysterious shade was still following them, floating along behind. Esha kept glancing back at it as well, making sure that her eyes never fell upon him.

"The building is going to be right around this bend, I'm almost sure of it." Esha pointed to the curve in the narrow street ahead.

When they rounded the bend, the street once again opened up onto a great square. The city was a bit like Venice, with its windy streets and open squares, but creepier and without the canals. Warren didn't like it.

"That's it." Esha pointed to an ornate building that sat across the square as the museum had. This one was far grander, however, a stone monstrosity accessible by an enormous flight of stairs.

They made their way across the square, and Warren tensed as they neared the stairs, expecting more shadows. When the wave of nausea hit him, he almost stumbled.

Nay. He'd just taken a pill. This shouldn't be happening. He swallowed hard and forced the nausea down, but it did little good as his muscles trembled.

They reached the base of the stairs and began to climb. When nothing swept out to stop them, the tension in his chest eased slightly. The souls must have been protecting the treasures and had no reason to be here. It took two of them to push open the great wooden door. Damn it, normally he'd have been able to do it alone.

"This is it," Esha whispered.

Again, the space was huge and silent, the windows streaming beams of light onto the brightly colored marble floor. The back of his neck twitched, and he turned around.

A horde of shadows, these darker and more human shaped than the last, hurtled at them up the stairs. He spun around and pushed Esha out of the way, back behind the wall so that she was out of the path of the shadows.

"Hide!" he yelled, but before he could turn to fight the shadows, something wrapped around his arms and legs and dragged him out the door. He struggled against the bonds, twisting around to see that shadows had caught him from behind. He strained to reach the dagger but his arms were held tight.

"Warren!" Esha hurtled out of the doorway. She ran down the stairs after him. His fear for her had been for naught. The shadows weren't attacking her.

She shot a blast of power at them, and they released him.

Warren crumpled to the ground, then surged to his feet. Before he could get his dagger, they rushed back, reaching for him once again, gripping his arms and legs with iron bands of strength that they shouldn't possess. From the corner of his eye, he saw the mysterious shade fly forth.

It charged into the group of shadows, scattering them. Esha's blast of power took care of the rest. In a flash of white light, they were obliterated.

"Esha, are you all—" Warren's knees collapsed out from under him once again, his muscles turned to jelly.

"Warren!" Esha fell to her knees by his side. "You're so white. Are you okay?"

"Pills," he gasped. "Left pocket."

"For what? What's wrong with you?" She scrabbled through his pocket and pulled the pills loose.

"One."

She pried the cap off and handed him one. He'd just had one an hour ago, damn it. They weren't fucking working anymore. He blinked up at Esha, who was running her hands over his body, looking for injuries. The sky was darkening behind her head and long shadows stretched across the square.

"We've got to get you back to the house," she said.

With her help, he struggled to his feet. His stomach still lurched like a ship on a rogue wave, but his muscles held long enough for him to stumble back to the house. Rage welled within him at being unable to move, to fight. This wasn't him, damn it.

It felt like hours had passed by the time they got back. Full dark had fallen, but a wave of Esha's hand lit the lamps in the entryway. He groaned in relief when he collapsed on the bed.

"What the hell is wrong with you?" Esha asked, her hand pressed to his forehead.

He drew in a ragged breath. "Whenever Aurora uses the power of my soul, it makes me ill. The witches gave me pills to fight it, but they've been failing. My body is becoming immune to them."

"Shit." Her worried gaze searched his face. "I'm going to the witches. You need more pills."

"Nay. You canna aetherwalk that far. It'll drain your power too much."

Esha stared down at Warren, her heart twisting in the most horrible way. He looked near death. This was what it was like to lose someone. It was everything she'd been afraid of. He shouldn't be mortal, but his body was giving out like one.

"I don't care," she said. "You need something to make you better. I can fuel up on power when I'm with the witches. Aetherwalking back will drain it more than if I came back the slow way, but I'll still have enough. There's no other option."

She yanked the covers up over him and said a brief prayer to whatever magic had kept this room in pristine condition since it had been abandoned so long ago. "Can I get you anything before I go?"

"Nay. Doona go."

"I don't see how you think I have a choice." She called the Chairman to her. When he pressed up against her leg, they disappeared.

It was dark and moonless on the university campus when they appeared and Esha prayed that all the witches would be together when she knocked on the cottage door. Not that she wanted to see them, but she needed a hell of a lot of power to make up for aetherwalking that distance.

She was in luck. There were at least twenty in the small cottage when the door swung open at her knock. She breathed a sigh of relief as their power flowed into her. The marmot witch stood on the other side, hand on the doorknob and frowning, as if she were the designated witchy butler.

"Warren's sick. Your pills aren't working. We need something else," Esha said.

"You don't have to be so bitchy," marmot witch said.

"He's sick. Really, really sick. I'm being urgent, not bitchy."

The witch huffed. "I can see that you're just scared for him, so I'll cut you some slack. And I like him. But there's nothing else safe that we can give him."

"He's so sick he can barely move," Esha said. "And I don't think he's going to get any better. We're desperate."

Marmot witch frowned, her eyes dark with worry. Unconsciously, she reached up to stroke the fat brown rodent who rode on her shoulder. Esha recognized the act as something she did with the Chairman and scowled at the similarities between them.

"Come on, I'm begging you," Esha said. Which was crazy, because she hated these witches. But she couldn't bear to see Warren so sick.

Marmot witch turned and joined two other witches in a corner. Esha couldn't stop her feet from tapping as she waited. They conferred in hushed whispers and after approximately a century, marmot witch went to a tall armoire and pulled out a tiny emerald glass bottle.

"Here." She thrust it at Esha, scowling. "That's *elictum erarus*. He'll feel no pain as long as he takes that. One drop of liquid per day, right on the tongue. No more, or he's dead as a squashed toad. But it will only last for five days, maybe four, before he's immune to it too. Then he'll be left in even worse straits than he is now."

"Worse?"

"Much. So get his damned soul back."

Esha nodded. "Thanks. Really."

Marmot witch shrugged. Desperate to get back to Warren, Esha didn't even bother to leave the front stoop before she aetherwalked. Upon arrival, a quick survey of her power supply felt like she was already down to half. Damn, that was a long way.

She ran up the stairs to Warren, who was sitting up but still white as a sheet. Her heart slowed its frantic, worried beat when she saw him alive. Gods, had she really been afraid he'd die on her like Brian had? Of course he wouldn't. He was a Mythean.

"Here. The witches gave me this." She held out the glass bottle. "One drop per day. Five days. Maybe four. Then you're worse off than you are now."

"Damn." He held out a hand for the bottle, but it shook so badly that she pushed it down.

"Let me." She sat next to him on the bed, and he tilted his head back and opened his mouth. She focused hard on squeezing the dropper the slightest bit. One drop of silver fluid fell onto his tongue. She tightened the cap on the bottle and looked up. His color had returned abruptly and his eyes had brightened.

"Bloody hell, I feel amazing," he said. He stood and flexed his arms, and her eyes shot to the muscles that bunched beneath the fabric of his shirt. "I feel completely normal. That's serious medicine."

"Not medicine. Magic. Strong magic."

"Well, it's fucking awesome."

His vitality was such a contrast his former pallor that it reminded her all the more of how sick he'd been. How sick he could become again.

She panicked. Obviously this was only going to end terribly. She spun on her heel and walked out of the room, saying over her shoulder, "I'm glad you're better. I'll see you later."

CHAPTER TWENTY-SEVEN

An invisible hand tightened on Warren's throat as Esha walked out, so there was nothing to do but follow her. Light spilled out of the room that she'd claimed as her own, dim enough that it was likely torchlight.

He stepped up to the cracked door and knocked, though he didn't wait for an answer before he pushed it open. Esha whirled from where she stood near the tall glass window.

"Is anything wrong?" she asked.

"Nay. I'm fine. Better than I've been, well, ever, really. But you doona seem all right."

"I'm fine. You should go rest. Just to make sure." She turned back to the window.

Warren was behind her in two strides, his hands gently gripping her arms. "Wait. You've been acting strangely. Distant ever since the night we kissed."

"Nothing is wrong. We're fine." She looked up at him and nodded encouragingly. "Go rest, Warren."

But she didn't pull out of his arms. Just being close to her made his heart speed up. Made something in his mind settle. If he'd had a soul, he'd have said something settled there as well.

She was afraid. He hadn't been able to stop thinking about how different her life was from his. Similar in that they were both loners. But he'd chosen his lifestyle. She hadn't. Not from the time she was a child and had been made an outcast at school because of what she was, and not now. He'd at least grown up within his clan, knew what it was like to be part of something.

All she'd known was rejection by the people she thought were her friends and the boy she thought she loved. He hadn't helped that by being an ass to her for a decade. Though she presented a tough front to the world, one in which she was happy with her life, the reality was bloody depressing. She thought so too, or she wouldn't be avoiding him after admitting that she knew she was an outcast. He was getting under her shell, figuring out the real Esha she kept hidden from the world, and she didn't like it.

He turned her around to face him, then reached up and brushed a swath of hair back from her face. Though she scowled, she leaned into his hand almost imperceptibly.

"We're friends, Esha."

"I don't really know how to *be* around friends. I've Ana, but what you and I have is very different."

"Aye," he said huskily. "I'd say that what I feel for you is more than friendship."

She shrugged and looked away. "Sex? Sure. There's that. I've wanted you for ages. Now you finally want me back, and frankly, I'm not entirely sure what to do about it."

Just sex? Far from it. She was becoming the light in his dark world. The only one who saw who he really was, yet kept coming back. "You're running." *From me.*

"No." She shook her head sharply.

"Then you're afraid."

"Of what?" Her voice challenged him.

"You're afraid of being close to another person."

"That doesn't make any sense. Everyone wants to be close to someone. I just don't want to be close to you."

"That's a lie. You're too clever for lies."

His gaze ensnared hers until he was all she could see. He *was* what she wanted, had been for years, and now he wanted her back. And it terrified her. He'd asked her what she was afraid of. She was afraid of him. Of his taking her up to the sun like Icarus's wings, then dropping her. Which he inevitably would, because someone like him wouldn't stay with someone like her. They were from two different worlds.

The thought gave her the strength to tear herself from his arms, to stride across the room. But not to leave. She couldn't bear to, because even though it hurt to be so close and yet so impossibly far from what she wanted, she couldn't break away. So she walked to the other window to give them space, to see what he would say.

But he didn't speak. Instead, she felt the heat and hardness of him at her back. One big hand was braced against the glass. So strong, with the scars to prove it, yet so beautiful. She wanted to reach up and touch it. She clenched her fist instead.

"Do you no' want to be close to someone?" His voice was rough at her ear, and the heat of his breath made her nerve endings sing all the way down her back. Though his heat and strength surrounded her, he didn't touch her. Always so close, yet so far away.

"Do you?" she asked.

"Aye. I want to be close to you."

She closed her eyes. "Why?" She wished she hadn't asked, but she couldn't help herself.

She moved to leave, to slip around him and out the door. As if he sensed her thoughts, he grasped her hands and pressed them against the glass at the level of her head. His hands trapped her, and the cold of the window only served to enhance the heat of him at her back.

"Look at me," he said.

"What?" He'd trapped her so that she couldn't turn. How was she supposed to look?

"Look up at the window."

A trick of the light allowed her to see their reflection, his head above hers. Only their hands touched, and the tension of being so close to him yet so far away made her tremble.

"I want you, Esha. For your courage, your strength, your wit and humor. You've ensnared me."

She stared at him, wide-eyed, as his eyes met hers in the glass.

"But I also want you for your body, for your lovely face. For the way you look at me when you think I canna see."

She gasped. Why was he telling her these things? Could he possibly mean them?

"I've had a taste of you, Esha, and I canna rest until I've had more."

He bent his head to her neck and dragged his lips along her skin. The contrast of soft lips and prickly stubble made goose bumps break out along her arms.

"It's just sex," she gasped.

He bit her once, at the slope where her neck met her shoulder, then looked up to meet her eyes in the glass once more. "You know it's no'. And I know it's no'. No' after that night on Mull, when I felt you hot and wet beneath my mouth. When your cries echoed in my ears and your hands fisted in my hair." His voice was darkly intense, his face more so.

She looked away, embarrassed. He released her hand to capture her chin, gently drawing her face back up until her eyes met his in the glass once again. She could have lowered her hand, could even have broken away and run for it, but she was caught in his spell. He returned his hand to hers, trapping her once more with nothing but a light pressure on her hands and the weight of his gaze.

"I'd do anything for that again. To make you mine in that way, when all the pretenses fall away and you're bared to me, unable to pretend you doona care."

"Warren, I—" She broke off when he pressed himself against her back, finally, *finally* making contact. The heat and strength of him were overwhelming, just enough to snap some sense into her.

"Aye, lassie?"

She shook her head. He pressed his hands against hers, enough pressure to let her know that he'd wait for her to finish. She couldn't keep herself from answering. "I care."

He grinned, a brief half smile that made her heart jump, then tilted his head to press a kiss to the top of hers. "Then doona move your hands," he said. "And doona look away."

The command caught the breath in her lungs, and she watched, entranced, as he moved his hands along her body. Slowly, as if cherishing every inch of her.

"I love your long, beautiful neck." His eyes held hers, almost painfully intense, as he ran a big, scarred hand down the front of her neck. His other hand gripped the side of her hip, as if to trap her because he was afraid she might run.

She was done running. She watched as he ran a broad hand down her chest to her breasts. He cupped one, gently testing the weight.

"They're too—"

"Perfect. Like the rest of you. Like your strong arms." His touch on the bared skin of her arms made her shiver, made her wish he'd touch the rest of her. He ran his hand down over her waist, slipping it beneath her shirt to rest on her stomach.

"Your skin is so soft. I want to kiss you and lick you here, teasing and torturing you for what's to come."

She had a vision of him on his knees, doing to her what he'd done before. Her own knees weakened, threatening to collapse, and he felt the brief shift.

"Nay. You'll stay upright for this." His eyes burned into hers as he spoke, compelling her to obey. To stay standing so that he could torture her some more. She could feel his strong chest against her back, the length of his thighs against hers. The steel of his cock pressed against her.

He wanted her. Wanted to be touching her, tasting her. The idea was thrilling, and so arousing it was all she could do to stay on her feet, desperate to see what he would do. There was something unbearably erotic about watching the two of them in the glass, watching as his fingers traced her skin and his eyes stayed rapt on hers.

His agile fingers began to undo her pants. She held her breath as he pushed them down, scared to do anything that might stop him.

Waiting.

Wanting.

Warren watched her in the glass, trying his damnedest not to grab her and throw her on the bed and fall on top of her like an animal. He'd accepted that she'd be the one with whom he broke his vow of celibacy—nay, delighted in it—but this wasn't about that.

Somewhere along the line, he'd begun to truly care for her. Enough to see that she cut herself off from the world and the people in it because she expected so little of it. She expected so little for herself. He wanted her to know how badly he wanted her, and for how many reasons.

"I could watch you like this for days," he said, as his hand returned to the juncture of her thighs. He repressed a shudder at the feel of her. "I could watch as my hands touch your body, all softness and heat. As my mouth traces across your skin, tasting you."

"Warren," she gasped, her head dropping back to his chest.

"Nay." His voice was harsh. "Look up. I want to see your face as I touch you. Want you to see mine."

She moaned, then tilted her head up until her fiery amber eyes met his. They were heavy-lidded with desire, her lush lips parted as her breath sawed in and out of her lungs. He teased her, skimming his fingertips over her pussy, letting her know what she could have, but withholding it. Just so he could watch her want him. Watch the desperate desire flash across her beautiful face and know that he'd put it there.

"You want me to touch you?" he asked.

She nodded.

"Where do you want me to touch you?"

Reluctance flashed across her face, just briefly. Enough to let him know that she wasn't lost in him yet. That she still held doubts. He couldn't bear it. He nodded at her, hoping she would answer his command.

"You know where," she gasped, her eyes hot on his and her breaths coming quicker.

"Aye, lassie. I do. Now spread your legs," he said, loving the way she so quickly obliged, toeing off her boots and kicking off her jeans.

When she was stripped from the waist down, her T-shirt riding just above her dark curls, he watched her eyes as he dipped his fingers into the heat of her, gently separating her folds to get to her glorious wetness.

"You're so soft here. So perfect." His voice sounded harsher to his ears, from the blood roaring through his head and the desire that clogged his throat. "So wet and slick and sweet."

He ran his fingers in circles over her clitoris, watching in awe as her face clouded with pleasure.

"You like that." It was more statement than question. She trembled in his arms, a woman whose strength astounded him. He moved his free hand to one of hers, holding it against the glass and not breaking eye contact.

"Tell me what you want," he said, wanting to hear it on her lips.

"I want you inside of me." There was no hesitation in her words, only desire.

"Here?" He teased at her entrance, pushing one finger gently inside. She nodded, and he fitted it fully inside of her. "Gods, you're perfect. I want to be inside of you."

"Yes." She moaned, her eyelids fluttering with pleasure.

He smiled, then rubbed her clitoris with his thumb and pushed his finger deeper inside of her. She moved her hips in a dance that made his cock throb with desire. Unable to help himself, he began to thrust against her, marveling at the pleasure.

"Warren!" She was breathless, the color high in her cheeks. "I want more."

"This?" He pushed another finger inside of her, marveling at the way she gripped him, and fucked her with his fingers.

"Yes. No. I mean... I want you." She pressed her ass back against him, and he groaned into her hair. *Yes.*

"No' yet. First, you're going to come in my arms. I want to see you. Feel you." He curled his fingers forward to focus on the bundle of nerves within her. When her weight sagged against him, he wrapped his free arm around her waist to support her.

"Look at me," he said when her eyes began to close. She snapped them open. "You're going to come for me now."

She had to. This damn idea would have him coming against her ass if she didn't reach orgasm soon. His control was near broken, the civilized part of himself stripped away until he was nothing but a shaking mass of instinct and desire.

He bit her earlobe, keeping his eyes on hers, and groaned when he felt her pussy contract around his fingers and a harsh cry spill from her lips.

"Gods, you're so perfect." He watched in awe as the pleasure swept over her face. She never looked away. Neither did he.

CHAPTER TWENTY-EIGHT

Esha surfaced from her orgasm to realize that Warren was tense behind her, his breath heavy and his erection throbbing against her ass. She met his eyes again in the window.

Animal need was stamped across his face, held back only by his iron control.

Celibate. No wonder he was near the edge. The idea that she'd be the first in a century made her pussy throb with need.

She turned, kissed him briefly on the mouth, but wiggled away when he reached for her. Instead, she dropped to her knees. The stone floor bit into them, but it was worth it for the look on his face.

"Oh, fuck," he breathed, his hands forming tight fists at his sides.

She loved how much he wanted her. Just as much, she wanted to take back some of the control she'd ceded to him. She was baring more of herself to him every hour, so much so that she might eventually lose her grip on everything that kept her separate. If she was to bare herself to him, he'd do the same.

"Take off your shirt," she said.

His hands trembled slightly as he tore it over his head, revealing broad planes of muscles and ridged abs. He felt even bigger this way, naked and strong above her. He dwarfed her in a way she'd never felt before. Not only was she one of the most powerful Mytheans, she wasn't a small woman. But with Warren, that all changed.

His muscle-roped arms dropped to his sides, his big hands returned to fists. To hold himself back. She couldn't be having any of that.

She tugged at his pants, undoing the fly and yanking the denim down to his ankles. Sculpted calves led to strong thighs and a jutting erection, the size of which made her pussy throb. It was laced with veins and topped with a broad head. Her mouth tingled with the need to run her tongue over all that soft skin and hard muscle.

She didn't hesitate, but took him wholly into her mouth, swallowing as much as she could. His harsh shout of pleasure shot a jolt of the same through her. His hand sank into her hair, then pulled away.

She reached up and moved his hand back to her head, giving him the permission he clearly sought. His hand fisted in her hair. She wanted to give him as much pleasure as anyone had ever given another.

A guttural moan drifted from his lips as she worked him with her mouth and hands. He was hot and hard beneath her tongue, yet smooth as silk. She licked as she sucked, delighting in the quick, helpless jolt of his hips.

He reached down and pulled her to her feet, then leaned his forehead against hers. His fist tightened in her hair and his other hand curled around her waist as if he couldn't bear to let her go.

"I want to be inside you," he said, his breath sawing. "May I?"

A shudder racked him when she stood on tiptoe and wrapped one leg around his waist. "Yes."

He yanked her up and pressed her back against the window. When she wrapped her legs around his waist, his hands bit into her ass and a harsh, "*Oh, fuck*," sounded in her ears.

Between her thighs, she felt him fist his shaft with a shaking hand and press the tip against the throbbing entrance of her pussy. She'd never wanted anything so badly.

"I've never wanted anything so fucking bad," he muttered against her lips.

"Now, Warren."

Slowly, torturously slowly, he pushed inside her. Then stopped. "Shite. Protection," he said, his voice tight.

"I'm on it. Please. Now."

He shuddered, then pushed forward. He was so big, so perfect, and he filled the empty space within her with pleasure. She dropped her forehead to his, squeezing her eyes shut at the perfection of connecting with him. Of feeling him pulse within her, deliciously hard and hot and male. She thought she was in control, but when she felt him, so overwhelming, inside her, she was lost.

The feel of Esha's pussy taking his cock, gripping him gloriously, made chills break out on Warren's skin. It'd been so long, but it had never been so perfect. This was something entirely different from any sex he'd ever had.

When he was fitted fully inside her, he tried to go slowly. Failed. His hips began to thrust, his mind and body taking over in a primitive rhythm that made pleasure surge from the base of his spine out over his body.

Her fingers dug into his shoulders, and he loved the bite of pain, the sound of her harsh breaths in his ear and the smell of her arousal.

"You're so perfect, I'm no' going to last," he muttered. Even like this, the pleasure, the wildness, crept in on him, taking over mind and body.

Her hand slipped from his shoulder and between them, her fingertips finding her clitoris. The idea of her touching herself short-circuited his mind and made impending orgasm start to tighten in his balls.

When her sex clutched around him, wet and hot and drawing him into her pleasure, he lost all control of his thrusts. His hips pumped as the orgasm ripped through him, tearing him apart and putting him back together, this time twined with Esha. It swept him up and along, blinding him to everything but her.

When the orgasm finally faded away after racking his body with shudders of pleasure, he turned and walked to the bed, Esha still wrapped around him.

He had enough energy to lay her upon the mattress before collapsing in a graceless pile next to her. With a weary arm, he dragged her against his side.

"That was amazing. Thank you." He pressed a kiss to her head. She'd given him that gift, even knowing who he was and seeing the shadows of all the evil that he'd done.

CHAPTER TWENTY-NINE

She was the biggest idiot in the world.

There was no question about it, Esha thought, as she crept out of the bedroom in the morning. Warren still slept in the warm bed she'd just left, but she needed some time to clear her head. She waved a hand at the torches in the hall, grateful that it took so little power to do so. She passed Warren's room and the Chairman perked up from where he sprawled in the middle of the bed.

Last night had been amazing. Stupid, but amazing. She was falling for Warren regardless of the fact that it was a terrible idea. It would end badly, as these things always did for her. It might not even last long enough for him to leave her, considering that he was determined to kill Aurora. For good reason too, with how sick she made him.

Her mind feel like it was squeezed in a vise, so she shook them away—or tried to—and went into the kitchen. If she was lucky, she'd face Aurora today.

After a cup of instant coffee and a granola bar for herself and a can of cat food for the Chairman—which she'd had to drag across the glacier because gods knew you couldn't forget the Chairman's wet food—she met Warren in the foyer. The sun was just now peeking over the horizon and the dim light shining through the windows highlighted Warren's face.

Esha didn't realize she was holding her breath, wondering if she would see regret there, until his smile broke out at the sight of her. For some terrible, crazy reason, that scared her even more.

If he had regretted it, sleeping with him would be a terrible one-off. A mistake she would no doubt cry over, but it would be done. Instead, he didn't regret it. But with everything ahead of them, now what?

"I think we're going to find Aurora today," she said. "I've got to ask you not to kill her. Not right away."

Disbelief flashed across his face. "No' an option, lassie. She's dangerous, and the longer she's left alive, the closer I get to being incapacitated and the more people she can hurt."

Fear sent her heart pounding. He was right, but she didn't want to hear it. "Maybe she doesn't know she's making you sick by using your soul. I know she's bad, and that she's done terrible things. But she did them during terrible times. Nearly every soulceress was killed during the Burnings—she was scared. I just need a chance to talk to her. One chance to see if I can convince her to give it back."

"She's too damn dangerous. I'm telling you it's no' an option." His face was harder than she'd ever seen it.

"I've never met another of my kind. You know about my life. Why this is so important to me. Just one chance."

"No' a chance in hell."

Everything she wanted—Warren and a chance to know another of her kind—was slipping out of her hands. She could feel it going, and it made some terrible, tragic monster surge inside of her.

"Ah, Esha. Doona cry, lassie." Warren stepped up to her and cupped her face in his hands.

She pulled back and sniffled, horrified to feel a hot tear spill onto her cheek. She scrubbed a hand over her eyes. "I'm not crying."

"I care about you, damn it," he said. "I doona want to hurt you. But I have to get my soul back. I'm a monster without it. And she is truly dangerous."

"I get that, I really do. I want you to get your soul back. Everyone should have their soul. But I just want to meet her and talk to her. Once. You don't have to be there, so you won't be at risk. I'll go to see her alone."

"The hell you will. I'm no' worried for me, I'm worried for you. I'd no' risk you like that. You doona know her. What if she really wants to take your power, as the witches said?"

"It's a risk I'm willing to take to meet her. I'm confident in my ability to protect myself. Why can't you be?"

"I am, but I'm the one who should protect you from problems I've created."

"That's not your choice. I care for you, Warren. I do. A hell of a lot more than I want to, but take this opportunity from me, and we're done."

She meant it.

But Warren didn't know how to fix this, because he wouldn't risk her. At some point, he'd become less concerned about himself and more about her. But this was the worst kind of argument. The kind in which each understood the other's perspective, but wouldn't budge. It would all come down to which one reached Aurora first. But would one of them do something that the other couldn't forgive?

"Let's go," he said, and turned to the door. They weren't going to see eye to eye, so they might as well get to work.

"Fine." Esha swept out the door in front of him into the cold morning air.

The gloaming lent a haunted aura to the city, especially once the disorientation hit him. They'd only walked a hundred yards up the narrow street when he noticed that the shade was following them again. Unlike the shadows that hovered in the windows and watched, or attacked mindlessly at the museum and temple, this one seemed to have its own agenda. But damned if he knew what it was. It had helped them twice, though, which was damned strange.

"We're close," Esha said.

His muscles tensed. He'd had no idea how close or far they were, which was weird as hell. Worse, the city's magic made him feel less capable of protecting Esha, and he hated it.

His hand went to the dagger in his boot when they stepped out into the square. They crossed quickly to the temple and Warren said, "Let's check for side entrances."

They circled the entire building, through the small alley on the left side, the street at the back, and another small alley on the right. But there were no more entrances.

"Looks like we're going up," Esha said when they reached the front of the building.

Warren nodded and they began the climb. Once again, they made it up the stairs without incident. When they reached the landing that led to the great wooden door, he spun around to face the square, waiting for the shadows to charge again. It was eerily silent.

"They're not here," Esha said. "Maybe we destroyed them."

He hoped so. They turned warily back to the door, and he pushed it open, this time having no trouble as he had yesterday at the museum. Damn, it felt good to be at full strength again.

They stood at either side of the door, behind the walls in case Aurora was within, and peered inside. The huge windows allowed light to shine in brilliant streams onto the rainbow marble. The ceiling soared overhead, arched stone as magnificent as any he'd ever seen. Stone pillars and arches supported it, creating aisles and walkways that led up to a huge platform at the other end of the temple. No question, the soulceresses of old had been talented and advanced beyond the ken of Mytheans and mortals.

"I don't think she's here," Esha said. "But this is the place. I'm sure of it."

"We'll search it."

They crept inside. Warren kept the dagger in his hand, ready for whatever flew out of the shadows at them. They walked along the silent aisles, looking for any kind of clue, but found nothing. It didn't take long for him to agree that the place was truly empty. Aurora wasn't here.

They reached the platform and began to climb. The air tingled, and he swiveled his head around, searching for the threat. A great crash thundered through the temple and a huge slab of ice slammed down between Warren and Esha, forming a transparent wall. Another crash, and slabs fell all around him, creating a giant maze of ice.

"Esha!"

She was trapped on the other side of the ice, but suddenly, there were dozens of her, emerging from the great frozen wall in front of him. The apparitions stomped toward him, gazes intense and mouths set. They converged upon him, pushing him back, tearing at his clothes and hair.

He struggled against them, shuddering at the tingly chill of them, but hesitated to strike out with his dagger. What the hell was this? Some kind of magic, but for what? One could be the real Esha, enchanted by Aurora. He couldn't try to kill them for fear of that, but they were strong. He'd be on his knees soon.

"Warren!" Esha screamed. She pounded on the great ice wall, her fists stinging with the cold. The Chairman scrabbled at the glass, his claws carving gouges that were no match for the thick ice.

"No! Stop!" she cried when apparitions of herself attacked Warren. She thought they hesitated when she screamed *no*, but they picked up again, dragging Warren to the ground. But he wouldn't fight back, not more than pushing them away, at least. Did he think she was one of them?

This had to be Aurora's magic. Until now, the shadows had always tried to repel him alone. Now, the magic let her in but barred him. Aurora really did want to see only her, but she didn't have to hurt Warren.

"Aurora, stop! Don't hurt him!"

The apparitions continued to attack, so Esha screamed again. Finally, she thought she heard the bored echo of a voice saying, "Oh, fine."

But the apparitions stopped, and Esha breathed a sigh of relief. Warren leapt to his feet and ran at the wall.

"Esha!" She couldn't hear his words, but she could read his lips as he pounded on the ice, fear for her plain on his face.

"I'm fine!" She screamed, then caught sight of a shadow behind Warren. "Behind you!"

Warren spun around and faced the shadow. It was the mysterious shade who'd helped them until now. He'd be safe with the shade. She read no evil in it, not the way she normally did, and had an overwhelming feeling that the two of them could face whatever came at them.

Knowing that she had no way to escape the ice except to turn around and continue across the platform, she did so. Her muscles tensed as she walked across the marble expanse that was now surrounded on all sides by ice. A great table, inlaid with marble of all colors, stretched across the back wall. Behind it was an archway that led into a small antechamber.

She skirted the table and cautiously stepped through the archway. The breath was sucked from her lungs, and her vision blacked out as she was pulled through space.

CHAPTER THIRTY

When Esha could finally breathe again, she opened her eyes to see that she was standing in the middle of a beach party. No, make that a beach *orgy*. Scantily dressed mortals were dancing—writhing, more like it—to thumping music pumped out of speakers the size of her car.

Hot sun sparkled on cerulean blue water that lapped in small waves at a white sand beach, so different from the frozen land she'd left behind. She turned to see that she stood next to an expansive marble patio, and behind it, a huge white mansion with gleaming glass windows.

What the hell? This was so not what she had been expecting. She glanced around for the Chairman. He wasn't there.

Holy shit. He'd been left behind. Her heart pounded faster. She was at half power without him. She readied herself for anything and pushed her way through the tanned, sun-oil slicked bodies of the partiers and stepped up onto the patio. The acre of white marble surrounded a huge pool, within which floated one woman on an enormous pool raft.

The woman leaned up and flicked her sunglasses up onto her head. "You're here!" She hopped off the raft and climbed out of the water in seconds. "Clear out, bitches, the party is over!"

She waved her hand and the crowd disappeared. Another wave, and the music turned off. Silence crashed around them.

It all happened so fast that Esha's head spun. The woman—who looked *so* familiar—strolled toward her. Esha gaped, remembering too late to snap her jaw shut. Aurora was as bright and golden as the sun. Golden skin, golden hair chopped short and tousled around her head, and most importantly, golden eyes that were far too familiar.

"Holy shit, we're related," Esha breathed.

"Of course." Aurora spoke as though it was the most obvious thing in the world. But it wasn't, not until you looked at their eyes. Their bodies shared no similarities. The other soulceress was shorter, with a more athletic build. Where Esha was a contrast of pale and dark, Aurora was golden.

Except for the black shadows that writhed around her, a mist that resonated with evil. They were the soul shadows of Warren and others. Esha didn't have any of those.

But her eyes. One look at her eyes and it was clear as the sparkling water surrounding this island that they shared a parent.

"How?" Esha asked.

"We're half sisters. Same mother."

The breath whooshed out of Esha's lungs, and she stepped back. No matter the broad smile that stretched across the face of the woman approaching her, she exuded danger and power.

Danger especially. As much as she wanted to believe the best of this woman—her *sister*, for gods' sake—she wasn't stupid.

"Where's my familiar? And Warren?"

"Back in the temple. Safe, since it seems you would no' come until I ended the magic. I thought it was quite clever."

"Why'd you enchant the portal so it didn't allow my familiar?"

"I figured you weren't out to hurt me, but if you were, I dinna want you having the extra power. You aren't out to get me, right?" Her sister arched a golden brow.

"Probably not, but I'm not sure yet."

"Fair enough. Want a beer?" Aurora plucked one out of a cooler.

"Um, no, I'm good, thanks."

"Come on." Aurora stood in front of her with an infectious grin that threw Esha off balance. She popped the top off the beer and stuck it out so that Esha had to grab it. "Took you long enough to find me. Let's go sit in those lounge chairs, get to know each other."

Esha stood dumbly, the beer in her hand, as she watched her sister saunter off. They were going to chat, with beers on the beach? This was too strange—it couldn't be right.

Esha's muscles tensed, ready to flee or throw a fireball or do whatever it took to protect herself. But she couldn't flee without the Chairman, there wasn't really anywhere to hide, and unless Aurora made a move on her, it wasn't smart to start something she wasn't sure she could finish. She decided to play along. And maybe Aurora wasn't as bad as her shadows might suggest.

She followed Aurora to the lounge chairs that overlooked the sea. It was hot as any of the hells, so Esha stripped off her jacket and sweater until she was left in only a tank top, then warily lowered herself to the lounge chair next to Aurora's. She glanced around surreptitiously for Aurora's familiar and finally caught sight of a sleek black cat lounging by the pool.

"Where the hell are we?" Esha asked.

"In the aether. I created this place."

Wow. It took some serious power to do that. But she'd been locked up for hundreds of years. How'd she know to add all the modern amenities, like the pool? Her magic must be greater than Esha had realized, which freaked her the hell out. "Why'd you enchant a portal to bring me here? Why the whole runaround to find you?"

Aurora shrugged and raised her purple-umbrella drink to her lips. "I wanted to find you, no' Warren. He's trouble for another day. When I sensed your presence at that damn place they imprisoned me, I wanted to meet you. But I had to be certain that it was you who found me and no' anyone else at the university—hence the *howf*, a place that only another soulceress could enter, and this city, a place that only another soulceress could find."

"Why me? And why didn't you just appear to me?"

"I wanted it to be on my terms, my turf. I won't be caught by the university and thrown into that prison again. And I've never really met another soulceress before, except our mother, so of course I wanted to meet you. And I wanted to see you specifically because there's a lot I need to know about the modern world, and you're the only one I can trust... since you're like me."

The breath whooshed out of Esha's lungs. Trust? The only one who really trusted her was Ana. Warren too, she was starting to believe. Now Aurora?

This was all coming too fast, too soon. She hadn't known what to expect from meeting Aurora, but not this. There was supposed to be more time to plan, to think about it. She'd have the upper hand, or at least an even footing.

But now she was totally out of her element on some tropical island, with no familiar, less than half a power supply, and she was being thrown for a loop by her unexpectedly friendly half-sister. Was she lulling her with a false sense of security so she could snatch her power away? Esha eyed the black shadows that hovered around Aurora. No matter how friendly Aurora seemed, she had a dark side that was all too obvious.

"How did you know I'm your sister?" Her voice was squeaky, surprised, and she flinched at the sound. *Badass. Esha, you are supposed to be a badass.*

"I thought you might be when I sensed you, but now that I see you, you're the spitting image of our mother."

"You sensed me?"

"When I was in the aether and you came to the witches' creepy little cabin to bind me there. Bitches and their awful prison." Aurora shuddered.

Esha nodded in commiseration. A prison in the aether was the worst, and it explained why Aurora was hanging out at a beach party on a sunny island. It was the complete opposite of the aether, which was vital to their world but had sections that were dark, cold, and lonely if you were trapped within it. The space between here and nowhere was like air, but not. Some reincarnated souls were held over there until they were needed and were reborn for their fated task. But if you were trapped there with your soul *and* your consciousness, it would be hell.

"Anyway," Aurora said, "when you dinna agree to their plan, I figured I could probably trust you. And you're my sister and all."

There was that T-word again. Esha tried not to let it warm her, but it was damned hard. She was here for Warren, not just for herself. As much as she wanted to grill Aurora for information about their mother, about their kind, about how she might possibly control her power collection so that she could have a normal life, she had Warren's soul to worry about too, and she didn't want to let him down. There would be time to learn about her mother later.

"There's something I wanted to ask you. Do you think you could give my friend back his soul?"

Aurora's friendly eyes hardened and the black shadows around her writhed more aggressively. A chill crept across Esha's skin. The fun lightheartedness that had radiated from Aurora was replaced by darkness, as if a switch had been flipped.

"No' going to happen." Aurora's voice was diamond-hard and her eyes had blackened.

Esha braced herself so she wouldn't flinch and asked, "Why not?"

"He's responsible for our mother's death." Rage twisted Aurora's features and dark clouds rolled across the blue sky. The water turned gray and choppy as a cold wind rushed across it.

Esha shivered as Aurora's shadows leapt and writhed. This wasn't the same Aurora. This was the Aurora that Warren had warned her about.

"The power of his soul is *mine*," Aurora said, her black eyes flashing. "He gave it to me of his own free will. I'd kill him if I could, but I'd have to give his soul back to do so and that is no' happening."

Oh shit. Aurora was deadly serious. This was not going to be easy.

The sleek black cat loped up to them with a grace that the Chairman could never dream of mustering and leapt up onto Aurora's lounge chair. It rubbed against her, purring.

Before her eyes, the shadows that writhed around Aurora calmed. Her face smoothed out and her eyes lightened to gold again.

Huh. Something was wrong with Aurora and her familiar knew it. Under the cat's calming influence, she came back to normal. So did the island, its blue sky and bluer water now bright and shiny.

But Esha wasn't similarly calm, not after what Aurora had just said. "Our mother's death?"

Aurora nodded, her eyes sad. Sad, but not black, and that was an important distinction that Esha was beginning to recognize.

"Before you were born, we fled the Burnings to live near the mortals, hoping we would be hidden from Mytheans who wanted to kill us. But the mortals hunted us, as well. Warren was supposed to help her escape Scotland, but he turned her over to the witch hunters. He let her die at the hands of bastard mortals." Her eyes darkened again, and clouds rolled back across the horizon, but her familiar frantically rubbed against her, purring like a jet plane. Aurora reached down to pet it, and her eyes cleared again.

"No," Esha said. "He told me about that. He tried to save her, but he was too late. He could only save her baby."

Holy shit. It hit Esha then, for the first time since Aurora had told her about their mother. *She* was the baby that Warren had saved and sent to America. She had to get back to Warren, had to ask him about it. And he'd spent long enough in that ice palace.

"Hey, I really need to get back. Can I come back tomorrow?"

"Sure. You will come back, right?"

"Of course."

"Good. Without Warren." Her eyes flashed dark and Esha scrambled up. "Just go back to that spot on the beach where you arrived. It will take you back. To get here again, you can aetherwalk with your familiar. Just think of me like you would think of a place and it'll work."

Esha said her good-byes and walked back to the beach. Getting Warren's soul back was going to be a hell of a lot harder than she thought. And it wasn't the only thing she had to worry about.

CHAPTER THIRTY-ONE

When the ice walls disappeared, Warren spun around, his gaze racing around the temple. The Chairman hurtled toward him, a black blur that dodged around the mysterious shade that had stayed by Warren's side during the thirty interminable minutes Esha had been missing. But where the hell was she?

"Warren!"

He whirled at the sound of Esha's voice and found her in the middle of the temple.

"Where the hell were you?" His voice shook with anger and fear. He had her in his arms before he realized he'd even moved. The terror in his heart was a live, wild thing that calmed only when he felt Esha's warm body in his arms. "I was so damned worried about you."

He felt her arms creep up around his back and squeeze. The cat had launched itself at Esha and was now twining about her legs.

"Sorry." Her voice was muffled against his chest.

"What happened?"

"She enchanted the altar platform. Made it so that I couldn't bring the Chairman in case I meant her harm."

"We need to get out of here." He dragged her out of the temple, then came to a stop outside the doors. "Damn it. I canna fuckin' navigate with whatever magic has been put on this place!"

"Come on." Esha grabbed his hand and led him through the city. He hated the damned feeling of needing her to do it, especially when all he wanted was to be the one to protect her.

"Fucking finally," he said when they pushed through the front door of the house. Frustration over his powerlessness in this soulceress city surged within him, making a toxic sludge with the fear for Esha that filled his insides. He'd never been this helpless, not when he wanted something so badly.

He rounded on Esha. "Damn it, Esha! You canna take risks like that again."

Her jaw dropped, then snapped shut. "Wait, what?"

"You canna see her again. She's too damned dangerous. You were never supposed to be alone with her. You were never supposed to fucking meet her."

"You were seriously going to try to keep me from her?" Her eyes looked stricken.

"Of course! Your life is at risk!"

"She's my sister!"

The ground felt like it dropped out from beneath Warren's feet. "What?"

"Oh, don't act like you didn't know."

"I dinna." He dragged a hand down his face. If they were sisters, that meant she was the baby he'd put on the boat to

America. It was fucking crazy. "Gods, it was so damned long ago."

She squinted at him, skeptical. "You really expect me to believe you didn't know."

"Aye. It was over three hundred years ago, and you were an infant. But it changes nothing. She's too dangerous for you to see again."

"She's not as bad as you think. She's ruthless, but I swear to you that she isn't evil." Her eyes pleaded with him to understand.

Dread washed over him like a wave of tar, followed quickly by a fiery spark of anger. "You don't know that."

"I think the souls have poisoned her. They're dragging at her mind with their desperation to leave her. Her familiar keeps her in check when she loses it, but I can persuade her to give yours back, I know I can. Especially if I can convince her she doesn't need to be holed up in her magical world."

The idea of Esha going back there, to face Aurora in one of her rages, made his head feel like it was going to blow off. "Out of the question! You canna see her again. I will no' allow it."

"You don't get to decide!"

"The hell I doona. Aurora must die. It's the only way."

"It's not that easy! She's more powerful than you can imagine. Convincing her to give it up is safer than a fight. And it could save my sister as well as you."

"She's no' really your sister, lassie! She's a monster. She's stolen souls and killed when it suits her. She's killing me as we speak."

"I just need time with her! Just half a day. You have at least three more days on your medicine. Give me half a day to try. "

"Never going to happen!"

"Fuck you, Warren." She glared at him, then turned and stomped up the stairs.

An hour later, Esha was still stewing over what Warren had said. Even the steaming water of the hot spring couldn't wash away her pissy mood. After stomping around her room in circles, she'd felt like the walls were closing in on her. So she'd come down to the basement, where she might be able to wash away some of her rage.

It hadn't worked, so now she was sitting on one of the big boulders with her towel wrapped around her, still gnashing her teeth over their conversation.

Who the hell did he think he was? She could deal with Aurora, she just needed one more try. Brute strength wouldn't work with her—she could already tell that her sister was stronger and more skilled than she. A bit of an ego-check, that was. But Aurora *was* older and powered by the souls she'd stolen. Esha didn't stand a chance in an outright fight.

No, the key was convincing Aurora that she didn't need Warren's soul, or any of the others. It was like—like heroin. A poison that Aurora was convinced she needed. As she was convinced that she was only safe holed up in her magical world. Getting rid of those shadows was the only way to save both Warren and her sister. She just needed to figure out how. Because when it came down to it, she'd pick Warren over Aurora, and this was the safest way for him.

"Esha." Warren's voice shook her out of her trance, and she looked up to see him stepping off the stairs. The dim torchlight glinted off his golden hair, and the shadows that he cast made him seem all the larger.

"What?"

He stepped through the steam that filled the stone room and stopped before her. "I wanted to apologize."

Her jaw almost dropped. "Really?"

"Aye. I haven't liked being in this city. No' being able to navigate or fight back against the souls... well, I've never felt so fucking helpless. With you in danger, out of my reach, I lost it."

She looked at him, standing so tall and broad, and realized that with his strength and skill, he was never at a disadvantage in normal life. Of course this had thrown him off.

"You were still an ass," she said.

"Aye. But you're precious to me. I only realized how much when you were trapped with Aurora. I couldn't live with myself if something happened to you. I lost it when I thought of you facing her alone." He walked up to her and cupped her face in his hands, his expression so heartfelt and torn that it made her heart ache.

"I was an ass too. If it comes down to it, of course I choose you over her. Giving me one more chance with her is the safest way. We don't stand a chance of winning in an outright fight. I just need a few hours."

"I won't let you risk your life for my soul."

Esha flinched even as her heart soared. He wanted her life more than his own soul? The thing he'd wanted more than anything else for centuries? It wasn't that simple, though. "But with your sickness, your soul is your life now. You won't survive if she keeps it. You'll just be incapacitated and in misery."

He shrugged, his eyes still on hers. "I've lived a long time. I won't trade your life for mine. I thought I wasn't complete without my soul, and maybe I'm no'. But losing you would take a bigger piece out of me than I'd be able to recover from."

A golden warmth spread through her at his words. She had no idea what to say, but she had to believe she could fix this with Aurora. He had to have his soul back, and soon.

"Come here." She pulled his face down to hers and kissed him. Not a kiss of desire, but of closeness. This was what she'd wanted for so long. Not the sex, not the flirting or the long glances, but the closeness and the caring. The kind that might last a lifetime. The idea took the breath from her. It was like a chance at sunlight after a life underground, but terrifying in that it might not last.

How could something so good endure? It wouldn't; her luck had never run that way. The only thing she could do was grab and hold on with both hands for as long as it lasted.

She was shaken from her dire thoughts when Warren's big hand ran up her back and cupped her head. The other wrapped around her waist. He held her so closely that she felt as though she were one with him, his heat pushing out the cold spaces in her heart that the hot springs hadn't been able to vanquish. His lips were firm on hers, stealing her breath.

Too soon, he pulled away and leaned his forehead against hers. The loss was palpable, the chill all the greater for having known warmth.

"We have to finish this discussion," he said.

She shook her head. "No. No." She kissed him. "Let it rest. Just for now. Kiss me. Please."

He groaned, a rumble from low in his throat, and pulled her mouth back to his. He slipped his tongue between her lips, his clever mouth making her moan, then pulled the towel from her.

"In the water," he growled.

She swallowed hard, then nodded. But only once he'd torn off his clothes and stood before her naked, with the golden light flickering off planes of muscle, did she turn around and step into the water.

When she reached the middle and it lapped at her stomach, she felt him behind her, his rough hands on her waist and his erection hard against her ass.

"You scared the hell out of me." His dark voice at her ear sent a shiver down her spine. Barely leashed control radiated from him, no doubt left over from his tension in the temple.

She jumped when his hand slipped between her thighs, his fingers stroking and finding the place that made her moan.

"Fuck, you're soft." The words were guttural, his need clear.

The stroking of his hands and the water blended to make her mind spin. When he pushed her forward so that she bent over and rested her hands on the rim of the pool, she parted her legs, tilting her ass up.

A shiver of anticipation racked her when his hands gripped her hips. The hot, hard length of him prodded at her entrance and she moved back, needing him to drive out her fear over the future.

His groan was harsh as he pushed forward, parting her flesh with the broad head of his cock. Her eyes slid shut in acute pleasure as she savored the feel of him, hot and hard against her. She cried out when he began to move, thrusting steadily while his fingers rubbed her clitoris. The slapping of water and flesh was a glorious and dirty accompaniment to the sound of his breath heaving in her ear.

"Come now, Esha." His voice broke on her name. "I'm no' going to last."

His fingers stroked her, making the tension coil tighter and tighter. But it wasn't until his thrusts lost their grace and his hand bit into her hip that it exploded into an orgasm that tore through her and took him over the edge with her.

Hours later, Esha gazed down at Warren, his harshly beautiful face peaceful in repose. She'd just woken after several hours of sleep to see that it was nearing two in the morning. After the hot springs, Warren had carried her up to his room. They'd fallen asleep nearly immediately.

Now, she lay on her side in the big bed and looked down at him. In all the time she'd known him, she'd never seen him looking so relaxed. He had so much weighing on him, so much at risk these last few weeks. He must be exhausted if he slept so deeply.

She couldn't, now that she'd awakened. Too many thoughts played in her head. A few weeks ago, she'd had so little in her life. Work, the Chairman—who was worth his furry weight in gold—and Ana. She was lucky. She was. But sometimes, the missing parts glared too brightly to ignore.

Then Warren asked her to help him, and everything had changed. She'd fallen for him. For all her big talk about keeping her heart separate and protecting herself, she'd failed miserably. How had she thought to resist this kind, strong, determined man?

Somehow, during the course of their search, his goals had become as important to her as her own. She had to get his soul back for him. And they couldn't agree on how to go about it, that was certain. She was grateful they'd been too exhausted to talk any more. He was so set on his path, but so was she. She just needed one more chance with Aurora.

If she couldn't convince Aurora this time, she'd agree with Warren, as much as it would hurt her to do so. But for now, she had the perfect time to sneak away and try again.

CHAPTER THIRTY-TWO

Twenty minutes later, Esha opened her eyes on the beach. Stars twinkled above, the moon a heavy orb hanging low over dark water. The silence was broken only by waves lapping at the sand.

Aurora was probably at the house, so she headed up onto the patio, around the twinkling pool, and toward the brightly lit floor-length windows of the white mansion. The giant sliding glass doors led directly into an expansive living room, where TV sounds blared. Knocking would be no use, so Esha pulled on one of the doors, unsurprised when it wasn't locked.

"Aurora?" she called over the TV. Hesitantly, she wandered through the white and blue living room and under the archway that led to the kitchen. It was an enormous space, with acres of white marble counters and clear glass cabinets. Every appliance was sitting out on the counters, plugged in and ready to go.

Aurora's familiar lounged on the island counter in the middle of the kitchen, graceful and sleek under the hanging glass lamps. When the Chairman's ears perked up and he stood a little straighter, she realized that the other familiar was definitely female. She watched in disbelief as the Chairman sauntered toward the lady cat.

Good luck, dude.

Aurora popped up from behind the island counter, headphones on her head and a big grin on her face. Her skin gleamed golden in the white kitchen, and she was dressed in a bikini with a sarong tied around her waist. The shadows still swirled around her like black smoke, but they were calm. She gripped a shiny steel toaster in her hand.

There were two different Auroras, that was certain. Goofy Aurora with a toaster, and deadly Aurora who came out to play occasionally. Esha hoped that it would be goofy Aurora in residence tonight.

"Esha!" she cried, yanking the headphones off her ears. The faint pounding beat of rock music drifted across the kitchen. "You're back. Do you know what this thing does?"

"Um, it makes toasted bread. Just stick the slices in."

"Huh. Okay, then." She put it on the counter and pointed to another appliance. "What about that thing?"

Esha stared at it, her brow scrunched. She wasn't much of a cook, but hadn't she seen one of those on an infomercial? "I think that one pops corn kernels into popcorn."

"What the hell is that?"

"It's a snack. Light and airy. Are you fond of cooking?" She gestured to the myriad appliances.

"Nay. No' if I doona have to. But I freaking love electricity. All the things you can do with it! And all these strange things for making food. Did you know there is a fire

264

that bursts into flame in my bedroom? All I have to do is push a button on a little box and poof! Fire!"

"Yeah, it's pretty nice." Aurora would really get along with Ana, Esha thought. They were equally entranced by technology—Aurora because she'd lived in a time without it, and Ana because she'd spent the last few thousand years stuck in Otherworld, where nothing had changed since the time of the Celts.

"Gods, I'm starving. Do you know how to make any food with this stuff?" Aurora said.

"Sorry, not much of a cook myself. Unless you've got frozen pizza in the freezer, we're out of luck."

"Pizza?"

"It's some fabulous food." Which gave Esha an idea. She wanted Aurora on her side, after all, and she really didn't want Aurora's shadows freaking out the way they had before. Esha was more convinced than ever that they were making Aurora crazy.

Food would be a good distraction. Because she was in the aether, it wouldn't take much energy to aetherwalk to get some. Distances weren't applicable in the here and nowhere, so she'd save her much needed power. She called the Chairman to her. He gave her a disgruntled look, but with one last longing glance at the female familiar, he came to her.

"Hang on. I'll bring some back," Esha said before they disappeared.

In the haze of sleep, Warren reached out for Esha and found only cold sheets. He snapped awake, his eyes taking an interminable time to focus on the dim room lit only by a single torch in the corner. She wasn't here.

His heart pounded a staccato beat as he leapt up, threw on trousers, and grabbed a flashlight from the floor near the bed. A frantic search of the three floors of the house revealed that his dire feeling had been correct. She wasn't here.

Damn it. She'd gone back to Aurora.

Fear made his chest feel too tight. He raced up to the bedroom and threw on a shirt and shoes, grabbed his sword and the dagger he'd taken from the museum, then charged down the stairs and out the front door.

The disorientation hit him immediately, a false confusion cast by the magic that protected the place. "Fuck!"

He looked from side to side down the narrow street. In the darkness cut only by a moon that was beginning to set, they looked identical, but he was almost certain that they'd gone left when they'd sought out the temple before. He stepped into the street and his certainty vanished. Every memory he had of traversing these streets was gone, and he knew as soon as he got out of sight he wouldn't know how to get back to the house. He could be wandering the labyrinthine city streets until he collapsed.

Bloody hell. Didn't have much choice, did he?

He stepped onto the street and turned left. He hadn't made it a dozen feet from the house before the shade that had followed them earlier appeared at his side. He glanced at it, realizing that it was more solid than he'd ever seen it, as if its strength surged and waned like Esha's. Perhaps it was the soul of a soulceress.

"Can you get me to the temple?" he asked.

The vaguely human shaped shadow didn't nod—he didn't think it could—but it drifted ahead of him as if to lead. He followed.

Twenty minutes later, Esha returned from London with her favorite pizza and some beer. Thank gods the place served so late or she'd have been out of luck.

Aurora was pushing the buttons on a blender when Esha appeared in the kitchen. She turned it off and looked up. "That smells great."

"Yeah, it is. That's a blender, by the way. It chops stuff up."

They spent the next twenty minutes eating pizza and drinking beer while Esha pointed out the various appliances in the kitchen. She had to guess about some, but for the most part, it was really nice to sit with her sister and just be... normal.

"So, I know all about these gadgets. Tell me about yourself," Aurora said.

"All right. I'm a mercenary."

"For souls?"

Esha winced. Did she mean, steal them? "No. I kill rogue Mytheans for money."

"Rogues?"

"Yeah. Like demons who get out of one of the hells through portals that shouldn't be open. They either aren't clever enough to run under the radar of mortals or they don't care. Either way, they've done something to earn a hit on their heads, and I'm the one who does it."

"My sister is a badass. I'm no' surprised."

Esha suppressed a grin. "Anyway, I live at the university."

"Why? With those assholes?"

"It's not so bad. There are a ton of Mytheans to draw power from. And they pay me. Works out well."

"Yeah, right."

"It's really not as bad as it was when you went to prison. I mean, the witches hate me. They don't try to hurt me, but they sure do hate me." She frowned.

"Eh, doona worry about it. Of course they're jealous. We can manifest our wishes with the flick of a hand. We're superior to them in every way. They need their stupid books and potions and crows' feet or whatever. But they work at the university too?"

Esha laughed—she couldn't help it. "Yes. In their own department. Lots of Mytheans work there. It's not just for classes and teaching. The university plays a bigger role in Mythean society than it ever did in the past. We're more civilized now. Mostly. The university sees to it that we keep law and order so that we stay under the radar of mortals."

"Fucking mortals, always causing problems. Sheeple. Spook them, and they all start running in one direction, bleating their hearts out."

Esha shrugged, not really agreeing since she liked mortals well enough. "How'd you learn all this slang? You speak almost like someone from this century."

"TV. I love this century. And some magic to help. Doona want to sound out of date. Weakness."

Esha nodded. Her sister took strength seriously. Aurora was one hard bitch, with a steel strength behind her eyes.

They could twinkle and joke as quickly as they could turn ice cold and ruthless. *Ruthless.* It was the perfect word to describe her sister. She'd do whatever it took to have her way, and fuck everyone else.

But it was a survival instinct, not evil. At least, not pure evil. Esha could recognize it in herself as easily as she could in Aurora. Only, once again, Aurora was a more extreme version of herself.

"Anyway." Aurora turned to her excitedly. A quick mood swing. "Give me all the gossip. What's going on in the twenty-first century? Mortals still doona know we exist, I got that. But what's going on with our kind? Any species fighting? The Fae were going after the Selkies big time when I was put away. How did that play out?"

"Probably okay, since they get along fine now. I haven't been in the UK long, so I'm not too up to date on the older conflicts."

"Ooh, a world traveler!" Her sister was back to being bright and bubbly.

"Have you always been this way? Fun and light sometimes, ruthless the next?"

"Doona forget bloodthirsty!" Then her face turned serious. "And aye. If I were a witch or some other species that wasn't despised, maybe I'd always be a basket of laughs. But I'm not. I'm a soulceress. I'll always get my power from other people's souls, and they'll always hate me for it. *Ruthless* is the only way for our kind to survive in this world."

Would Esha be as ruthless had she been born before the university had established order? She might get nasty looks or comments and be a bitch right back, but at least no one was trying to burn her at the stake.

It was a thought that led to her mother. She hadn't wanted to jump right in with the questions, but she and Aurora were getting on well now.

"About our mom," Esha asked. "What was it all like then? Did she take souls like you do?"

Aurora's face turned dark and her knuckles whitened where they clutched her beer bottle. "Nay. She believed it was wrong to do so, and so did I. Until the mortals killed her, at least."

"Why did she let herself be captured and burned at the stake? I don't get why she didn't use her power to free herself."

"She couldn't. She was pregnant. Pregnancy is dangerous for soulceresses. All our energy goes to the baby, so we canna use our power."

"Pregnant with me?"

"Aye."

The bottom of Esha's stomach dropped away. "So I killed her."

Aurora's head swung around and she met Esha's gaze, her own shocked. "No, idiot. That's not how it works. You didn't do it on purpose."

"But if I hadn't been born, she wouldn't have been targeted."

"You need to work on your guilt complex. And probably your self-esteem. Respect our mother's decision. She wanted you. *I* wanted you. Everything else that happened was bad luck and evil people. Not you."

Esha felt like an idiot, but that seemed to be pretty common lately. "You're right. What happened next?"

"She had to escape on foot when the witch hunts and the Burnings came to our doorstep. We lived amongst the mortals because Mytheans were out for our blood, every one of them. They finally had mass hysteria on their side, the only thing that could make a bunch of otherwise reasonable beings commit genocide. Stupid mortals and their paranoia. If they hadn't gone crazy over their idea of mortal witches, the fever never would have spread to Mytheans. But Mytheans finally had a chance to get rid of us. So we went to live near the mortals, where there were none of our kind to threaten us. But we were low on power because the mortals doona have enough to speak of unless you take their souls."

"And they turned on you?"

"Yes, they targeted our mother. Her pregnancy advanced freakishly fast for mortals, but normal for soulceresses. They thought it made her a witch, so they were going to put her on trial. But mother wouldn't let me help her escape. The mortals hadn't targeted me, you see. She thought I would be safest if I stayed. The journey to the New World was so dangerous at the time."

"What about our dad?"

"I doona even know if we share one. I never met him, and she never spoke of him. Gods know he dinna help us when the mortals came for our mother. But I had my vengeance." Her voice and her eyes darkened.

"You took their souls."

"No. I killed them. They deserved it for burning her. Then I went to Spain and stole Mythean souls because they're more powerful. And it is awesome. Power. Unlimited power and you doona have to be near other Mytheans. Except that I was caught for breaking some rules."

It did sound awesome. Esha shook herself. Bad! Of course it was bad. She'd seen how Warren had suffered without his soul. She couldn't do that to someone. And she'd seen what it had done to Aurora. Her soul shadows still circled her, but she stayed calm.

Wanting a lighter subject to put Aurora in a good mood, Esha turned the conversation from their dark history to their lives and interests. She really liked her sister. They had a lot in common, if one ignored the fact that her sister was an unrepentant soul-thief being driven crazy by the power she so loved.

With Aurora and Warren in her life now, she had not only a friend in Ana, but a sister and a boyfriend. Which reminded her of her primary goal. As much as she loved chatting with Aurora, and despite the fact she'd started this journey hoping to learn more about her own kind and herself, she had a more important task now. She had to retrieve Warren's soul and get Aurora off this island, and she was afraid she only had this one chance.

"Why do you need the power so badly now? The Burnings are over," Esha asked.

"I canna leave this realm or I'll get thrown back in that prison. I need the power to maintain my world. And even if I could go out and stock up like you do, I would no'. You know as well as I do that for a soulceress, strength is everything. Giving up my souls would be weak." Her eyes darkened and her familiar raced over to snuggle up to her, which seemed to work. Aurora said, "Whether or no' you've actually got any power, survival depends on other Mytheans being afraid of you. I've got to have titanium ovaries or no one will fear me. If no one is afraid of me, they'll come after me again. Then I'll end up back in that damned prison."

"Not if you don't do anything wrong!"

Aurora laughed and gave her a pitying look.

Esha's face heated, knowing she was right. When other Mytheans were afraid of you, they wouldn't wait for law or right on their side before they tried to screw you.

"So you would never consider leaving this island?" Esha asked.

"No way."

"Come to the university with me. There's plenty of power there. Hundreds of Mytheans, and the city is full of people. It's the opposite of the aether. You'd love it."

Aurora shook her head, then looked out at the darkness through the big windows over the counters. "This place is great. I've got everything I need, I control who can come and go. I'm no' leaving."

Esha stared at her sister, comprehension dawning. "You're scared."

"What? No!"

"Oh my gods, you are. You're scared to go back to Scotland." Of course it made sense. When Aurora had been free in the seventeenth century, she'd been hunted. Then she'd been locked up. There were only bad memories there. Here, she had complete control.

"Come on!" Esha cried. "You're better than that. You're a freaking soulceress! We aren't afraid of anything." Which was a lie, because she was afraid for Warren. But it was a lie that had gotten her through a lot of hard times in her life, times like those Aurora was going through.

Aurora suddenly looked smaller sitting next to her, and her heart clutched at the sight. For Aurora to let her see her like this, without her hard shell, meant Aurora really cared for her.

Aurora straightened. "I'm no' afraid, I'm smart and wary. There's a difference. I broke out of prison. They'll throw me back in if I return to Scotland."

"What if I can get you a pardon?" She'd need Warren's help, and Aurora would definitely have to give up her souls. But she'd wait to mention that part.

"I'm no' interested."

"Yes, you are. You've got to be bored here. But you're scared to leave. I could never really understand what your life has been like. But I understand being afraid of what I am because other people fear me. But I know you, Aurora. You're like me. You'll hate yourself for cowering here. This isn't you. Prove me wrong. Come back with me."

Aurora's soul shadows were now vibrating. Were they becoming agitated? Should she be nervous? No. She was no longer afraid of her sister. Aurora was volatile, dark and light, with a serious ruthless bent. She was older and stronger. But it didn't matter. Because Aurora wouldn't fight her. She was her sister. Anyone else would be right to be afraid of her, but not Esha.

"Come on," Esha said. "Come back with me. I'll get you a pardon, and you can rub your power in the witches' faces. You can even work with me at the university—there's an awesome salary, by the way—and it will be great."

"Great? Great to be back among people who hate me and want to toss me in jail? I suppose the price for their grudging tolerance is for me to give up my souls as well." The soul shadows vibrated more quickly.

"Warren really needs his soul back. It makes him ill when you use it. If it goes on long enough, he'll be worse than dead. Just give it back. You can get power the way I do, by borrowing it."

"You care for him!" Aurora's eyes blackened. "How could you? After what he did?"

"He tried his best to save her! It wasn't his fault." Esha had no doubt of it. He was too good to have let her mother die.

"No' hard enough!" Aurora leapt off the counter and backed away. Her familiar ran to her, no doubt trying to calm her, but it did no good. Aurora's short hair was now whipping around her head as her shadows writhed and swirled around her. "Our mother is dead because of him. And you want me to give up his soul? To become powerless?"

Esha flinched as the lights in the room flickered and thunder boomed outside. The Chairman hissed and arched his back.

"They're making you crazy, Aurora! Soulceresses aren't meant to possess so many souls. It's driving you insane! Your eyes are black. And look at the house!" Esha waved her arm. The appliances were rattling on the counters, dancing with excess energy thrown off by Aurora's rage. It was really starting to freak her out. "I'm just making suggestions, and you're flipping out. It's not normal!"

"We're no' normal! We're soulceresses. I'm just doing what soulceresses are supposed to do!" She waved her arms in front of her and a blast of power sent the appliances off the counters and threw Esha against the wall. The Chairman howled.

Aurora grasped her head and shook it, as if she were trying to silence the voices inside. The floor shook, marble cracking beneath her feet. Glass shattered in the cabinets as the walls warped.

Oh, shit no. "Chairman, come here."

He hurtled toward her, a black flying blur. As soon as he reached her, she envisioned their base in Iceland, and they disappeared.

When she opened her eyes in the main foyer of the house, she grabbed the Chairman and hugged him to her, soft and warm and alive. She set him away from her and stared hard at his furry little face, lit by the soft dawn glow through the windows. He looked disgruntled but uninjured.

What the hell had happened back there? Aurora had been overcome by her shadows. The sister she'd gotten to know had been completely consumed by her madness.

Esha had spoken too soon when she'd declared herself unafraid of Aurora. Perhaps she'd been right—Aurora wouldn't hurt her. But when she was overtaken by the madness from housing too many souls? She was an entirely different person.

That was the Mythean that Warren had warned her about. In that moment, when Aurora had been in the depths of her rage, she hadn't been her sister. She hadn't even been Aurora. She'd been a Mythean with unimaginable power who was completely unpredictable and totally under the influence of the madness of the souls she'd trapped.

Esha's shoulders drooped. What would she do now? Convincing her would never work. Was killing her really the only way to get back Warren's soul?

She shook the horrible thought away and ran up the stairs to the bedroom, only to pull up short when she saw the empty bed. A quick search of the house revealed that Warren was gone. *Shit!*

CHAPTER THIRTY-THREE

It felt like an eternity, but eventually Warren and the shade arrived at the square. His shoulders sagged with relief. "Thank you."

The shade ignored him and drifted forward, up the steps to the temple. Warily, he followed, keeping his guard up for the shadows that had attacked them the first time. He made it up the stairs without incident and pushed open the heavy doors. The blade of his flashlight cut through the dark, cavernous space until it hit the platform at the other end where Esha had disappeared.

He gripped the dagger and headed straight for it. The shade appeared in front of him, blocking his way. He sidestepped, and it did too.

"What the hell?"

It was herding him toward the wall on the left. He could just step through it, though it would probably feel like shite, but the shade clearly wanted him to go left. It had led him correctly thus far, so he strode over to the wall. He'd give it one minute, then he was going through that portal.

"It's just a wall." It was made of gray stone blocks that rose forty feet above him. He stepped back toward the platform, but the shade blocked him again. Frustrated and ready to get to Esha, he tried to step through it, but was propelled back. "Damn it!"

The shade pushed him back farther, and he reached for his dagger. He didn't want to hurt it if it had helped him, but it wasn't giving him a lot of choice. Out of the corner of his eye, he caught sight of great sweeps of color across the stone wall, illuminated by the glow of his flashlight.

This was what the shade wanted him to see. He hadn't noticed before because of the dark. "Fine. I'll look."

He ran his light over the wall. It had been painted with figures in rows starting at the top. It was a story, or perhaps recorded history. He squinted and began to read from the top to the bottom. Some of the tales he couldn't decipher, but the one about souls being trapped in the city made him frown. The shade hovered by the bottom portion of the tale, where the temple was destroyed and the souls were set free.

"You're trapped, and you want to be freed," he said.

Though it didn't nod, he could almost feel its desire.

"But it says I have to destroy the temple. I canna—the portal to Aurora's world is here. I need it to get to Esha."

Frustration now vibrated from the soul, making his skin prickle.

"If I can get her back safely, and my soul from Aurora, I'll do it. I'll free you."

He couldn't tell what the soul felt now, but it advanced on him and he stepped back instinctively. It glided by him down the wall a few feet to another panel of paintings. It hovered near one and he stepped closer, his light and his gaze racing over the images.

"Oh, fuck," he breathed. He raised the dagger in his hand and laid it against the wall next to the depiction of an identical one. These images, more detailed than even the story about the souls trapped in the city, showed the life of a soulceress who had stolen souls from others. Her crazed eyes gleamed with madness in one of the last panels, no doubt taken over by the pain and misery of the souls trapped within her body, trying to escape.

In the next panel, another soulceress stabbed her with the same dagger he now held and the trapped souls flew free. Finally, both soulceresses rose to their feet. The crazed one now had normal eyes and the wound in her belly had healed.

He gazed at the dagger in his hand. Could this really be the answer to his problems?

If he used this against Aurora and it worked as it had in the painting, she would live. Was he willing to risk that her madness and cruelty were due only to the souls, as Esha said?

Uncertain of the answer, he turned and strode toward the platform. The soul now let him pass, as if it had shown him the final painting as a reward for promised help.

He slowed when he reached the steps and climbed cautiously, his muscles tensed and ready for the appearance of the ice walls.

Nothing crashed down. A one-time spell, then. He prayed that the portal still worked. He hadn't seen her enter, but it only made sense that it was the archway to the anteroom behind the great marble table.

He skirted the table and came to a stop before the archway. The sickness hit him without warning, the nausea and aching muscles nearly knocking him over.

Shite. In his fear for Esha, he'd forgotten to take the medicine.

With shaking hands, he struggled to search his pockets, praying that the vial was still there and hadn't fallen out onto the floor of the bedroom. Finally, after an eternity of trembling and sweating, his hand closed over the tiny glass vial. It took several tries to get a drop on his tongue, but within seconds, his strength and steadiness surged back.

He shook himself, clearing his mind, then tucked the vial back in his pocket. With the dagger gripped tightly in his hand, he stepped through the archway and was sucked through the portal.

When he opened his eyes, he stood on a tropical beach at night. His gaze was drawn immediately to the brightly lit mansion that stood back from the beach. The windows were all broken and great crashing noises sounded from within.

Dread surged within him as he raced across the sand and up onto the marble patio. He stifled the desire to call out for Esha and pressed himself flat against the wall of the house. His only chance to stab Aurora would come with stealth, and he couldn't blow it.

He peered through the broken glass door and saw only a living room, the marble floor cracked and the furniture upended. Noise crashed from the back. Heart in his throat, he crept silently through the living room, his back flat against the wall, and peered through an archway into the kitchen.

Shattered appliances littered every surface and Aurora stood within, her eyes wild and black, her short hair waving about her head. Her familiar, a sleek black cat, hissed at her from its perch on the counter.

Esha was nowhere to be seen, but pizza boxes and shattered beer bottles littered the countertops. She'd been here, because there was no way that Aurora could know about something as modern as carry-out pizza after being locked up for so long. Though that didn't explain how Aurora had ended up in a place with all the conveniences of modern living. The thought flitted from his mind. He had more important things to be concerned with.

Aurora pulled at her hair as if voices echoed inside her head and Warren took his chance, sprinting across the kitchen and vaulting over the island. As he landed behind Aurora, he struck out with his dagger, aiming for her back.

She spun at the last moment, taking a slice to the arm before knocking his hand away. He saw his death flash in front of his eyes as she raised her arm and threw a blast of fire at him.

He flew back into the wall, his front blackened and steaming. Though he was burned to hell, he couldn't feel it because of the potion the witches had given him. Thank gods, or he'd be incapacitated.

With a growl, he pushed himself off the wall and threw the dagger at Aurora, hoping to nail her in the chest. She disappeared as the blade came at her, too fast for it. But a second later, Warren appeared on the other side of the room, his hand gripped around the hilt of the dagger where it was sunk into the wall.

What the hell? He'd just aetherwalked using the dagger. He shouldn't be able to do that, but soulceress magic was strong. He flung it again at Aurora, and though she disappeared, he was transported across the room until his hand was wrapped around the dagger's hilt again.

This was a trick he could work with. Another blast of fire hit him unawares, and he was thrown back into the wall. He blinked and shook his head, making out the raging form of Aurora across the kitchen.

This time when he threw the dagger, he didn't aim for her, but rather for a spot several feet away. She didn't aetherwalk because it wasn't coming at her, so he yanked it free from the wall when he appeared next to it and lunged for her.

Esha appeared in Aurora's kitchen in time to see Warren attempt to stab her sister in the back. Before Esha could throw off her shock, her sister spun and threw a bolt of power at Warren so strong it tossed him across the room.

"No!" she screamed as Warren's back hit the counter and he crumpled.

He was on his feet a second later, charging Aurora. With predatory agility, he ducked under one blast of lightning and had nearly reached her when another knocked him off his feet and he crumpled in a pile of twisted limbs and burned flesh.

An electric shock of fear spiked in her blood. Aurora looked utterly insane, her black eyes rolling in her head and power glowing from her skin. The shadows that circled her writhed frantically, reaching out, then being sucked back in toward her form. When her familiar arched its back and hissed at her, shit was clearly about to roll way downhill.

Desperate to get Warren and herself out of there before Aurora imploded—and possibly took the enchanted island with her—Esha lunged across the kitchen and grabbed Warren's prone body. The Chairman had hurtled behind her and when she felt his warmth against her legs, she envisioned the house and they disappeared.

"Oh shit," Esha breathed when she opened her eyes to see Warren's broken body. She crouched on the floor of the foyer, Warren in her arms. Midmorning sun shone through the windows and highlighted patches of his skin that were blackened and burned. His forearms were twisted at bad angles. The lightning that Aurora had thrown at him would have killed a lesser Mythean.

Thank gods he couldn't die. She'd been too terrified and too stupid to aetherwalk them directly to the bedroom, so she took them there now, using a bit of levitation to get him up onto the bed.

With a wave of her hand and the thought of light, she lit the torches in the room. In too-bright detail, they revealed the extent of the damage to Warren's flesh and bones, and she swallowed hard, trying to force down the fear and panic. This was far past her ability to heal, but she didn't know any healers and she didn't have enough power to aetherwalk all the way back to the university to get one.

"Gods, Chairman, what do we do?" She spun in a frustrated circle, then stopped.

She wasn't alone and helpless.

Esha ran to her room and dug down into the bottom of her bag. Relief rushed through her as she yanked out a cylindrical cardboard container that had once held maps. She popped off the plastic cap and slid out Ana's arrow. Thank gods Ana had repaired it, and she'd remembered to bring it. This would make two times in one month she'd used it, but then, these were extenuating circumstances.

"Here goes," she said, then snapped the arrow in half.

Ana appeared immediately, this time in clothes. "Esha! What's wrong?"

"Warren's hurt." Her voice broke. "Can you heal him?"

"Where is he?" Ana glanced around the room.

"Come on, he's in the other room. My sister blasted him with something that broke his bones and burned his flesh. He's in terrible shape." She led Aurora down the short hall to Warren's room.

"Holy cow," Ana breathed.

"Can you do anything?"

"I can try funneling some of my power into him, see if that speeds up his natural healing process."

"You're a god—that should work, right? Try it." And if it failed, Esha now had enough power from Ana that she could aetherwalk back to the university for a healer.

"Okay." Ana removed Warren's clothes to get a better look at the damage.

The sight of more burned skin and great purple bruises made Esha wince. A shuddery breath escaped her lungs as Ana sat on the side of the bed, laid her hands lightly on the broad expanse of Warren's chest, and closed her eyes.

Esha watched as Ana tried to heal Warren's various wounds. It didn't look like much, but as Ana removed her hand from each burn or broken bone, smooth, healed skin was revealed. It was working. The terrible tightness in Esha's chest eased.

Eventually, Ana rose and turned to face her. "That's all I've got."

Esha rushed to Warren's side and ran her fingertips gently over his chest. It rose, steady and even. Nearly all the bruising and burns were gone. His limbs were all straight and he slept peacefully.

"His body can take care of the rest." She spun and threw her arms around Ana. "Thank you."

"'Course. What happened?"

They walked over to the doorway so that they could talk without waking Warren. In a hushed whisper, Esha told her all about Aurora and Warren.

"Maybe it's not as bad as you think. Maybe he wasn't trying to kill her. Just trying to protect himself," Ana said.

"I guess it's possible." Gods, she'd been scared when she'd seen Aurora blast Warren. She'd worried initially that Aurora might use her love for Warren against her, but never that she'd actually try to kill him.

Esha's mind skidded to a halt. *Love? Did I just think the word love?* She swallowed hard, her head reeling. She scrubbed a hand over her face. Gods, she was a mess. She couldn't actually love Warren, she just liked him a lot. Less now that he'd tried to kill her sister. But then, Aurora wasn't innocent herself. There was no question now that Warren was right and she'd been blinded by her desire for a sister. Aurora was too dangerous.

"Are you okay?" Ana asked.

"Yeah, I'm fine, I just—"

Warren shifted, and her eyes locked on him.

"I think he's waking," Ana said. "I'm going to go explore. I've never been to a place so weird. I'll be back in a while."

"Thank you again." Esha hugged her friend, so desperately grateful.

"Esha." Warren's scratchy voice made her let go of Ana and run to his side.

She dropped to her knees next to the bed. "Hey."

He sat up on the bed and said, "What the hell happened?"

"You and Aurora tried to kill each other." The boiling tar of anger surged within her at the memory, spurred on by the stress and frustration over everything that she couldn't control. "You faced her alone, when she's insanely powerful and could take you out. She could take anyone out!"

"Hey, hey." He reached out and gripped her arms, trying to calm her. "I wasn't trying to kill her. And hell, Esha, you did the same damn thing! You went there alone."

"Don't turn this around on me. And what the hell do you mean, you weren't trying to kill her?"

Warren glanced over the bed and the floor as though he was searching for something. "I was no'. Where's the dagger I had in my hand?"

"Um, I don't know." She searched her memory. "I think it's on the floor downstairs in the foyer. Why the hell does it matter?"

"It's a soulceress weapon that I found in that museum. The painting on the wall of the temple says that dagger will remove the stolen souls from a soulceress, but it won't kill her."

Shock left Esha temporarily speechless. He hadn't been trying to kill Aurora? Finally, she said, "What?"

"The shade who's been following us helped me get to the temple, then showed me the painting."

"That's how you navigated."

"Aye, without it, I never would have made it. The soul wants to be set free. It's trapped here until the temple is destroyed."

Understanding dawned. "Oh, crap. I've heard of souls like that, but only briefly and I didn't make the connection. When soulceresses who steal souls die, their own souls can't pass on to their afterworld because the stolen souls are tangled up with their own. It pulls them in so many different directions that they can't leave earth. So they come here."

"If we destroy the temple, they'll be freed."

"I guess so, if that's what the painting says. But first we have to deal with Aurora. You really think that dagger will work?" Hope was a bright light in her chest, beating back the despair that there was no way to help both her sister and Warren.

"Aye, according to soulceress lore. It's our only choice."

It really was. Esha stood no chance of convincing Aurora to release his soul, and Warren had two days left at most before the medicine stopped working and he was entirely incapacitated.

"How the hell are we going to manage this, though? When she's enraged, her power is immeasurable—and right now she's out of control," Esha said.

"We should wait a bit. Give her a few hours to calm down and for me to heal up. Then I'll go back."

Esha glared at him. "I'm going too."

He stared at her for a moment, no doubt trying to think of a way to keep her safe, then nodded. "Aye. It's your fight."

"Good. We only stand a chance if there are two of us." She frowned, recalling the sheer strength of Aurora's power when she was in the grip of her madness. "Maybe not even then."

CHAPTER THIRTY-FOUR

A few hours later, the creaking of the foyer door pulled Esha out of her doze. She untangled her limbs from Warren's and slid out of bed, the cold of the room immediately reminding her how warm he'd been. He was sleeping more heavily than normal, no doubt still recovering from his injuries. She threw on her clothes and met Ana in the foyer. She'd just returned from her exploration of the city.

"This place is amazing!" Ana said. Her cheeks were pink from the cold, and her eyes were bright with excitement.

A small laugh escaped Esha despite her stress. "It's really not. You just like anything that isn't Otherworld."

Ana shrugged. "True."

"Can I ask you for another favor? A dangerous one?"

"My favorite kind." Ana's hand went to the bow strapped to her back and her eyes hardened. "We're going after Aurora, aren't we?"

Esha nodded. "Come into the kitchen. We'll talk about it there and grab a quick bite. We should go after her soon."

"Okay. I'll have to be back in Otherworld before the other gods know I'm gone."

"Of course."

Esha cobbled together sandwiches from their supplies and sat with Ana just as Warren arrived, clean from a bath in the hot springs. She nodded to a plate next to hers. "That one's yours."

"Thanks." He sat and reached for the plate.

"Tell me what we're up against." Ana bit into her sandwich.

"Aurora has created a world in the aether. It's a huge Mediterranean-style mansion on a tropical beach."

Ana shrugged. "Makes sense, considering the prison the witches had her in. She must have envisioned a luxurious place that's the opposite of where she's been. No surprise she ended up in a villa in the Med."

"Wait, what do you mean? She's in the aether, no' the Mediterranean," Warren said.

"Sort of." Ana spoke around her bite of sandwich, then swallowed. "She's in the aether, but she needed something to work with as a starter. There's got to be a real island with a real house on it that she's using as a base for her world. That's just how the aether works—even with all her souls, she's no' powerful enough to create a whole new world. If we could find the island, we'd find a house in the real world. But she wouldn't be there. It's sort of like another dimension, a construct of her mind that she's made real within the aether, yet it's partially based in the real world in a place that suited her specifications. She's in the aether like you think, just not entirely."

"Of course. That's why there are so many appliances and modern conveniences there that she didn't recognize. And probably how she got the mortals there for her party," Esha said.

"Exactly." Ana popped the last bite of sandwich into her mouth. "What else do I need to know?"

"She's pissed as hell and nearly invincible. When I left her, she was tearing her house down around her," Esha said. "She has complete control over her environment when she's in her world. We've got to drag her out if we're going to have any chance against her, but I don't know how we'll get close to her."

Ana frowned thoughtfully. "I think I can help with that. We've got to destroy her world. My arrows can tear through the aether."

"Really?" Esha asked.

Ana shrugged. "I *am* a god. There's got to be some perks. That's one of them, though it took me a few centuries to figure it out. I can't completely destroy the aether, of course. It's too big. But her world is so small. If I fire into it—like the walls of her house—I bet I can get her illusion to collapse. I'll break apart her reality until she's in the normal world."

Esha finally felt something a bit like hope. "That's really good. Get her in the real world where we're on a more even playing field."

"In the real world?" Warren asked. "What about the mortals?"

"It's unlikely that her island is inhabited in the real world. If there were people using the same space, it would take an unbelievable amount of power to maintain her world. Dollars to donuts that it's been abandoned by people."

"It was a tiny island," Esha said. "No other houses on it that I saw."

"Then we'll hope for the best," Warren said.

Half an hour later, after the last of Warren's injuries had fully healed and they'd collected their weapons, they reconvened in the kitchen. It was nearing dusk, and they hoped to hell that Aurora had calmed down some.

"Ready?" Warren asked as he checked his weapons. Knives in his boots, sword at his hip, and the soulceress dagger in his right hand. Practice weapons for so long, they'd now go into true use.

"Looking forward to it," Ana said.

Esha nodded, her jaw tight, then held out her hands for both of theirs. Though Ana could aetherwalk, she didn't know the location of Aurora's aether hideaway. Esha would lead her, and as usual, she'd bring Warren along because he couldn't travel in this damn soulceress world.

He reached out for her hand. Within seconds of contact, he was sucked through space until he stood on the dark night beach of Aurora's island home. Ana split off immediately, but Warren pulled Esha close until her face was inches from his.

"You mean a hell of a lot to me." Worry roughened his voice. "If it comes down to my soul or your life, take your life, damn it."

"Fuck you, Warren. I'm not leaving you behind." She kissed him hard and fast and then spun to join Ana. The Chairman trotted after her.

They made their way quickly up to the patio, ghosts in the dark night. A raging party spilled out of house, the music manic and tension hanging over the crowd that danced and drank as if they were under a spell. Even the night breeze that drifted across the palms vibrated with an otherworldly energy.

"Aurora's trying to make it normal," Esha whispered.

"But her shell's cracking," Ana said, then skirted around the side of the crowd.

They followed, scanning the writhing bodies for Aurora. A great booming noise shook the ground and a bright light flashed from the left side of the house. The light faded to reveal a smoking black crater and a shriek of rage rent the night.

Ana had started firing.

And Aurora had figured out they'd arrived.

Warren and Esha took up posts behind Ana as she raced around the front of the house, firing her arrows into the walls and tearing apart the reality of Aurora's world. Aurora's shrieks of rage competed with the booms of Ana's arrows and drew Warren's eye to the window. Within, Aurora shot blasts of light from her hands at the holes that Ana had created, no doubt trying to repair them.

Her black gaze met his through the window. The rage in her eyes flared as she waved a hand at him and Esha. He threw himself in front of Esha to protect her from the blow, but none came.

What the hell had—

A wave of bodies poured from the doors and crashed through the windows, heading straight for them. Fuck. *This* was what Aurora had sent. She'd turned the partiers to monsters, shells of their former selves propelled by her will. Their skin had become pasty white, and their eyes great gaping holes of black.

He drew his sword as Esha threw a huge blast of earth at the advancing figures. The great wave that she'd drawn from the earth bowled over a dozen. The Chairman fought at her side, a blur of fur and fangs that bowled over monsters and tore at their throats. He was still no larger than a housecat, but he was fierce as a lion and nearly as strong. Warren clashed with others, swiping his blade against necks and bellies until blood ran red in the grass.

Bile rose in his throat at the sight. It reminded him of that night so long ago when he'd slain his kin and why he'd vowed never to take another life, but he tightened his grip and continued to hack at them. There was no other way. If he didn't cut them down, Esha and Ana would be swallowed by the mob. They surged toward them in waves, too fast and too strong to be natural, and soon his skin ran with blood from their teeth and nails. He'd lost sight of Esha, and fear tightened his skin. She could take care of herself, but it didn't mean it didn't scare the hell out of him when she was up against a mob.

"I'm close!" Ana screamed. The light of her arrows brightened the night, the booms a cacophony like thunder. "The walls of her world are falling!"

Warren fought his way toward Esha, who stood at Ana's back deflecting the monsters that clawed to reach her. His chest loosened when he saw her safe and sending another blast of earth that buried a wave of Aurora's creatures.

Together, they fought their way toward the side of the house, protecting Ana from the crush of bodies. They rounded the corner, and an explosion from the side of the house rent the night. When the dust settled, Aurora stood framed in a gaping hole in the wall, her arms stretched out at the ground beneath their feet.

The earth shook, then rose up, a mountain carrying him and Esha toward the sky. The Chairman yowled from below, where he'd been left on solid ground. Ana slid on nimble feet down the far side toward the patio, shooting arrows as she went. He jumped away as the ground split between them.

Esha fought a small horde of the ghostly pale former revelers, unaware of the three approaching from behind. Warren leapt across the chasm in the dirt, reaching them in time to take the head off one and fell the other two with swipes across the abdomen.

"The dagger, Warren!" Esha screamed. "I'll aetherwalk."

He nodded, and knowing that she'd get to safety away from the rising earth, he turned to Aurora and flung the dagger at her chest. She disappeared and it flew through. When it thudded into the wall behind her, Warren was sucked through space to join it.

He arrived with his fist gripping the hilt and pulled it free. From within the house, the damage was illuminated. It was a mess. The walls wavered like the apparition they were, great holes to the real world blasted into them. His gaze raced around the destroyed living room, hunting Aurora.

Nowhere to be seen. He sprinted out onto the back patio, just in time to see Aurora shoot a jet of the pool water at Esha. Thousands of gallons bowled her over, and he roared, charging Aurora.

A crash of thunder and a flash of light, and the world went black. He stumbled, then righted himself as the light of the true moon illuminated the scene before him. Aurora's world had melted, leaving behind a destroyed mansion and a dried-out pool. Esha was rising from the giant puddle on the beach, and Ana was running to her, no doubt to ensure that Esha benefited from the power of her soul rather than Aurora. Both soulceresses would need a power boost after what had just gone down.

Aurora stood on the destroyed patio and shrieked, her hands clutched in her hair. Her wild black eyes flickered over the mansion. The monstrous revelers had disappeared. Her familiar sat at her heels, hissing at her as if it knew something was terribly wrong. She whirled on Warren. "You destroyed it!"

She raised her hand to throw some kind of magic at him and instinct had him hurling the dagger at a tree to her left just to get out of its way. He appeared, hand on the hilt, as a bolt of lightning incinerated the spot where he'd been standing.

Shite, that was close.

"From behind!" Ana's scream dragged his gaze to the left in time for him to see some kind of sea monsters crawling from the waves on the beach, weeds and barnacles clinging to their misshapen forms. Celtic *fomori*, famed for razor teeth and vicious appetites. Christ, had she called them all the way from the Celtic Sea?

Focus on Aurora. He jerked his attention to her as she was hurled to the ground by a great rush of wind thrown by Esha. She leapt to her feet a second later, her black eyes crazed and her hair whipping unnaturally about her head. She thrust out her arm, and an enormous wave rose from the sea behind Esha. In less than a second, Aurora's eyes flashed from black to gold. Shock and regret streaked across her face. She waved her arm again and the wave crashed down too soon, spraying Esha but not drowning her.

Aurora was flashing in and out of sanity. And she didn't want to kill Esha. No sooner had the realization struck him than Aurora spun from Esha and caught sight of him. Her eyes blackened again, and she threw a blast of fire at him that was too big to escape.

He threw the knife, knowing it was futile, as Esha sent a jet of water from the sea. Steam rose up at the collision of fire and water and the tail end of the flames seared his flesh as he was transported to the knife, his hand grasping the hilt where it stuck out of a palm tree. He yanked it out with a burned and blackened hand, knowing that if he hadn't been under the influence of the pain-relieving potion from the witches, he probably wouldn't have gotten it out of the tree.

Esha threw another gust of wind at Aurora, hoping to give Warren enough time to reach her. Gods, she needed Ana's help with Aurora, but the sea monsters kept coming. Their growling and the clicking of fangs was an eerie accompaniment to Aurora's screams and the blasts of power that rent the night.

Warren halted and flung the dagger, avoiding Aurora's strike of lightning. He popped in and out of existence as he made his way closer to Aurora, who could dodge his knife like a pro, while Esha tried to hold Aurora off. Water to stop her fire, wind to knock her down. If only she could throw a killing blow, this would all be over, but she didn't want to kill her only family, no matter how crazed she was now.

But gods, she was running out of power. She'd been siphoning it off Ana, who was now likely as weak as herself. Thankfully Ana had her skills as an archer to fall back on. Esha had nothing without her power except a mean right hook, and that wouldn't be of much use against Aurora.

But Aurora was slowing too. No longer bolstered by her magical world, she didn't have infinite power. She'd burn through it and have to wait for the souls to regenerate.

Please, gods, let her run out before me.

"Warren!" Esha screamed when he appeared near some fallen *fomori* who had just started to rise.

He was quick with the dagger and one was on the ground seconds later. Aurora shot a bolt of fire at him while he was killing the second, but Esha deflected most of it with another jet of seawater. Thank gods his healing was so fast, and he didn't feel pain, else he'd never have made it this far. Aurora was obsessed with taking him down, even though she couldn't kill him. Rage had clouded her mind.

Aurora stood with her back to a copse of palms and shot another stream of fire at Warren. He'd already taken aim and heaved the dagger. It sailed past her and into the tree at her back. He disappeared as the fire hit the spot where he'd been standing and reappeared behind Aurora before she had a chance to register the maneuver. He yanked the dagger from the tree, spun, and plunged it into her back.

Her shriek rent the night air, an unholy howl that was joined by the wailing of the souls that flew free from her body. They streaked into the sky, shadows rising toward freedom and their former owners. Warren's soul flew straight back into him and he fell to his knees.

"Ana! Chairman!" Esha screamed. "Home! Now!"

The *fomori* had begun to slink back into the ocean, Aurora's spell broken. Ana sprinted to Aurora and Warren. Esha met her there, desperate to get the hell off this miserable island.

Esha wrapped her arms around Warren, who'd just surged to his feet, while Ana did the same with a collapsed Aurora. The Chairman pressed himself against Esha's legs.

"Wait! Her familiar!" They couldn't aetherwalk without Aurora's companion. Just then, a sleek black blur streaked from the trees near the beach and curled up against Aurora's prone form. No doubt the cat had fled when Aurora had lost her mind. "Let's go!"

CHAPTER THIRTY-FIVE

Esha appeared in the foyer of the house with her arms wrapped around Warren. Ana arrived next to her, collapsed on the floor with Aurora's crumpled body in her arms.

"You're good?" she asked Warren.

"Aye." He was blackened and burned, but he was whole.

Relief rushed through her, and she spun to kneel at Aurora's side. She looked like hell, her golden skin sallow and her eyes closed.

"Aurora!" Esha shook her gently. "Come on, wake up. You have to be okay." The wound in her back seeped blood, but not enough to be fatal. Right? Even without the souls, her sister shouldn't die from something as small as that. "Come on!" She shook her again.

"Hey, chill out!" Ana said. "Give her a second."

Esha drew in a shuddery breath and realized that fear was making her a bit crazy. She was appearing in the foyer of this house holding broken bodies far too often. "Let's get her up to the bedroom."

She wrapped her arms around her sister and aetherwalked them to her bedroom. By the time she got her sister up onto the bed, Aurora was stirring. A second later, she popped upright and shoved Esha away.

"It's okay! You're safe!" Esha shouted.

Aurora leapt to her feet and threw out her arm, but no power hit Esha. Esha's shoulders relaxed. Her sister must be tapped out, and with Ana downstairs, she couldn't refuel.

"What the hell happened?" Aurora demanded, her eyes wild but her color turning golden again. She swung her head, searching the room for threats.

"We took your souls."

"I know that! But why? You betrayed me!" Aurora backed into the corner, her hands raised as if to fight.

"I didn't. I helped you! The souls were making you crazy. It was only going to get worse. Eventually, you'd be trapped here like all the other soulceresses who stole souls. A shade stuck in this miserable city."

"What? Where am I?"

"The old soulceress city. The one with the temple that led to your world. I had to do it, Aurora. It was killing Warren, and it was killing you too. We aren't meant to own souls."

"Damn it, that's how I protected myself!" Aurora's eyes gleamed with anger and desperation, but not the black madness that had haunted her when she'd been influenced by the trapped souls.

"The world isn't that bad anymore. You'll be fine. I'll help you be fine. You'll be with me. And don't you feel better without them weighing on you?"

"I doona know. Everything feels wrong!" Her sister's brow wrinkled. She looked so desperate and confused it made Esha's heart ache.

"I'll help you, Aurora. I promise. Everything will be fine." Esha backed up to the wall and slid down onto the floor, trying to look nonthreatening and helpful. Her sister mirrored her, sinking down to sit against the opposite wall.

After a while, Aurora's breathing calmed, and the frantic glaze to her eyes eased. She finally seemed to believe that Esha wouldn't hurt her. She said, "I suppose I do feel a little better. No' torn in so many directions. And my mind feels clearer. But damn it, Esha, what the hell am I supposed to do now?"

"I'm going to figure that out. You're still a powerful badass. It'll be fine."

"I know I'm a powerful badass, damn it. I just need to get powered up. But the future doesn't look so bright from here."

"Sure it does. You're not being driven mad by souls or hiding out like a hermit on your island."

"I liked my island." Aurora glared at her.

"The world is better. Come on, we'll go get cleaned up in the hot springs. You'll love them."

An hour later, once her sister was no longer freaking out, Esha went in search of Warren. It was getting so late, and she'd only slept a few hours the night before. Exhaustion dragged at her shoulders like ten-ton boulders. She found him in the bedroom he'd claimed as his own for their short stay, standing at the window and looking out at the city. He was standing straighter, and most of his wounds appeared to be healed, probably with Ana's help.

"Hey," she said.

He turned around and she gasped. In the craziness of stabbing Aurora, she hadn't really seen him since he'd received his soul.

He was so different. Golden. Perfect.

She'd always thought him perfection before, and it had kind of annoyed her even as it had intrigued her. But not having his soul apparently had physical ramifications as well. He was so handsome that he made her head swim. So strong, honorable, kind. So *everything*.

Or maybe it was just that she could see him fully now.

She'd fallen for him so quickly, and so hard. It had crept up on her while she'd been busy pretending she wasn't affected. And gods, it was scary. She couldn't bear the thought of ever losing him, not now that she'd finally found him. He was her reward for so much misery earlier in her life.

He started toward her, and she walked into his arms, sighing when he pulled her tightly against his broad chest. His strength and vitality reassured her. He'd be fine.

"Gods, I'm glad that's over," she said.

"Me too."

"How do you feel?"

"Whole."

"And I don't deplete your power now that you have your soul back?" Could this be possible?

He shrugged. "Doona think so. I feel fine."

She grinned, too happy to wonder about it, and followed him when he pulled her over to the bed. He lay down and dragged her with him. When he wrapped his arms around her, she put her head on his shoulder and sighed, relaxing into him.

"I really like you, you know," she said.

Lie. She loved him, but it was hard enough to confess it to herself, much less him.

"Likewise." He leaned down to kiss her hair, and she grinned. But it faded when she realized that he hadn't used the *L* word she'd been hoping to hear. She shook it away.

"Good. Where's Ana? Did she go back?"

"Yeah. She was worried the other gods would notice she'd left." She paused. "Warren?"

"Aye, lass?"

"I'm going to need your help."

"With what?" Warren asked.

"Aurora needs a job at the university."

He tensed. He hadn't been expecting that. "What?"

"She only wanted to keep your soul and the others for the power they gave her to protect herself. Without the souls, she has nothing. I promised her that she could work with me hunting rogues. That way, the university can keep an eye on her, but she'd have a place to go and a way to fuel up her power. Mytheans aren't out to burn us anymore, but it's still too dangerous out there for a soulceress alone."

"Nothing is too dangerous for your sister, even without owning the souls."

Esha grinned. "You're right. She's ruthless and strong as hell, and I like that about her. I want her to come to the university for me. I want her with me."

Of course she wanted her sister with her. After everything she'd done for him, helping him find Aurora and retrieving his soul, it was the least he could do.

"Warren?" Her worried tone made him realize that he'd been silent too long. "You wouldn't have to see her much."

"That's no' my concern. Most of her evil was because of her situation during the Burnings and because she was polluted by the souls. She's no' my favorite person, but I can tolerate her. And I did offer you a team of your own if you agreed to help me on this."

"Yeah, but then you realized no one would work with me." She leaned up and smiled wryly, then her eyes brightened. "Wait, does this mean you agree?"

"Aye. I canna control where she goes. And honestly, it's my job to keep an eye on her. She's no' wholly evil, as you said. So she isn't a rogue, and we canna kill her. No' that I'd ask it of you," he added quickly. "What I mean is, I took an oath when I agreed to lead the Praesidium. More important, I made a promise to myself that I'd no' let my own desires rule my decisions. Offering her a job at the university is the obvious course."

Esha pressed a hard kiss to his lips. "Excellent. I can't wait to tell her."

"Aye. But first you'll sleep. Your voice sounds halfway to bed as it is."

He felt her lips move and the warm puff of breath when she yawned hard against his neck. "But Aurora..."

"Is probably in her bed as well."

"Yeah, you're right." She snuggled closer to him and his chest tightened at the sheer rightness of having her against him.

CHAPTER THIRTY-SIX

When Esha walked into the dimly lit kitchen at dawn the next morning, she found Aurora playing with a flashlight.

Aurora looked up and said, "Ready to do this?"

"A thousand times yes." She was so ready to get out of this damn city. All they had to do was destroy the temple and free the souls, and she'd be able to leave. She and Aurora were both powered up, courtesy of Ana, and Esha had a feeling they'd need every damn bit of it to see this through.

"Good. We need a plan."

"Sure, when Warren gets—"

"I'm here."

Esha turned at the sound of his voice and reached for his hand. When his rough palm gripped hers, she stifled a grin. It was weird, but so wonderful, to be with him like this. After calling herself all manner of fool, she said, "We'll go to the temple as soon as the sun is up. Aurora and I will disrupt the foundations of the building so it collapses. That's what you saw on the painting, right, Warren?"

"Aye. When the temple collapsed, the souls were released. No doubt it's holding them here."

"Aye," Aurora confirmed. "Mother said the temple is the center of our power. It calls to the souls when they canna pass over. Destroying it should work."

"Good. Just one loose end, and we're done here," Esha said. Then she could start the rest of her life, one that contained Warren and her sister and would be so much better and fuller than the one she'd left behind when she'd started on this adventure.

"Are you sure you want him to come?" Aurora nodded at Warren, her brow wrinkled.

Esha frowned. "Why wouldn't he?"

"All that falling stone—it's going to be dangerous, and he's mortal."

"What?" That didn't make any sense, but the mere possibility made the air heavy, as though it were pressing in on her. Warren shifted next to her.

"He's mortal now," Aurora said. "I thought you knew that."

"No." Fluttery wings of panic beat inside her chest, and there was a low humming in her ears that couldn't be normal. "No, he's not. He's part of the Praesidium. He's one of us."

Aurora frowned. "Nay. Now that he has his soul back, he'll age and die like a normal mortal. He was never really a Mythean to begin with."

Esha looked at Warren, whose brow was furrowed, and shook her head frantically. "No. No. That's not possible. Did you know about this?"

His gaze heavy, he said, "I suspected."

"No. No. No." The buzzing in her ears grew louder. "I don't believe you."

"I'm sorry, Esha. I'm pretty sure it's true. I wasn't sure how to tell you." Concern wrinkled Warren's brow, and his green eyes searched hers.

"No. Just no." She was repeating herself, and it was crazy, but she couldn't help it.

He looked at his feet, then withdrew a knife from the sheath in his boot and made a small incision in his palm. She watched in horror as the blood welled. Kept welling. As the wound refused to close.

The breath whooshed out of her lungs. "After everything I told you? You let me love you, all the while knowing you would die? How could you do this to me?"

"I dinna think—"

She shook her head and backed away, her throat closing up. *Mortal.* He would die on her. She would stay with him, grow to love him more every day. To rely on him for her happiness. He was part of her. He would become an even bigger part of her as the years went on. And she'd have to watch him age and sicken and die. She couldn't do that. How could anyone be expected to do that, knowing that they'd have eternity alone afterward? Without the one they loved?

She spun on her heel and tripped through the door out into the street. She took a left, not knowing where she was going, and finally stopped near an alleyway. With a ragged sob, she sank down onto her butt and buried her face in her knees.

A boulder lodged itself in her throat, and her eyes burned as she tried to hold back the tears, but finally they burst free and she wept—bitter, horrible tears that made her previous freakouts over Warren look like a joy ride. Once, she'd have thought them pathetic. To be weeping like this over a mere man.

But he wasn't just any man. He was Warren. He was her love. A mortal. She clutched her arms more tightly about her legs, desperately trying to rock the pain away. The Chairman's meows did nothing to comfort her, and even when he rubbed up against her leg, it was like she couldn't feel it at all.

When her sobs ran dry, she realized how silent the city was. Shadows peered out at her from their windows, ghostly remnants of soulcerers and soulceresses trapped forever in this cold stone labyrinth. The warmth that had once filled this city was long gone, leaving only shadows of the past that weren't meant to be here.

Their job here wasn't nearly over. And no matter how much her future was going to hurt, she couldn't fall apart like this. It just wasn't her. She wouldn't let it be.

Esha shook her head violently, and it cleared a bit. She rose to her feet and headed back to the house. When she reached the front door, she scrubbed her hands over her eyes to get rid of the damning wetness and reminded herself of every shitty thing that had happened to her.

"This isn't that different from everything else," she said to the Chairman. "I've been left before and suffered loss, and I've been fine. I'll be fine now."

He meowed, and though she had no idea what he meant, she took it to a be *I'm with you*. She nodded resolutely and climbed the stairs to the house. The hall was dim as she made her way back to the kitchen, hoping for Aurora.

She got Warren instead.

"We'll head to the temple now," she said, trying her hardest to keep any inflection out of her voice.

He reached out to her. "Esha, I—"

"I'm going to get Aurora." She turned and left the room, unable to look at him. Did she blame him for not telling her? Not really. But she also couldn't look at him right now and keep her shit together.

There were too many unanswered questions. Would she be able to be with him, knowing that he would die? Or should she try to end everything now and save herself greater pain later?

Hell if I know. She huffed out a dejected laugh and climbed the stairs to the top floor. Aurora walked out of Esha's room and met her in the hall.

"I was waiting for you," Aurora said. "Are you all right?"

"Fine."

"You're no'."

"I know. But I don't want to talk about it. I can't."

Sympathy gleamed in Aurora's eyes. "So you doona know what you'll do?"

"No. It doesn't matter now. Not until we destroy the temple and get out of here." She clung to that. A job. As long as she had that to accomplish, she didn't have to think about anything that hurt.

"Okay. Any ideas how we'll do it?"

"Some. We can talk on the way. You ready to go?"

Aurora nodded and followed her down the stairs. Warren waited in the foyer, which meant she couldn't leave him behind.

He stepped toward her. "Esha, can I talk to—"

"I don't want to talk about it." No, she *couldn't* talk about it. But even explaining the nuances of that was a field fraught with land mines. Even though it was stupid to ask, desperation made her open her mouth. "Stay here. Please. We don't know what could go wrong with this. Please stay here."

"You know I canna do that. There's no way in hell I'll stay behind when it could be dangerous for you. And I canna stay away from every potentially dangerous thing because I might die. That's no life." His jaw was set.

"For me?" A crazed laugh escaped her. Did he have any idea how dangerous it would be for her to *lose* him? What that would do to her?

Clearly not. And he was the type of man to throw himself into danger on her behalf, no matter the consequences to his mortal body. It would kill him.

They weren't going to get anywhere with this because there was no way she could convince him. She turned and headed out the door. The sun beat down weakly from overhead, illuminating windows occupied by soul shadows that watched them. Did they have any idea what was coming? That they'd soon be free to go to their afterworld?

She walked next to Aurora as they made their way to the temple, and though she could hear Warren's footsteps behind her, she didn't look back. When this was all over, she'd have to make up her mind. But even this small task of destroying the temple—which she doubted would be all that dangerous—made her skin tighten with fear for Warren's mortal life.

Could she face that for all of her days? *No.* She shook the thought away and went to work plotting with Aurora how they would destroy the temple.

"Do you think you could make the floor crack like you did back in your world?" Esha asked her sister.

"Nay. I could do it because I created the world. The ground beneath the temple is too great a space for me to modify if it's no' already my creation."

"What about forces of nature?" Esha asked.

"Well, lightning and fire are out because it's made of stone."

"So is flood. These days, it's just bad form to melt a glacier." Esha couldn't laugh at her own dark joke.

"And I doona think I can muster enough wind to blow it over."

"What if you think smaller," Warren said from behind. "Remove key stones from the temple so that it topples over."

His voice sent a pang through her, but her mind latched onto the idea. "That could work."

They arrived at the square a few minutes later and took up positions. Esha and Aurora stood about fifteen yards back from the temple at the north and west corners. Going into the alleys on either side had been deemed too dangerous once the building started to collapse, so they stood in the square.

Warren took up a position just behind her, no doubt to protect her from whatever might come at her, and she tried to ignore him. She looked up to check the sky, pleased to see that a great grouping of winter clouds had begun to fill the blue. It gave the whole square a gloomy feel, but they'd be perfect.

"Ready?" Aurora yelled.

"Yes. North corner first!" Esha returned her attention to the sky. Once she felt the Chairman's warm little body lean against her leg and saw Aurora's familiar do the same, she focused all her energy and power on the clouds. When she could feel Aurora doing the same, she yelled, "Now!"

She forced a great blast of wind toward the clouds. Her breath grew short with the strain, but eventually the clouds gathered together in a group so dense and heavy that they turned the color of charcoal. Together, she and Aurora forced them into a whirling funnel, smaller than a tornado but just as deadly.

When the sky shrieked with the force of it, she and Aurora directed their cloud tornado toward the north corner of the building. It collided with the stone and great chunks of granite exploded into the air. Esha's chest vibrated with the reverberation.

Aurora dodged, barely escaping a huge boulder that crashed down next to her, cracking the ground. Her broken concentration withdrew her power and the tornado faltered. Esha pushed everything she had into keeping it going, and finally Aurora scrambled to her feet and rejoined her.

"West corner!" Esha yelled. It'd been stupid to start with the side closest to them, but they were no demolition experts, and hindsight was twenty-twenty.

With a heave of joined power, they directed their tornado to the far west corner. A great crash sounded and one whole side of the temple began to collapse in on itself, blocks of stone tumbling as great plumes of dust rose into the sky, blending with their clouds.

They'd turned their cloud tornado to the east corner when a great shrieking flowed through the streets, growing in volume and ferocity. Her attention broke from the tornado just long enough to see a horde of souls flowing through the streets into the square.

Shit. They couldn't stop the tornado or they'd never get it started again.

Warren cursed when he saw the mass of souls rushing toward them, clearly intent on saving the temple. They were a surging wave of black shadow, a force of destruction racing toward them.

Didn't they know the soulceresses were trying to help them? Or were they just shadows of themselves acting on ancient instinct, as they had at the museum?

"Aurora! Get closer to Esha!" he yelled and drew the dagger that had freed Aurora from her souls.

Aurora ran toward Esha, still controlling the tornado, and he clashed with the first of the souls, protecting the soulceresses while they destroyed the east corner of the temple. The shade joined him, along with several other shadows. He got the impression that they'd died more recently and still had their minds instead of merely instinct.

When the dagger passed through the shades, they flew off into the sky as Aurora's had done, freed to go on to their afterworld. But it didn't stop the horrible too-wrong chill when they touched him or the force of their determination that pushed him back toward the soulceresses.

"Warren! Stop! Too dangerous!" Esha yelled.

She feared for his mortal life. And she was wise to. Contact with the souls weakened him, as if they sucked out his life force. But he hadn't a choice. They'd be on Esha in seconds if he quit.

He struck harder and faster, sending souls toward the sky with every swipe of his blade. But a new soul always filled in the gap left by one he'd freed, and dozens pressed in on him and the souls who fought by his side. With every brush of their shadowy forms, a chill raced through him, followed by a shot of weakness.

Every strike of his blade or movement of his feet came slower and slower as the endless tide of souls brushed against him and stole a bit of his mortality, as if they tried to steal the power of his soul as they had before they'd died. He'd sent dozens to their afterworlds, but the hundreds that still surged forth from the side streets would be the end of him.

He had no doubt that he'd stay and die to protect Esha. So he and the shades continued to battle the souls, warding them away from Esha and Aurora. The weakness dragged at his muscles and weighed at his bones until he nearly went to his knees. Force of will alone kept him upright until he heard the crashing roar of the final corner.

A billowing plume of dust rose up into the sky as the rubble settled into itself. Finally, the shrieking of the souls stopped, leaving behind a sudden eerie silence. The shadows shot for the sky, rising out of the city and toward freedom. The mysterious shade that had helped him through this journey hesitated. It flashed from shadow to solid form, revealing a woman he hadn't seen in centuries. Avera.

"Mother," Aurora whispered.

"What?" Esha asked.

A smile flashed across Avera's face, love and gratitude shining through, before she too returned to shadow and flew up toward freedom. The rising souls darkened the sky until there was nothing left but settling dust from the temple.

They stood alone in the square with the ruins in front of them. Warren could hear Esha and Aurora whispering about their mother. Her soul must have recognized them and helped them through the city. When he tried to catch Esha's eye, she looked away.

"Holy crap, look at the city," Aurora said, changing the subject from her mother.

Warren dragged his gaze away from Esha and glanced around. Everything was dingier, with stones tumbled here and there and the windows broken.

"It's aged," Aurora said. "The souls must have been what kept it from decaying."

"It's time to get out of here," Esha said, already turning and heading back to their base camp to pack up.

The streets were eerily silent as they walked, and it became clear that the souls were truly gone. The city felt genuinely abandoned for the first time, not just because of the absence of souls, but because of the ancient state of the buildings, their windows broken and stones worn and crumbling.

Esha was backing away from him, as surely as the souls had retreated from the city. They reached the house in record time, Esha setting a fierce pace with her familiar trotting at her heels. When they entered the foyer, it was no longer brightly decorated and inviting. The tapestries, drapes, and carpets had all faded and worn through, beige shadows of their former glory.

It was truly an ancient house now, no longer protected by the soulceresses' souls. It was cold, too, no doubt because the magic had fallen from the hot springs below, and they'd returned to their normal course far away from the city and the glacier.

"I'm going to grab my stuff, then we can get out of here. You can share my snowmobile on the way back, then we'll aetherwalk home. I've got just enough power. Do you?" Esha asked Aurora without looking at him.

"Aye, I can get out of here."

"Good." Esha turned and started up the stairs while Aurora headed for the kitchen.

"Wait." Warren reached out to Esha.

She stopped on the stairs, her back stiff, and spoke without turning around. "I can't, Warren. Today, when you fought the souls, I couldn't bear it. I was so worried for you that I could hardly keep my attention on destroying the temple. I'm glad you have your soul back and can have the normal life you've always wanted, but I can't watch you die. I'm used to being alone. I'm not used to loving someone and losing them. It'll tear me apart. Don't ask it of me." She ran up the stairs, a harsh sob of breath the only indication that she wasn't fine.

Something hard and horrible tightened in Warren's chest. Watching Esha back away from him earlier today after he'd been declared mortal, her eyes wide with horror, had felt like having an ice pick driven into his heart.

This was worse. More final. Not just a panicked reaction on her part, but a final cutting of ties because her past was too much to overcome. She'd avoided mortals for decades. Now he'd become one.

His soul, the thing he'd wanted more than anything else, now cut him off from her. He'd lain awake nights, thinking of how it would feel to have his soul back. To be mortal again and have his destiny in his own hands. He'd vowed never to lose it again. He'd hold fast to his soul, the most important, valuable thing he could ever have.

Until Esha. Having his soul back made him feel normal. Having her made him feel extraordinary. Yet he couldn't have both. He'd always thought that when he finally got his soul back, everything would be perfect.

How wrong he'd been.

CHAPTER THIRTY-SEVEN

Esha dragged her hand over her eyes, wiping the tears away. She just had to find her clothes and pack them. Then she had to go down and meet Aurora. Then they would get Warren and go home. Then—

A sob broke free of her attempt at normalcy. Nothing was normal now. She loved a mortal. Warren.

And she wouldn't be able to stay away. She'd be drawn back to him, like a fish on a line, unable to help herself. But it would be a bittersweet happiness, always overshadowed by his looming death, followed by an eternity of loss.

A banging sounded on the door. She wasn't surprised. Hastily, she scrubbed away the tears right before Warren burst through.

"Warren." She turned from him. "Can you give me a minute?"

"Nay." He was in front of her then, wrapping her in his arms and pulling her to him. She collapsed into his warm strength, then shook with more tears. To know this, and know that she'd lose him?

"You're no' going to leave me," he said, his words muffled in her hair.

She shook her head. She wouldn't. As much as it would hurt to watch him die, she'd be drawn back to him, unable to help herself.

"And I won't leave you either."

She pushed out of his arms and looked up at him. His eyes were fierce. "You can't control that. You're mortal now. You'll *have* to leave me."

"I doona have to stay mortal."

"You can't become a Mythean." She reached up to run her hand down the side of his cheek, her heart cracking more as she did so. How would she ever bear this? Their lives would be terrible with this always hanging over their heads.

"Nay. But I can stay a mystery monster." A tender grin kicked up the corner of his mouth at the reference to one of her earlier insults.

"What?"

"I'd like to make you a deal," he said.

Gods, he's handsome when he looks at me like this. Golden and good, with eyes like a midnight forest and sincerity and strength radiating from him. "What do you mean?"

"I'd like to sell you my soul."

She jerked backward, horrified. "What?"

"Soulceresses can buy and keep souls. If you buy mine, I canna die. I'll live as long as you do."

"No." She shook her head frantically. "Your soul has been all you've wanted for centuries. It's your *humanity*. You said so."

"I was wrong. I thought it would fix whatever was broken inside of me, but I was wrong. Losing my clan, my family—that's what broke me. I've been hollow since then. Living for so long is a burden once you've lost those you love. I couldn't do that to you. To be with you, to keep you from having to suffer the pain I did when I lost my clan, I'd sell it in a heartbeat."

"Me?"

He shook her lightly. "Of course, you."

"You care for me, I know that. But I'm a soulceress. I just—I don't—"

"I doona *care* for you. I *love* you. There's a difference. A damn big one. You've saved my life, saved my soul, woken me from the coma of existing but no' living. And I love you. You're strong, brave, determined, selfless, funny. You're everything I've ever wanted but dinna realize. You're what makes me whole now, no' my soul."

"Wow." Her mind scrambled to absorb everything he'd said. All the words that she'd never expected to hear said to her. That she'd needed to hear them. A dark place in her heart that she hadn't realized existed was filling up with light.

"As long as I'm alive, I know that I won't be able to resist the urge to protect you," he said. "I know you can protect yourself, but I canna help myself. Except, I'm mortal. No matter how good a warrior I am—and I'm damn good—I won't live long against magic. If I want to stay in this world with you, I can't be mortal. I'd trade my soul in a heartbeat to have a life with you and be able to protect you."

"Oh my gods." She couldn't believe he was saying these things.

He took a deep breath and pinned her with his gaze. "I've seen what happiness can be, and it's with you. You already have my soul."

Her head spun. "But you'll be sick if I use its power."

He shrugged. "You'll just have to be careful. Stay fueled by borrowing power like you do now. And it won't drive you mad as it did Aurora, because my soul will want to be with you. I can guarantee it."

Holy hell, he meant it. And it would work. If he was willing and she was careful, it would work. She threw her arms around his neck, hugging him close, her mind still buzzing with happiness and confusion and awe at the turn her life had taken.

"I couldn't have borne watching you die, and then having to live so long without you," she said against his neck.

"I know. Because I couldn't have borne it, either. I love you, Esha."

She pressed kisses along his neck, up his jaw, until she finally met his mouth. Perfection. It was perfection. *He* was perfection.

She leaned away. "What do you want in exchange for your soul, if you sell it to me?"

"Just your love."

"That, you can have." She grinned up at him, hardly able to believe the life that lay before her. She threw her arms around Warren and kissed him, every sad or lonely moment from her past banished by the light of their future.

EPILOGUE

Immortal University, Edinburgh
Christmas Eve

"Can you believe it, Chairman?" Esha asked as she all but hopped down the hall of the Praesidium. Of all the buildings on the campus of the Immortal University, the Praesidium was the most decked out for the holidays, and it suited her mood perfectly.

The Chairman meowed his agreement, the low yowl cutting through the sound of Christmas music echoing down the hall from the holiday party in the historian Lea's office. Garlands of evergreen and strings of lights lined the hall, and Esha sent a zap of magic at one of the glittery red plastic ornaments. It fell off the garland and bounced across the floor. The Chairman chased after it, on the hunt.

Esha laughed, joy as she'd never known filling her being. She swore it radiated out from her skin so that she sparkled like the Christmas lights above. With a bit of help from Aerten, she'd done it. Warren would never know what hit him.

It'd be the best Christmas gift ever.

The Chairman returned, the sparkling ruby ornament dangling from his mouth.

"You've got your prize?" she asked.

He made a low noise in his throat, and she grinned. She almost zapped him with a bit of magic to give him a festive green bow tie to match his eyes, but she resisted. He'd hate it, and he was so happy with his ornament right now. He normally only liked his fluffy green snake, but he made an exception for Christmas ornaments.

"Come on. Let's go to the party. We're late."

He followed her down the hall toward the music and smell of food. The door to Lea's office was open, and Esha slipped into the huge library-esque space. Mytheans from all departments drank and chatted and danced, the Christmas lights sparkling above.

"Esha! Thanks for coming!" Lea, the nearly transparent hostess, gestured her farther into the room.

Esha had always liked Lea, who'd never given her any shit about being a Soulceress. Esha had no idea what Lea was, but she knew the historian hated being called a ghost.

"Thanks for having me. Happy Christmas!" She smiled at Lea and barely resisted dancing about anxiously. She *really* wanted to see Warren. "I'm going to find Warren. I've got something to tell him."

She ran off before Lea could say goodbye and slipped through the crowd gathered near the punchbowl. Out of the corner of her eye, she caught sight of her sister shooting green sparks at some witches, but ignored her. They'd exchange gifts and celebrate tomorrow.

There! By the towering Christmas tree stood Warren with his friend Cadan and Cadan's wife, Diana. She hurried over and hugged Warren.

"Hey." He leaned down and kissed her, then smiled. "You're late."

"I had something to do." She glanced at Cadan and Diana, who were smiling at them. Diana was the reincarnate of the Celtic warrior Boudica, but she looked like the historian she was right now, wearing a red dress that somehow managed to look killer with her red hair and little black glasses. "Happy Christmas, guys!"

"You too!" Diana said.

Esha opened her mouth to make polite conversation, then realized there was no way she'd be able to stand still. She turned to Warren. "We have to go. I have something to tell you."

"Stay, the party just started. I'll get you some mulled wine," he said.

She tugged on his hand and couldn't stifle the huge grin that stretched across her face. She didn't even want to try. "Really, Warren. Come on."

"You'd better listen to her, mate," Cadan said.

Warren grinned and nodded. "All right. Let's get out of here."

Esha tugged him out of the room, catching sight of the Chairman making eyes at Aurora's familiar in the corner. He still hadn't dropped his ornament. She grinned and left him to it. He'd follow behind them shortly.

"What's this all about?" Warren asked as they made their way down the hall.

"Let's get back to the house first."

They pushed through the big wooden doors of the Praesidium and out into a winter wonderland of fat snowflakes and a full moon peeking out from behind clouds.

"Let's take the short cut." Esha tugged Warren's hand and they set off running across the lawn, now blanketed with white snow. She laughed and the sound echoed through the quiet night. Fairy lights twinkled in the trees and reflected off the snow.

Panting, they climbed the spiral stairs to her tower. She pushed open the door and grinned at the sight of the Christmas tree in the corner. With Warren here, this place no longer felt like the outcast's tower. *She* no longer felt like quite such an outcast, as if Warren and her sister had healed something in her.

Now, she had something to give back to him. She turned and pushed his mussed hair off his forehead. His cheeks were red from the cold, and he was so handsome that her breath caught.

"What is it?" he asked, then pulled her close and pressed a kiss to her lips.

"I spoke to Aerten." The words tumbled free. "She's going to see if you can be made into a Mythean Guardian."

"What? That's not possible. They don't take applications. They do the choosing. And they haven't chosen a new guardian in centuries."

"They're going to make an exception. It's not a sure thing yet, it still has to be approved by the council, but there's a good chance they'll make you a guardian. You've been leading the guardians for so long that you're an obvious choice. When you're immortal as a guardian, I can give you back your soul!"

It was the best plan she'd ever had. Mythean Guardians were immortal. Warren had never been made into one, even though he served the Praesidium because he'd already been immortal without his soul. It'd taken constant petitioning and not a little begging, but she'd convinced Aerten and the council to consider Warren's application.

"But I told you," he said. "I don't need my soul back. I have you."

"You might not need it, but you want it. And I want you to have it. This will work, Warren, I know it will."

He pulled her close and kissed her again. He pulled back and looked into her eyes. "I have what I want."

"I know. Me too. But you'll have this too. There's a first time for everything. This is my first Christmas tree—" she gestured to the sparkling tree in the corner "—and you're going to be the first Mythean Guardian selected by application. It will work, Warren."

"I love you. With all my heart. If this works, that'd be great. If it doesn't, I don't care. I'm happy."

Esha's body filled up with so much joy she couldn't contain it. She threw her arms around Warren and kissed him. She had everything she'd known she'd been missing and more than she ever could have dreamed.

-The End-

THANK YOU!

Thank you so much for reading *Soulceress*. I loved writing this story and hope you enjoyed reading it!

I love to hear from readers, so if you'd like to get in touch or to know when my next book is available, you can...

- Join my new release newsletter at http://linseyhall.com
- Connect with me on twitter at @HiLinseyHall
- Or find me on Facebook at https://www.facebook.com/LinseyHallAuthor

Reviews help other readers discover books. I appreciate all reviews, both positive and negative, and I really appreciate the time you take if you choose to leave one.

If you liked *Soulceress*, the next book in the series is *Rogue Soul*. Book 4, *Stolen Fate,* will be available December 8th. More will come in 2015! If you'd like a peak at how Andrasta and Camulos are getting along, turn the page.

ROGUE SOUL: EXCERPT

CHAPTER ONE

The Caipora's Den
Edge of the Amazon River, Brazil
Present Day

Andrasta, Celtic goddess of victory, swallowed hard, her gaze transfixed by the man in the makeshift boxing ring. *Was he that handsome when I tried to kill him? Or that brutal?*

She honestly couldn't remember. It had been more than two thousand years since she'd seen him last, and she barely recognized him. Dim spotlights gleamed off sweat-slicked muscles and highlighted the feral brutality with which he pounded his opponent. No gloves protected his big hands, just white fabric wrapped around knuckles. They were spotted with blood.

She swallowed hard again, unable to look away.

She'd known she would find him here when she'd strolled up to the Caipora's Den, a little dive bar perched on the edge of the Amazon River. But she hadn't expected the outdoor boxing ring surrounded by a horde of cheering Mytheans or that her prey would be inside it, pounding his opponent into a sack of broken bones.

She'd never before been to the bar, which catered only to the supernatural beings who lived secretly alongside mortals. The building itself was ramshackle, and she had a feeling that it was just as run-down on the inside. The outdoor lot in which she stood was pressed between the building and the river. It housed the boxing ring and nearly a hundred Mytheans, most of whom looked human even though they weren't. They screamed and cheered as punches landed with fierce smacks.

"All right, that's enough," hollered the ref, a big ugly brute who stepped forward to end the fight. The man she'd come for stood over his collapsed opponent, his heavily muscled chest heaving. He was declared the winner—no surprise, considering his opponent didn't look like he'd be getting off the floor anytime soon.

She sank back into the crowd when he turned to exit the ring. Though she wanted to watch him, to devour every hard inch with her eyes, she didn't want him to see her before she could approach him on her terms.

Their past was a pit of snakes, so confusing that even she couldn't figure head from tail though she'd lived through it. She wouldn't be surprised if he was pissed as hell, considering the arrows she'd sent through his heart the last time she'd seen him. Not that he hadn't wronged her. He had. He'd started the nightmare that had ended in her stealing his godhood for herself. Worse, they'd cared for each other. Until it had all gone to shit, at least.

And now she needed his help.

She turned and pushed her way through the crowd, toward the small bar pressed against the outside of the building. She needed to buy herself some time to recover from the sight of him but didn't want to do it inside the bar where she might lose track of him. Seeing him again made her shaky, even though it had been so many years. She just needed a minute to catch her breath, that was all.

She squeezed between two Mytheans of indeterminate species and reached the bar—which was more of a table with some liquor bottles and a cooler, but it would do.

"A beer," she said to the bartender, a beautiful brunette who had the slightly feral face of some kind of shifter. Ana had never been any good at identifying Mytheans since she rarely got away from her own kind.

The bartender handed over a sweating glass bottle and hissed, "On the house."

Anaconda Incantada. The sound of her voice gave away what her features did not. She was a snake shifter.

And it had better be on the house. There had to be some perks to being a god, since everything else had been a disappointment. Although Ana never tired of Mytheans fearing or bowing to her. Some watched her warily even now, and she appreciated it all the more for not having had it when she'd been mortal.

"How often does this happen?" Ana asked the bartender, hiking a thumb at the ring.

The shifter shrugged. "Every night."

"Know anything about the fighters?"

"Not the loser. But the winner, he's never lost. Fights pretty often. Seems to like it. Keeps to himself otherwise."

Ana nodded and turned to look for her prey. The beer slid refreshingly down her throat, and she sighed in pleasure at the smooth taste of the infrequently allowed delicacy. Focusing on the taste helped calm her nerves just a bit. She was raising the bottle to her lips a second time when she spotted him standing off to the side of the crowd near the jungle that crept up to the dirt lot.

It had been two thousand years since she'd seen him last, when she'd thought she'd killed him and taken his place as a Celtic god. Those years had been kind to him, considering that he was still alive. Almost as kind as the way-too-hot woman draped around him, sucking on his neck while he unwrapped the bloody cloth from his hands.

Ana stifled the strange little twinge in her chest. She'd cared for him once, and he for her, but that was so long ago the memories had gone to dust. Or so she told herself. She took one last swig of the beer to chase them away.

Now or never. If she wanted a permanent escape from Otherworld, the land of the Celtic gods and what felt like her eternal prison, there'd be no more dawdling, no matter how nervous she was about his reception or willingness to help her.

She needed him. Admitting to it scraped something raw inside her. But after two thousand years, she wanted out more than she wanted her pride.

Ana sucked in a deep breath and wound her way through the crowd. When a *lobisomem* got handsy as she passed, an elbow to the gut halted his straying paws, and a glare stopped another. Fancy Brazilian name or not, they were dogs like the rest of their werewolf brothers. Within moments, she'd reached the edge of the crowd and stood before the now-kissing pair.

She squashed her nerves as she gazed at the strong profile of the man she'd never been able to forget—whose mouth was glued to the woman's. He was a bruiser, even from the side, a contrast of hard features and short ginger hair. He looked rougher than she remembered. Bigger, too.

"Camulos," Ana said. She glanced dismissively at the sultry woman now trying to swallow his tongue.

"Cam," he said absentmindedly as he drew his face away from the woman's to look at Ana. His brows shot up, his gray eyes widening the barest fraction. A scar sliced through one of the brows.

"Recognize me?" she asked, absorbing the fact that he no longer went by Camulos.

"Andrasta," he rasped, shock plain on his face.

Did she hear his breath catch?

Hers certainly did. He looked every inch the god he'd once been—strong and powerful, with broad shoulders and big arms that looked like they'd been cut from steel. A man comfortable with the mantle of worship, even if he no longer carried it.

Ana shot a pointed glance at the other woman.

"Luciana," he said, drawing the woman's mouth away from where it had suctioned onto his neck.

Ana's eyes zeroed in on the huge hand that cupped the back of Luciana's neck, then looked back to realize that he'd kept his gaze trained on her own face.

"You need to go," Camulos said to Luciana.

Luciana pouted at him, then turned to look at Ana.

"A goddess?" Her brows shot high. She no doubt noticed the small glow emitting from Ana's skin and marked her as one from Otherworld. Her lips twisted in a sneer. "I thought you Celtic gods never left your cold realm."

She'd be right, Ana thought bitterly. Cold and emotionless, that was Otherworld, and she was trapped there except for a few times a year when she could sneak out without the other gods noticing. But that's what she wanted to change.

"Beat it, sister," she said, trying out some earth slang she'd seen on a TV show. Sneaking a laptop into Otherworld and firing up movies with her magic was one of the few ways she stayed sane.

The woman pouted, gave one last longing glance at Camulos, and then moved off into the crowd.

Camulos gave her a hard, searching look, his shock now masked. He didn't make a move to kill her—which was good. Not that she'd let him. But still, it was promising. He might have cared for her once, but after what had happened at the end, she wouldn't be surprised if that had been pushed out by anger.

"Come on. Let's get a seat inside." He jerked his chin toward the ramshackle bar.

Ana nodded and turned to lead the way. This time, with the huge male of indeterminate species following closely behind her, the crowd parted in waves to let her pass. Camulos was so close on her heels she swore she could feel the heat of him. It made the fine hairs on her arms stand on end. She tried to ignore it.

The smell of sweat and stale beer assaulted her nose when she walked into the bar. It was even more crowded than the outside, with dozens of volatile Mytheans partying and fighting in the dark, smoky space lit only by bare, dangling light bulbs.

She blinked. Wow. This was so different from Otherworld. Gross, definitely, from the smell to the cleanliness of the occupants.

But it was great. It was nothing like Otherworld, and she *loved* it. There was one small unoccupied table in the corner, but it was far enough from the main crowd to suit her.

They hadn't so much as settled at the table when a beer appeared in front of Camulos, carried by a smiling waitress whose eyes didn't stray from him. He ignored it and spared her only a curt nod.

"How the hell did you find me?" he asked when the waitress slunk away.

His rough voice sent a shiver down her spine. That first tingle of attraction hadn't been a fluke, after all. Damn it. This was what had gotten her in trouble so many years ago. Insane attraction that had blinded her to the danger she'd stepped into.

She dragged her mind back to the present. "More importantly, how the hell are you still alive? I thought I killed you."

His big hand clenched on the table. Scars sliced across his knuckles.

She tried not to squirm in her seat as his eyes roamed from her face down to the hint of cleavage she knew peeped above the top of her leather breastplate. She always wore it, but then she spent most of her time in temperate Otherworld or Scotland. It was damn hot in the jungle.

Finally, his gaze dragged back to hers. The sight hit her straight in the solar plexus. Damn, he looked good, no matter how wary or how harsh his gaze. His short reddish-blond hair glinted in the dim light that struggled to illuminate the seedy bar with its sticky seats. He still looked like a damn god, no matter what he'd turned into.

"You didn't kill me," he said, one corner of his mouth hiked up.

"Then what the hell *are* you? How are you immortal?"

"Why would I tell you that?"

So it was going to be this way? A game of chance where neither showed their cards? But it suited her too, since she had no idea how she felt about him. She glared at him as a Jurassic-sized fly buzzed around her head, as annoying as the questions hanging in the air between them. She still didn't fully understand everything that had happened those many years ago when she'd taken his place as a god by sending an arrow through his heart. Twice. She flinched at the mental image that came with the thought—him dying in the snow, his blood soaking through the knees of her dress.

"Aren't you afraid of me?" he asked.

"Nope." If she was going to be afraid of anyone, it would be him—with his huge body, scowling face, and potentially deadly grudge against her. But she wasn't. She could take care of herself, damn it. Being afraid was a thing of the past.

"Cocky."

"Yep." She wasn't the same girl he'd once cared for, however briefly. After they'd gotten caught in the crosshairs of the gods and her whole life had gone to hell, she'd changed.

"Anyway, it worked out for the best." He raised his smudged glass in toast to her.

"Really?" Her brows shot up. He truly thought their past—trading places so that she became a god and he went to earth—had worked out for the best?

He nodded, but she had a hard time believing him.

"Why? You should have loved Otherworld. You're a god," she said.

"Not anymore."

"Yeah, but you get what I mean," she said. "Otherworld, the coldness there, shouldn't have bothered you since you were born a god. The power, the perfection. It was all yours. Without all the downsides."

Like the soul-sucking loneliness of a place with no emotion. No one could care about anyone else. She was a fluke, a god with the ability to feel because she'd once been mortal. But there was nothing to feel there. No joy, no love, no fun. No way to distract herself from the misery of being trapped. All the other gods, they were perfect for it. Automatons in their impeccable world. But not her.

"So why would it be better for you on earth?" she asked when he didn't respond. He had less power here and had to hide from the other gods. And earth was messy and miserable compared to Otherworld. But it was that ability to be miserable, and alternately joyful, which made her want to return. "There's nothing for you here."

His gray eyes darkened, his expression effectively closing the subject. "That's my business, not yours. Why the hell are you here?"

"I want out."

"Are you kidding? Do you know what will happen to you when the other gods figure out you've tried to run?"

What was it about his voice that made her want to squirm in her seat? The mixed accent from his long life sounded exotic somehow and a hint of roughness dragged across her skin.

She shivered. "I've snuck out before."

"For a few hours maybe, and not with the intent to flee." He nodded smugly and she knew he must see acknowledgment in her eyes. "When they figure out that you're gone and don't intend to come back, you'll end up chained to the most desolate tor in Blackmoor for a thousand years while ravens circle for dinner."

Ana swallowed hard. The knowledge of the great rock formations where lawbreakers were punished was something she'd tried not to focus on when she'd decided to run. Blackmoor was the most desolate place in Otherworld, all scrubby ground punched through with granite tors and howling wind and rain. She had about a day before the other gods figured out she was gone. At that point, she'd be considered a deserter and they'd hunt her down.

"I'm aware of the risks." She tried to make her voice hard. "I want out."

"What the hell do you expect me to do about it?"

"You cared for me once." She didn't want to play that card—not after how it had ended between them—but she was desperate.

Truth flashed in his eyes, then his jaw hardened. "It was a long time ago."

It had been. But seeing him was dredging up emotions she'd forgotten she'd ever had. She tried to force them to the back of her mind and focus on her goal. "I want to know how you became mortal."

"Not mortal."

"Damn it, you know what I mean. I just don't want to be a god anymore. You stole my life when your obsession with me attracted the attention of the other gods. I want my life back."

"I don't owe you a thing." He raised his glass and his strong throat worked as he swallowed, drawing her eyes to it. She couldn't help but notice the way his worn shirt stretched over his broad chest. She scowled at her own interest. Long ago, that same interest had gotten her into trouble.

"Fine. I'll just have to convince you," she said.

He didn't respond, just smiled and folded his muscled arms over his chest. She sighed, then tensed when he swung his feet up onto the chair next to her.

Her breath caught in her throat. She could almost feel the heat of his thighs close to hers. Her leg tingled, her skin prickling. Something low in her stomach tightened, and it reminded her that this was one of the reasons she wanted to be back on earth.

Fates, her nerves were on edge, and he wasn't helping matters. She'd spent nearly every day of the last two millennia in Otherworld—the dullest, loneliest place in all of creation. As much as she loved the hustle and bustle of the Mytheans and mortals on earth, there was way too much of it in this bar. Her senses were on overdrive, and the air fairly buzzed with emotion from the dozens of volatile Mytheans carousing around her.

She swallowed hard and met his eyes. His smile reappeared, as if he knew what was going on inside her head. Inside her body.

"I need some air." She jumped to her feet. "Come on."

As soon as he stood, she spun and headed for the front door of the bar, hoping it would be quieter than the fighting ring out back. She had to cool down or things were going to get out of control.

AUTHOR'S NOTE

Though *Soulceress* is set in the present day, I couldn't help but try to stay as true to history as possible when writing Warren and Esha's past. This meant timing everyone's birth to the Great Scottish Witch Hunt of 1661-1662. It was one of several large witch trials during the 17th century, and this was likely the period during which the most people were tried for witchcraft in Scotland. These are the witch hunts that inspired the Burnings. Warren was born in 1630, which would have made him 31 at the time he rescued an infant Esha in 1661.

Books by Linsey Hall

Braving Fate
Soulceress
Rogue Soul
Stolen Fate

ABOUT LINSEY

Before becoming a romance novelist, Linsey Hall was a nautical archaeologist who studied shipwrecks from Hawaii and the Yukon to the UK and the Mediterranean. She credits the historical romances of the 70's, 80's, and 90's with her love of history and her career as an archaeologist. After a decade of tromping around the globe in search of old bits of stuff that people left lying about, she settled down and started penning her own romance novels. Her debut series, the Mythean Arcana, draws upon her love of history and the paranormal elements that she can't help but include. Several books may or may not feature her cats.